1.
Lola

CU01507753

I don't think blowing your boss appears very often on those clickbait listicles about how to nail your first day at a new job. But I've always been an outside-the-lines kind of girl.

"God, Lola," Coach Will groaned, running his fingers through my hair as I swallowed his release. He leaned his head back and closed his eyes, and I buttoned his pressed khakis and stood, propping a hip against the edge of his desk.

"You were saying something about the new players," I said, smirking at him. I flicked my tongue over my bottom lip and dragged it between my teeth. He stared at my mouth for several seconds, then blinked and cleared his throat.

"Right. The big shots touched down last night. Everybody's at practice now. We should probably make an appearance." He winced guiltily. He'd left his assistant coach, a neurotic dynamo named Huck Hart, to steer the ship while he came up to his office for a… meeting…with me.

I knew we were asking for trouble, but I'd been drawn to Will like a magnet from the first day I met him.

I got the call three days before I was supposed to report in Casper, Wyoming. I packed my life into four suitcases without a second thought and returned to my hometown to start my dream job.

Well, this was step one of the dream, anyway. When I graduated with my degree in sports massage therapy, I had visions of working for some glitzy, high-dollar professional team with a state-of-the-art facility. The Ice Hawks arena was…not that.

I followed Will through the twisting, chipped cinderblock hallways to the rink, stepping behind him into the refrigerated room. Immediately, I could hear the shouts and chirps of the players on the ice. It was a practice game, two lines in red jerseys and two lines in white, going head to head.

"The new guys are in red," Will said in my ear as we approached the white team's bench. Huck's arms were crossed tightly over his chest. He scowled at the movement on the ice, which was almost too fast to track. The red team was clearly superior. They were scoring on the white team every time they got the puck. I could hear the white team's goaltender hurling insults at the red team whenever they came within earshot.

Huck cast us a dark look as we walked up together, and then he clenched his jaw and turned his attention back to the ice.

Where Will was tall and sweet and open, Huck was stormy and brooding. He was shorter than Will, but still a head taller than me. He had dark hair, piercing blue eyes, and a razor-sharp jaw that was always twitching with what I could only assume was annoyance.

He was…intense. But I was fascinated by him. He'd been a rising star goalie in the major leagues until he broke his back in a car accident, a drunk in a pickup truck that drifted over the double

Puck It Up

A Reverse Harem Hockey

Romance

by

Cameron Fox

Puck It Up: A Reverse Harem Hockey Romance © 2023
by Cameron Fox
All rights reserved. No part of this book may be reproduced in any
form or by any electronic or mechanical means, including
information storage and retrieval systems, without permission in
writing from the author. The only exception is by a reviewer, who
may quote short excerpts in a review.

Cover designed by Cameron Fox
This book is a work of fiction. All names, characters, places, and
incidents are products of the author's imagination. Any resemblance
to actual persons, living or dead, is purely coincidental.

yellow line and destroyed any chance Huck had had at a professional hockey career. From what I'd read online, it was a miracle he was alive and an even greater miracle that he wasn't confined to a wheelchair. He didn't even walk with a limp.

I'd spent the last two evenings falling down search engine rabbit holes, finding out everything I could about the team I now worked for and its players.

There was one player I knew more about than I particularly cared to. My eyes tracked the guys on the white team, bulky he-men coasting back and forth in a strangely graceful dance. One of them was Reid Wright, the erstwhile love of my life and still the record-holder for my most painful heartbreak yet. But the practice sweaters didn't have names or numbers, and their helmets made the men-on-ice as indistinguishable as plastic foosball players. Maybe I would recognize the guys eventually by their body language, their stature, once they'd become more than strangers. But right now, I couldn't have picked out any particular player if you paid me. Which was a shame because as pissed off as I was at Reid, I was dying to lay eyes on him. I hadn't seen him in five years, since he left town to play as a second-line defenseman on the University of Wyoming hockey team. He'd single-handedly taken that team to the playoffs in his third year. That much I knew without having to boot up my laptop.

I knew before I came back to Casper that he'd taken a position on this team right out of school to be close to his sister, my childhood best friend and current roommate Hope. The Ice Hawks were the development team for the Denver Prospectors, and he'd been drafted to play for that team. He was supposed to play a year here and then move on to the major league. But that hadn't happened yet. The year he was drafted, the team missed the playoffs by a nose. My internet search had filled me in on how he'd fallen apart the second he hit the ice as a professional player. Gone was the verve and pizazz he'd shown in college. He was clumsy, with a hair-trigger temper. He spent more time fighting than skating. His fellow draft picks left for Denver at the end of the season while he stayed put and sharpened his blades for another round in minor-league development hockey.

After a couple of minutes spent observing them, I started to suspect that I did know which skater was Reid after all. One of the white team's first-line defensemen was racing up and down, elbowing red sweaters out of his way, protecting his centers and wingers as they flew across the ice. This guy was one of the most dynamic players in the rink, a force to be reckoned with. But he was all raw power, no finesse.

Which described Reid Wright to a fucking T.

The red team executed goals with surgical precision, one right after the other. At one point, the white team's wild defenseman went chest-to-chest with the other team's first-line center, and I was sure the gloves were about to come off, and fists were going to fly. But after clacking helmet guards, they skated away from each other as the striped-shirted official blew his whistle. The game was over. I winced as I read the score on the board.

6-1.

The red team's lead center took a victory lap around the ice, and as he passed him, he collided shoulders with the man in the white sweater, who I was now convinced was Reid. The player in the red sweater said something under his breath that made the white team's defenseman lunge toward him, but a teammate was there to pull him back as the new center skated off with a laugh.

The white team's defenseman had switched shifts less than anyone else, and hadn't bothered to take off his helmet during his brief breathers on the bench. But now he was skating right at me, pulling the helmet off his flowing, dirty-blond hair. He shook the mop out of his face as he coasted right up and jumped off the ice. I was standing directly behind the bench, Coach Will's hand lingering at the small of my back, when Reid's dark gray eyes met mine. He froze. His jaw tightened, and then he turned and threw himself onto the bench. He slung his stick and his helmet down at his feet. Will leaned forward, clapping him on the shoulder, but he didn't look back.

I tugged on Will's sleeve. He looked at me, and I jerked my head toward the double doors that led back to the locker room.

"You headed out?" he asked, straightening up. I swear I saw Reid's shoulders tense even under those thick pads. Maybe it was silly to think that I could read his emotions by watching the back of his head, but I'd managed to pick him out of the crowd by his body language and the position he was playing, so anything was possible. I knew him with a part of myself that lived deep down inside, buried under the layers of protective armor that I'd spent the last five years building and reinforcing.

But everything that had happened in the intervening years flew out the window when Reid and I locked eyes.

We were kids again, with skinned knees on the playground, he the older brother teasing his younger sister and me, her best friend. I hadn't thought that coming home again would be easy, but it had already been much more difficult than I'd expected. I'd made the ill-advised decision to go out with my boss after orientation, and then I'd given in to my lizard brain—the shrill, demanding voice that lived inside my head and that, all throughout dinner, screamed *Fuck him! Drag him to the bathroom and fuck him right now! Get under the table and milk him dry!*

She was a horny little bitch. Insatiable, even. I'd spent years trying to deny her, shying away from my scorchingly hot libido in favor of safe, vanilla boyfriends who left me chronically unsatisfied. But as my life rearranged itself around me, I'd realized that maybe she was on my side. Maybe it was okay to explore my desires.

And explore them I had, in the front seat of Coach Will's sedan and then again in his plush king bed, in his big house on the outskirts of town. He'd been a big shot in the show and his digs reflected that fact.

We feasted on each other all night, and then I had to be back at the arena first thing the next morning to set up my massage studio and fill out the rest of my HR paperwork, all while hiding the fact that the coach had railed me absolutely goddamn senseless the night before.

There was this one point, when we were both stretched out on the rug in front of his crackling fireplace, our legs tangled together…

"Lola?" Will's voice derailed my train of thought. I blinked at him. "You headed out?" he repeated, and this time the words sank in. Afraid to look at the back of Reid's head again, afraid that I wouldn't be able to tear myself away without some kind of loud, shouting confrontation, I swallowed around the lump in my throat and finally nodded. Will's dark green eyes searched my face, his brow furrowed. I put a hand on his arm, but then dropped it back to my side just as quickly. Touching him made me want to kiss him, which was definitely a no-no here in front of the entire team. His eyes crinkled in a smile that his lips barely acknowledged. Then he gave my hand a subtle squeeze and let me go.

I somehow managed not to break into a sprint as I approached the swinging doors, as I closed the distance between me and my escape route from this ice box. And from Reid. I shoved through them, sudden tears prickling behind my eyes.

At the mere sight of Reid, everything I'd been trying to hold at bay had rushed over my walls and drowned my heart. I had to put as much distance between myself and him as possible so I could work through those emotions without doing something stupid. But seconds later, I heard the doors shush open again behind me and the clunky, long strides of a man hurrying after me in ice skates. I stopped, closing my eyes, trying to gather myself as the voice in my head switched between cursing and unhinged laughter. I'd thought I could handle this, that I was ready to see him again, but I'd clearly been very wrong.

"Lola Fucking Rey." The voice behind me was unmistakably Reid's, dusky and grinding like tires rolling slowly over a gravel road. I turned to face him and he was on top of me in an instant, his big, bulky body pinning my small, soft one against the wall.

I looked to both sides, afraid to be seen, and more afraid to meet his scorching, steely stare. "What are you doing here?" His breath was hot against my cheek. Now I did raise my eyes to meet his, my lips parting in surprise. He glanced at my mouth, his stormy eyes hot enough to singe my skin.

"H-Hope didn't tell you?" I asked, and then I swallowed hard. *Let's try that again, and this time, engage your spine.* "I took a job here as the team's new sports massage therapist. I'm surprised you don't know that already, given that I'm living with your sister." His eyebrows snapped together. He slammed his hand into the wall and then pushed away from me, shaking his gloves off and raking his hands through his luxurious mane of hair. When he turned back to me, he was laughing. But there was no humor in his eyes as they swept from my head to my feet and back up again.

"You're going to be working here. For this team."

"That's right. Something about a final push to see if you guys are worth a damn before the owner decides if he's going to fold the Ice Hawks, or replace every last one of you with skaters who can actually find the net."

His nostrils flared as he fought to maintain control. He took a towering step toward me, glaring down at me with those thunderclouds he called eyes. I ignored the guilt that threatened to drag me under. It was the simple truth. Maybe he needed to hear it. The team was in danger. The players were going to have to wake up to that fact if anything was ever going to change.

Reid glanced away from me down the hall. Then he braced his hand on the wall beside my head again, pinning me with a burning stare.

"Fine," he ground out. "Whatever. Just stay out of my way." I gaped up at him, amazed that he would have the balls to talk to me this way after how he'd ended our relationship. Ghost City.

What the fuck?

I raised my hands up between his chest and mine, palms out. A gesture of surrender.

"Don't you worry about that," I assured him, my lips twisting into a sneer. His eyes searched mine as the air between us grew taut with tension, and then he shoved away from the wall and clomped back through the double doors into the rink.

2.
Lola

"You didn't think to tell your *fucking brother* that I'd moved in with you? Or that I'd be working for his team?" I demanded, my eyes bugging out at Hope. She smirked at me around the strawberry she'd been raising to her lips when I came bursting through the front door. My hair was standing on end from the way I'd forced my hand through it a hundred times during the short trip home as I shouted out all the things I should have said to Reid instead of just taking his shit like always. My manic, one-sided conversation with Imaginary Reid had done nothing to calm my nerves. If anything, it had whipped me up into an even greater frenzy.

Hope leaned back against the kitchen counter and crossed her arms, the half-eaten strawberry dangling, its leaves still pinched between her long fingers.

"It's better this way, *trust me*," she said. I just looked at her. Trust her? She set her brother up for an ambush today and sent me in blind to do the sniping. "I don't talk to you guys about each other," she shrugged. But her eyes were sparkling.

I dropped my bag in one of the kitchen table chairs and then stalked to the cabinet to get the biggest wine glass we had. I filled it half-full from the omnipresent box of rosé in Hope's fridge and then kicked the door shut behind me, rounding on her.

"Make it make sense," I ordered, taking a very undignified slug from my glass.

"You know Reid," she said, eyeing me warily like she'd just figured out that I was actually upset about the situation. "I love the guy. He's my brother. But you know as well as I do that when things get sticky, Reid bails." I stared at her as she spoke, really taking her in for the first time since I'd landed in a whirlwind a week ago. I'd already spent several nights at Will's, and with everything going on, I realized that I had only talked to my best friend in the world for a grand total of twenty minutes since she picked me up from the airport. That took the edge off my indignant attitude. "Plus…he's been a bit cagier than usual lately." I frowned at her.

"What do you mean?"

For a second, she didn't answer, like she was thinking every word over carefully in her mind before speaking. She was as gorgeous as Reid, a year younger but they could have easily been fraternal twins. They had the same big, pillowy lips and wide gray eyes ringed with criminally long, thick lashes. Hope's hair was a shade darker than Reid's, a light honey brown streaked with shimmering natural highlights in every shade of blonde. I think stylists call hair like hers *expensive brunette*, but Hope was all-natural. A fucking knockout from the day she was born.

She and her hunky dickhead of a brother won the genetic lottery. Both looked like movie stars with their chiseled jawlines and high cheekbones, and both had been star athletes in high school who made their sports look effortless to those of us who were perpetually on the sidelines. Both were exhilarating to watch, Reid on the ice and Hope on the track, dusting her competition to set school records in both the 800 and 1200-meter races.

She still had the body of a runner, and still took long, meandering jogs through town when the weather was nice. But unlike her brother, she'd chosen a career field that didn't have an average retirement age of thirty-five. One that wouldn't leave her body a broken mess with no other skills or education at the point in her life when she should be at her peak. She'd never been the type to dream of Olympic gold or a shiny cup. After we graduated, she'd happily hung up her cleats and applied to the culinary school down in Denver.

But Reid had always had his heart set on playing major league hockey, from the first time their dad strapped him into a pair of skates and handed him a stick. I couldn't understand why he was choking now, when he'd made it all the way to the threshold of his greatest dream. All that was left was for him to turn the knob and walk through into the big time. But instead, he was stuck in the doorway, spinning his wheels.

Hope sucked in a shaky breath and then blew it out again, ruffling the fringe of hair around her face.

"I think he's depressed," she said at last, in a defeated kind of voice. "Dad took him on a fishing trip this summer, trying to figure out why he'd had such an awful season after his stunning run at UW." She shook her head. "But he couldn't get through to him. Reid drank all the beer and went on and on about hockey, but anytime Dad tried to bring up a touchy subject, he shut down. They had a pretty big blowout, apparently. He's just been getting angrier and angrier. I kind of hoped…that seeing you might jolt him out of it." She rushed out the last part. I crossed my arms and cocked an eyebrow at her.

"Well, it didn't. If anything, I was just gasoline on a wildfire. Seriously, I thought he was going to fight their new center, and that was before he'd even seen me."

"Nate the Great," Hope said with a bite in her voice. "Yeah, he's a world-class prick. That's why the owner exiled him down here in the development league, to punish him for blowing off practices and team meetings and just being an all-around entitled asshat." I snorted, the tightness in my chest loosening. I should have made the time to reconnect with her sooner.

"Tell me how you really feel."

She spared me a smirk and then dropped the top of her strawberry into the garbage disposal, ran the water, and flicked the switch to chop it up.

"Basically, Reid was already having a really rough time before these hosers from the show came in. He thought he could turn it all around this season, pull his reputation out of the toilet, but now he's just worried about getting play time."

"His reputation is not in the toilet," I said, rolling my eyes. "He's so dramatic. So he had one bad season. So what? Another year on the development team never killed anybody. And it seems like the owner is throwing a lot of money at the Ice Hawks to try and get them out of their rut."

"They've definitely never had a masseuse on staff," Hope said, raising her eyebrows. "I thought that fancy stuff was just for the big-time pro teams." I shrugged.

"I go where I'm called. And for some reason, I've been called back here." It was a fluke of the universe, my first real job taking me right back to the place where it all began. Where I'd been a girl, rubbing out the knots in Reid's shoulders and Hope's calves. With my insatiable hunger for science, I learned as much as I could about the human body and how it worked. I'd never played a sport in my life, but being best friends with Hope meant that I spent more days than not hanging around after school, watching some practice or other.

I'd existed on the periphery of their popular jock crowd, blending in well enough with my "all-American girl-next-door good looks" (Hope's words, not mine). But all of the real friends I had, aside from the Wrights, were honors class nerds like me. Still, I was in with Hope and Reid, two of the brightest stars Casper High had ever seen, and that meant I was in with the droves of people who were clamoring for their attention and approval.

Or, at the very least, I was tolerated. I might be the only science geek alive who wasn't bullied in school, thanks to the umbrella of protection my friends cast over me.

The timer on the oven went off. Hope jumped like she'd forgotten where she was. A delicious smell had been slowly but surely permeating my senses as my embarrassed shock and anger at her had ebbed away. When she opened the oven, a cloud of it wafted out, and my stomach rumbled loudly.

So Reid was a mess. That much was obvious. He'd been shitting the bed since pretty much the moment he was drafted, according to the internet. What I couldn't figure out was *why*. What had changed between his senior year of college and here, now, to make him such an unpredictable and uncontrolled presence on the ice?

Hope pulled a spinach lasagna out of the oven, my favorite, and my last remaining annoyance with her dissipated on the spot.

We ate from deep bowls on the couch, watching old re-runs of our favorite sitcoms. I marveled at how it felt like nothing had changed, even after four years apart. We'd kept in contact during that time, but we hadn't curled up together in our pajamas on her couch to binge mindless television since senior year.

A cozy feeling settled over me like a warm blanket fresh out of the dryer. A certainty sank into my bones, an awareness of the thing I'd been denying and trying to ignore but no longer could.

For better or worse, I was home.

3.
Reid

I was going to kill my sister. Actually kill her. The time for idle threats was past.

How long had Hope known that the bane of my existence and the love of my fucking life was about to waltz right back into Casper like she never left? She hadn't even given me the courtesy of a heads-up so I could prepare myself. And now I'd shown my ass, showed Lola exactly how much power she still held over me. She could still twist me up in knots with a single glance.

Her teenage beauty had sharpened into the stunning features of a woman. Long blonde hair that, even in a ponytail, nearly brushed her pert, round, bouncy ass…

Get a grip, Reid.

But it was no use. I was in the shower in my apartment, rinsing off another shitty day in paradise, and the image of Lola was bumping and grinding and bucking and writhing all around in my brain.

I glanced grimly down at my painfully hard cock. I'd have to go to Copper's soon and find a poor, unsuspecting girl to take my frustrations out on.

Maybe one with a long, blonde ponytail that I could wrap around my hand while I stuffed my cock down her throat…

I groaned, giving up and grasping my throbbing shaft tightly. After seeing her, I was ready to explode. We'd been *this* close to each other…

I leaned forward against the wall and closed my eyes, letting myself fall into a fantasy of her.

On her knees, taking me like a good girl, licking the tip of my cock before swallowing me straight down her throat and sucking me within an inch of my life…

Lola's dark, glinting eyes, challenging me. The stubborn set of her little chin.

Fuck.

I was in some serious fucking trouble.

I pressed my forehead to the cool tile, thrusting my hips forward, fucking into my fist and imagining that it was her mouth, those sweet pink lips sliding up and down. Up and down…

I splattered come all over the wall, shuddering as I drained every last drop into the water swirling at my feet.

My knees were shaking as I settled back into myself.

I groaned, turning my face into the hot shower spray.

When I was clean as I was ever going to be, I climbed out and toweled off, then went to the fridge for a beer.

Hope had offered to let me live with her in the room where I assumed Lola was now sleeping. But the team offered free housing, and I liked my space.

Plus, my best friend lived in the apartment right next door. We were living out an extended college fantasy, crashing in the dorms and walking down to the bar most nights.

I didn't exactly want my sister to wake up to the sounds of me plowing some puck bunny or three that I'd brought home from the pool hall.

Not that I'd been doing much plowing lately.

I clenched my jaw, popping the tab on the can as I ruminated.

And another thing.

Was it just me, or was she standing way too fucking close to Wild Bill Manners?

4.

Lola

Will's text lit up the screen of my phone right after I turned out the lights and climbed into bed. I picked it up from the nightstand and stared at the simple question that had a very complicated answer.

What was that with Wright today?

I could pretend to have already been asleep when it came in, obsess about it all night and then respond in the morning. Or I could bite the bullet now.

It was nothing, I replied. Then I followed up with, *We have a bit of history, but it's really nothing.*

The three dots bounced on Will's side for a minute, but when the message came through, it was brief.

A history, huh?

I bit my lip, debating whether I should lay all the gory details on him or play it all off as a silly fling from half a decade ago. But deep down, I already knew it was no use. If our interaction today was any indication, my past relationship with Reid wouldn't remain a secret to the team for long.

It's kind of a long story to text. I stared anxiously at the words for a beat before I pressed send.

    Then come over.

My stomach swam with a heady mix of desire and nerves.

I'm already in bed, I replied.

Three bouncing dots.

    I didn't ask where you were. I told you where you need to be.

The swimming feeling sank lower, damp and fluttery between my legs. I didn't bother replying to his last message. I was too busy lacing up my tennis shoes and throwing my work clothes into an overnight bag.

He answered the door looking like he'd nodded off while he was waiting for me. His hair was adorably mussed, his eyes squinted half-closed. But when he saw me, his face split in a wide grin.

There was no need for words then. I stepped inside, dropped my bag, and jumped into his arms.

Will caught me easily, wrapping my legs around his waist as he backed me up against the wall and captured my lips in a soul-stealing kiss. He ground his hips against mine, and I could feel that he was already hard for me. Groaning into his mouth, I ran my hands over his shoulders and up into his thick crop of sandy hair, pulling him closer. He leaned back with a low swear. Then he spun around and carried me through the house to his bed.

He threw me down and pounced on top of me. We tore at each other's clothes like we hadn't seen each other in weeks, even though I'd just had his cock in my mouth a few hours ago. My need for him was all-consuming. It eclipsed everything else, even Reid, and I managed to forget about him as I tugged Will's shirt over his head. I dipped down to press a kiss to his collarbone, earning a guttural groan.

Then he was inside me, filling me to the brim and then some. Will was an unusually big man, even for a hockey player. He loomed over me in the dark, his hands digging into the mattress on either side of my head as he sank himself into my pussy inch by inch. He took his time with me, which was typical. I was curvy, solid and strong, but I was still a petite girl. Will always handled me gently at first, warming me up so that he could rail me without doing damage.

When he was buried to the hilt inside me, he let out another low swear.

"Damn it, Lola. You're too fucking perfect, baby," he said in a hoarse voice as he stared down at me, his eyes shining through the darkness. I reached up and cupped his face in both of my hands, pulling him down and pressing a burning kiss to his lips.

He relaxed into me, his chest expanding as he took a deep breath.

Then I arched my back, pressing myself against him. And we were off, moving with a frantic need, like we would never get enough of this giddy weightlessness we felt when we were together. He rolled over onto his back, bringing me with him. I sat up, straddling him, and circled my hips with his cock planted firmly inside me. His hands shot out and grabbed my waist, driving me down onto him in a relentless rhythm until we were both gasping and ready to explode.

We'd known each other a week, but we were already intimately familiar with each other's bodies. I could tell that he was getting close, and he could tell the same about me.

Every stroke was electrified, the sensation incredible as he stretched me around his thick shaft, bucking up to meet me every time he pulled me down.

We locked eyes, our mouths open in mutual awe as the tidal wave rose up and dragged us under.

5.
Lola

My first full day at the arena was the following Monday. I'd lingered at Will's house through Saturday, meaning to go home that night, but then he'd convinced me to stay until Sunday morning. I tried to sneak out at dawn because I had a lot of work to do to get ready for my first day on the job, but Will caught me and held me hostage with the fluffiest pancakes I'd ever eaten. Then he bent me over the kitchen table for another hard, fast fuck before he sent me home with his come leaking into my panties.

When I walked through the door, Hope glanced up from the couch, where she was curled in a ball with her nose buried in a thick book. She gave me a wry smile that didn't quite meet her eyes, but I refused to feel guilty. Hope may want me to marry her brother so that we could be sisters-in-law and best friends forever and all that. But the first time he'd seen me in five years, Reid Wright had looked at me like I was something disgusting he'd discovered on the bottom of his shoe.

Hope might be holding her breath for a reconciliation, but I wasn't. I had a hunky coach to keep my mind and body occupied, and I felt no shame about the earth-shaking orgasms I was receiving from him on a daily basis.

I had a minuscule office at the arena. I was pretty sure was just a repurposed broom closet. Next door was a slightly larger room where I'd set up my table, a stereo to play plinking spa music, and a collection of incense burners and candles. I probably wouldn't ever actually light them, but they gave the room a heady, floral scent that was just right. Pleasant, but not overpowering. Their main benefit was that they somewhat masked the odor of stale socks that eked out of the locker room and permeated the entire building.

Along with hiring me and sending down some problematic but powerful players from the Prospectors, the team's owner had also launched a renovation project. Fresh paint, new carpet, a revamped dining hall menu, and updated dorms. Mr. Branson was really throwing his weight—and by weight, of course, I mean money—behind the Ice Hawks, giving them an honest, fighting chance to redeem themselves after the last few abysmal seasons. He seemed to have faith that they could turn around their streak of bad luck. I tried to use his faith to shore up my own, because I was dreading the thought of moving to yet another new city next year if the team folded.

But I couldn't worry about the future now. I was holding open office hours for the first time today, and I needed to be fully present. Anyone on the team could come in for a quick massage, let me get a good look at their trouble spots, and we'd work out a course of treatment together that would fit into their schedule. The therapy was optional, but I assumed that all of the guys would want to take advantage of the perk.

Ten o'clock rolled around, and my door still had not been darkened a single player.

At least Hope had thawed out a bit by dinnertime the previous evening. We could both be overly sensitive, but our friendship always outweighed our petty grievances in the end.

I glanced at my phone screen to see that I'd missed a message from her—her cartoon avatar holding a banner that said GOOD LUCK! I smiled, firing back prayer hands in response. I would wait until I saw her to complain about the entire team giving me the cold shoulder.

Switching to my music app, I scrolled idly through the playlist I'd made with the most relaxing music I could find. Nature sounds laid over flutes and ringing harps, the reedy whistle of a recorder lilting underneath gentle tantric chanting. I turned up the volume on my phone, hoping that the strange sounds would draw someone in.

Like magic, a knock sounded at my door. I glanced up to see a large, burly man hovering in the doorway. He flashed me a charming smile, and I saw that he was missing his front teeth.

"Are you Ms. Rey?" he asked. "The massage therapist?" He hadn't used the word *masseuse*, and just for that, I liked him already. I gave him a smile of my own.

"That's me," I said. "You can call me Lola. Come on in."

The big man sidled into the room.

"Lars Skinner," he said. "Third line."

"Nice to meet you, Lars," I said, repeating his name a few more times in my head for good measure as I smiled up at him. I was a long way from having memorized the names of every player, but now that I had his broad, sweet face to connect to his name, I wouldn't forget about Lars any time soon.

I moved to the table, smoothing the sheet draped over it. I still wasn't sure exactly why he was here, but my hands were itching to get to work. "How can I help you?"

"Well," he took a hesitant step into the room. "My lower back goes out at the start of every season and what do you know?" He gave me a thin smile, closed-lipped this time. I could tell that this was his more common smile, the one he showed to the outside world to hide his missing teeth when he wasn't wearing a flipper.

"Hop up here and I'll take a look," I said, patting the padded table. "Just sit for now."

"Should I take off my shirt?" he asked shyly. I swallowed a laugh. I didn't want to make him more self-conscious than he already was, but he was downright endearing, like a giant kid.

"Shirt on and sitting. We'll start there and mix things up if we need to."

He nodded, looking relieved, and climbed onto the table. As he did so, he flinched like the motion had caused him discomfort.

"What's your pain level today?" I asked, standing behind him and palpitating his lower back gently with the tips of my fingers, pressing here and there, feeling for knots.

I didn't have to feel around for long. This guy was all tied up, his lower back a tangle of spasming muscle tissue.

"Four," he said with a shrug.

"Four?" I repeated skeptically. "By the feel of you, I'm surprised you're walking around on your own two feet and not laid out in a bed somewhere." Lars stilled, and I could practically hear the gears in his head turning as he weighed his options.

"Okay, maybe it's a six."

"I need you to be honest with me, Lars," I reprimanded him softly as I pressed with my thumbs on either side of his spine and stroked both up toward his shoulders. He grunted, relenting.

"It's a six as long as I'm sitting still and doing nothing."

"And if you're moving around?"

"Nfmp," he mumbled.

"I didn't catch that."

"Nine," he admitted at last.

"Well, that's quite a difference from four."

He was silent for a few seconds, long enough that I was afraid I'd offended him. I opened my mouth to clear the air, but then he spoke.

"I know I'm not a big-name player on the team or anything, but I don't want to get benched if I can help it. And it's really not that bad, most of the time."

"But right now, it is," I said. He didn't argue.

"Okay, shirt off and lay down with your face in the hole." He snorted, and I could tell that he'd only just stopped himself from making a dirty joke.

He did as I asked, settling himself face-down on the table. I ran my hands up and down his back, warming his skin and getting him used to my touch.

"Any music preference?" I asked. He hesitated. "Doesn't have to be hippie music."

Lars chuckled, then listed off a couple of heavy metal bands I'd heard of but hadn't ever listened to. Some massage therapists didn't like to use loud or high-tempo music, afraid that it would cause the client to tense up inadvertently. But I subscribed to a slightly different school of thought. I believed that a person's favorite music was the best choice. Playing Enya for a bunch of rough-neck minor-league hockey players probably wouldn't have the same relaxing effect it had on wealthy middle-aged housewives. So I added a dozen songs from the bands Lars had named to a playlist and hit shuffle.

The stuff really wasn't half-bad. I'd never been a big metalhead, but I could see the allure. The raw power and emotion, the passion behind the raspy, wailing voices. I couldn't help but wonder if some of the knots in Lars's neck were caused by head-banging.

As I worked, his body eased, loosening under my hands. When he was thoroughly warmed up, I started to dig in. He hissed, tensing up again, as I pressed forcefully with my thumbs against the biggest knot I'd found, just to the right of his spine.

"Breathe through the pain," I coached him, applying even more pressure until the tangle of tissue started to relax, the wad of tension dissolving under my touch. He forced out a shaky breath, and then another. Massage therapists, myself included, had brought bigger men than Lars to their knees with our freakishly strong, well-conditioned hands. A certain amount of force was necessary to break up knots as inflamed and tight as the one I was currently rubbing out of his lower back. I'd seen grown men weep on the massage table many times, both from the release of the emotions they'd been suppressing and also the relief from the low-level pain they'd been carrying around with them, doing their best to ignore with a stiff upper lip for months or even years.

I had a feeling that with Lars, we were talking decades. His rusty hair was salted at the temples, and despite his still-boyish face, he had faint lines around his eyes and mouth. He was one of the career minor leaguers who was dug in here and had no plans to leave. No major league aspirations. Some third- and fourth-liners had stepped down from brief stints in the show, and others never made it there. They'd bought houses in Casper, had families. They'd put down roots. If the team folded, they would be the ones in trouble. They had the most to lose.

A lot of people considered guys like Lars to be the least valuable members of a hockey team. But they're the foundational building blocks of a powerhouse franchise, reliable grinders, defensive muscle that could do some serious damage to the opposing team during their forty-five seconds on the ice. On the third and fourth lines, egos usually took a backseat to work ethic and team morale. This was in stark contrast to first and second-line players like Reid Wright and Nate "The Great" O'Ryan, who were fueled by blind ego, buckets of testosterone, and the poor judgment that came from being hit in the head a few too many times.

"Shhh—damn it!" Lars checked his language mid-outburst as he did the Worm on the massage table, trying desperately to get away from my elbows. But I just leaned in harder, applying the majority of my one hundred and forty pounds to the small of his back through the two blunt pressure points. This was the best method for breaking up a particularly stubborn knot, but I was starting to worry that I would have to strap Lars to the table to finish the session.

"Breathe, Lars," I said brightly, gritting my teeth and grinding my elbows in tiny circles over the big, angry knots that swirled like twin hurricanes on each side of his spine. He groaned weakly, going limp under me as the muscles in his lower back finally calmed and smoothed out. I knew that he was feeling the heat now, all of that stored energy dumping into his bloodstream.

Deep tissue massage was painful and difficult, and twenty minutes was more than enough to get Lars started down the road to recovery.

When I was finished, and he was a formless ball of putty on the table, I left him languishing in a delicious, achy, post-massage bliss as I went to the freezer in the break room and pulled out two long, narrow gel ice packs. There were at least a dozen stacked along the top shelf, ready for injured players and overworked muscles.

I wrapped the packs in thin cloth and carried them back to my studio, where I laid them vertically down Lars's back, framing his spinal column. Then, I left him alone again with his favorite music for ten minutes of cold therapy. The type of massage I'd used on Lars could cause some serious next-day soreness, so much so that some clients felt like they were just trading one agony for another. But it would hurt less with time, and the benefits would be enormous.

At the end of our session, I suggested a core-strengthening workout for him to do every day, gave him a printout of gentle lower-back stretches to try, and sent him along with a skip in his step, looking a thousand pounds lighter.

A few minutes later, as I was gathering my things to go to lunch, another knock sounded at the door. I turned, and my soul momentarily left my body when I found myself staring into the deep, dark eyes of Nate O'Ryan.

Though football was more my sport, I'd grown up around hockey, plus I always kept an ear out for news about Reid. So, even before my research, I'd heard of Nate the Great. He'd already led the Prospectors to two Stanley Cup victories before Mr. Branson kicked him back to the minor league for what sounded like a *much*-needed attitude adjustment.

But if I was being completely honest, standing alone in that cramped space with him, I could kind of understand why he thought he was the king of the world. He was so hot it was like his entire body had been digitally blurred and resized into some perfect action-figure version of a human being. He was tall with broad shoulders and a tapered waist, countless rows of abdominal muscles narrowing into a sharp V that disappeared under his towel. Which, as far as I could see, was all he wore.

He looked like a fairytale prince, with thick forearms and a thicker swoop of black hair that hung over his brow into his eyes. His granite jaw was dark with five o'clock shadow, and his pouty lips, currently curling into a wicked little grin, were so fucking kissable I was afraid I would drop dead on the spot if I didn't taste them.

You should *taste them. Throw yourself at him right now. Tear that towel off his body and go to town!*

I begged my inner voice to shut the fuck up.

"Nathan, right?" I asked, breaking the silence that had gone on so long it had become awkward. He nodded, raising his thumb to brush it back and forth across his bottom lip as he looked me up and down. I was wearing a black athletic-fit crop top and high-waisted leggings that hid my small stomach pooch and accentuated my curvy hips. My long blonde hair was tied back in a high pony that brushed against the small of my back. I knew I was attractive, but I also knew that guys like Nate the Great were more interested in quantity than quality. I'd heard some mind-boggling body counts for professional hockey players. "I'm Lola."

"I know who you are," he said with another quirk of his lips. He stepped into the room and closed the door behind him, his eyes never leaving my body. I knew I should be annoyed, maybe even pissed, but for some reason, heat was spreading between my legs as he watched me like a jungle cat stalking its prey.

"Are you here for massage therapy?" I asked lamely. This guy was so handsome my throat was about to close up. When he shut the door, he'd sucked all of the air out of the room.

I seriously needed to get a grip.

On that dick.

Please. Shut. The fuck. Up!!

He crossed his arms over his chest and smirked at me.

As hot as he was, I could already see a glimpse of what people meant when they said he had an attitude problem. He acted like he was in on some joke, like he knew some secret about me. But then again, maybe that was just his face. He could have played the role of the villain as well as he could play the prince. There was something dangerous simmering under his beauty, something I couldn't put my finger on just yet.

"Yeah, I'd take a massage," he said at last, smiling at me with the corner of his mouth. I gestured to the table and then rocketed my eyes to the ceiling when he dropped his towel. He sauntered forward, big dick swinging between his legs, and…God help me, I'll admit it.

I peeked.

"Um," I said, walking around the far side of the table to pick up his towel as he lowered himself facedown onto the fresh sheet, putting his tan, peachy ass proudly on display. My mouth went dry. What I meant to say was, "I think you dropped this."

I'm really not sure what came out instead. Something along the lines of, "Dropped, you think?"

What??

It doesn't matter! For the love of God, cover the man before you climb him like a tree and get fired on your first day. But earmark that memory for later…

Face flaming pink, I pinched the towel, shook it out, and draped it over his backside.

"It does no harm to look," Nate said, his voice slightly muffled by the cushion supporting his face.

"Well, you don't need to be nude for our sessions together. Athletic shorts are fine."

"And if I want to be nude for our sessions together?" he asked. I could hear the lilt of a laugh in his voice. I shook my hands and then dipped them in oil and rubbed them together. I brushed them lightly down his back, feeling for knots as I considered his question.

"You can't always get what you want," was what I landed on. "Wear shorts next time."

He pushed up on his elbows with a huff, tossing a dark look at me over his shoulder. The muscles in his back stood out, winding and twisting under his olive skin. I let myself enjoy the feel of him even as I rolled my eyes, matching his annoyance with a healthy dose of my own.

I planted a hand between his shoulder blades and pushed him down flat on his stomach, then slid it up his spine into his hair to hold his head in place on the cushion, his face firmly planted in the hole. He didn't say anything, didn't resist me. Just let me hold him there.

After a couple of seconds, I let go, tracing both of my hands back down his spine, probing and pushing, searching for problem areas. Nate the Great had me all flustered, and though I'd been touching him for several minutes now, I had no idea whether I'd felt any knots.

"There aren't a lot of girls who would complain about getting a free show from a guy like me," he muttered after a couple of minutes of silence.

I almost laughed out loud. I couldn't believe he actually just came right out and said it like that. I knew most hockey players, especially big shots, felt this way. Of course they did. But I'd never seen one pull the *Do you know who I am?* card so shamelessly.

Welcome to the big leagues, where the dicks are big and the egos are huuuuge.

I dug my thumbs in at the base of his spine, just above the pelvic bowl. Almost everyone who wasn't a newborn baby carried stress and tension right…there. He groaned and shifted, lifting his hips up a bit and then laying down flat again.

"I'm not a puck bunny, Nate. And I don't give happy endings, if that's why you came in here. I'm a massage therapist." I replaced my thumbs with my elbows, walking them up either side of his spine as he groaned. "This isn't the spa. It's not a parlor. So be assured, if in the future I need you to disrobe, I'll let you know. Otherwise, keep your shorts on. Understand?"

"Fuck! Yes!" he shouted, twisting away from me. I planted my elbows in the small of his back and held him in place.

I wasn't applying any more pressure than I would have otherwise, nowhere near as much as I'd given Lars. But this time, I did get a bit of a vicious thrill when Nathan squirmed under me.

I straightened up, giving him a brief reprieve as I walked around the end of the table to work on his shoulders. As I reached down, his hand shot out and closed around my wrist. When I tried to pull away, he rolled up onto his side and raised his eyebrows. His cock was fully erect and pointing at me.

"You're telling me you don't want to touch it?" he asked with another smug smirk. "Not even a little bit?" He thrust his hips at me, and this time I did laugh. Caught off guard, his grip loosened, and I jerked my arm free.

"If I can still see your dick in three seconds, I'm calling security," I said, stepping away from the table and crossing my arms over my chest. He stared at me for a beat and then scoffed and sat up, pulling his towel over his lap. Fully covered, he held his hands up in a defensive gesture.

"All right, damn. I'm sorry. Boldness usually works."

"Just because it gets you laid doesn't mean it's okay," I countered flatly, cocking an eyebrow. He had the decency to duck his head. Maybe he wasn't a completely lost cause after all.

But attitude adjustment was an understatement for what Nate needed. He needed a personality transplant. It was a crying shame for that divine physical form to go to waste on an arrogant jerk.

He slid off the table, securing the towel around his waist as he straightened up to his full, considerable height. He gave me another dark look, then turned on his heel and stalked to the door.

Swinging it open, he screeched to a sudden halt. His eyes were fixed on something I couldn't see. I watched his face in profile as his gaze dropped down and meandered back up. Then he grinned that shit-eating grin, adjusted his towel in an obvious way, and ambled off in the opposite direction.

A second later, Reid stepped into the doorway, leaning his arm against the top of the jamb and looking at me with those stormy eyes. A muscle in his jaw was twitching. He shot a poisonous look at Nate's retreating back, and then he stepped inside and closed the door.

"Do I have to take my pants off?" he quipped. He wasn't smiling, but he wasn't anywhere near as hostile as he had been on Friday, either.

"You need a massage?"

"Hey, if somebody's giving out free massages, sign me up," he said with a noncommittal shrug. His surfer boy hair was tousled like he'd just come in from the beach. We were more than a thousand miles from any ocean. But the wind on the plains could be twice as strong.

I was gripped by the urge to reach up and smooth it away from his face. My thighs clenched together reflexively.

I cleared my throat.

"Are you having any particular problems?" I asked, fighting to keep my voice steady. Emotions warred in my chest. I hated him, and I wanted him.

I may even still love him. Was it possible to love one person your whole life?

I'd never believed in that sort of thing, but with Reid standing in front of me, I realized that I'd only buried my feelings for him. I hadn't killed them. Not by a long shot.

"Just the usual stuff. Stiffness, low back pain, a crick in my neck every other week."

He'd always been the type to downplay his aches and pains. A trait shared by most hockey players.

"Uh…just let me just change the sheet and clean the bed since Nate had his dick out." I jerked the linen off the table and then picked up the spray bottle of cleaning solution and a rag. Reid made a strangled sound behind me. I looked back to see that his face was completely red.

"Nate…had his…dick out…" It wasn't a question. I nodded, pulling a disgusted face. His dick may not have been gross, but his behavior was.

Reid spun on his heel and grabbed the door's knob, wrenching it open so hard he nearly ripped it off the hinges.

"Reid!" I gasped, surprised. "What are you doing?"

"I'm going to break that fucking weasel's neck," he said, bolting out into the hallway. I chased after him, grabbing his wrist and digging my heels in to stop him. I didn't even slow him down. He'd pulled me halfway down the hall before he realized that I was still hanging onto his arm.

"What are you doing?" I whispered frantically. "Come back!" He continued to pull against me for a second. Then he went still, threw my hand off, and stalked back into the studio.

"Did you tell him to…?" he started, rounding on me as I came in behind him and closed us in again with a quiet click.

I put my hands on my hips and leveled Reid with a frosty glare.

"Do you really think I asked Nate the Great to take his dick out… what, so I could give it a rub down?"

He snorted without humor.

"You and Coach seem awfully friendly," he said, giving me whiplash with his sudden segue. His face was unreadable as he waited for my response. All of a sudden, my heart was pounding in my ears. I was somehow cold and sweaty at the same time.

Were we that obvious? Our chemistry was off the charts, sure, but I thought we were hiding it well enough to avoid attention.

"And?" I asked casually, refusing to blink. I was determined to win our impromptu staring match. "Do you need a massage, or are you just here to berate me about my hypothetical love life? Which, by the way, is exactly none of your business."

Reid narrowed his eyes and then looked down, shaking his head. I wanted to scream and rage and beat my fists against his chest.

I'd known this big, hard man when he was a soft little boy who loved to catch turtles and then set them free, who teased his little sister but also watched after her like a hawk.

Who held me one summer under the stars every single night and whispered in my ear about all the things that we would do together once we got out of this town, once we were free to be ourselves out in the world.

The life we would have, the two of us.

Empty words.

My heart gave a wretch, a groan of pain.

I slammed the door on it then, and locked it away in its well-guarded tower far out of Reid's reach.

The only problem with that plan was that he had carved his name into the soft, bleeding tissue long before that summer when we lay naked and all tangled up in the bed of his pickup truck, him pointing out and naming the constellations that spun over us as I nibbled gently on the lobe of his ear.

The Reid Wright who had claimed my heart as his own was a little boy, knobby knees poking out of his cut-off jeans, helping me hop across the big river rocks to the other side of the creek.

6.
Reid

My heart was kicking like a jackrabbit against my ribs, fighting to get free of my body and fling itself at her feet.

Lola Rey was my everything. She always had been. When there were hundreds of miles between us, I could ignore the ache. I could file her away with all my other warm and fuzzy childhood memories. But now that she was standing here in front of me, even the *thought* that she might be letting some other man touch her made me want to burn the whole goddamn arena to the ground.

It was taking everything I had to stay where I was, not to cross the room in two strides and pull her hard against my chest, force her head back, and kiss her until she gave me everything. My everything.

My Lola.

"Didn't you tell me to stay away from you?" she asked with a dangerous glint in her eye. "That's what I've been doing. So why are you here?"

"Because my neck is all tight," I grumbled.

A lie.

I was there to see her. To have her put her hands on my body.

I knew I was playing with fire. I wanted to get burned. Maybe she could bring me back to life after all these years that I'd spent floating around like a zombie, living the life of a college hockey star, playing my part, blowing through puck bunnies but never being able to forget her or truly move on.

I was the one who blocked her and left town, so I figured I'd done my level best. But I could see now that I'd just been hitting snooze on an alarm that wasn't going to stop ringing until I woke the hell up.

She lowered the massage table a few notches and waved a hand toward it.

"Have a seat," she said without looking at me, her tone business-like. I wanted to scream. I always fucked everything up.

She was right to ask. Why *had* I come here? Did I even know? Was it to confront her and demand answers? Beg her to take me back? Piss a boundary line around her office to make sure the rest of the guys on the team knew that she was *mine*?

Yeah, that would go over really well.

Seeing no other option, having backed myself into this corner, I sat down on the padded table and stared straight ahead at the wall as she stepped up behind me. At first, she didn't touch me, didn't move. She just stood there. I was going crazy, not being able to see her face, but I refused to look back.

After several more agonizing seconds, I felt her fingertips brushing lightly over my shoulders. Even though the material of my T-shirt, I could feel the electricity in her skin.

She was sending out signals in a language only my body could understand.

7.
Lola

The first few weeks of the season were a whirlwind.

I was locking down the names of all the guys on the team and had even mastered a few of their nicknames. They called out appreciatively when I came into the locker room or when I got on the bus for an away game.

Reid was giving me a wide berth, and I wished Nate would do the same. But he'd kept up the smirks and the hooded glances, and the comments muttered under his breath to his friends, the three slick guys who had flown in with him. One was Dallas "The Tank" Cash, an injured goalie who kept to himself but hung around in the shadow of his fellow exiled Prospector teammate. Xander "Xaddy" Bardi was the definition of tall, dark, and handsome, but I wasn't sure he was even of legal drinking age yet. He was the youngest member on the team by far, a rookie draft recruit here to spend his first year in development playing defense for the Ice Hawks before he shot straight to the major league and took the world by storm.

That was his plan, anyway. Nothing got him down. He kept his chin up and an unbothered smile on his face, even when he was brawling. And he was an absolute dynamo on the ice. Occasionally I caught him smoldering in my direction, but we hadn't had much contact beyond that.

Erik "Moose" Bouchard was another new recruit and a powerful wingman. His nickname served him. He was as big as Dallas but a little bit younger. He had a sort of clumsy, ambling gait on land, but once he hit the ice, he defied gravity. He was fast and agile, zipping back and forth in a blur from one net to the other, circling, driving the puck into the goal alongside Nate, who was our new star center.

The four of them stuck together and kept to themselves for the most part, sitting at their own table in the dining hall on the rare occasions when they actually ate there. All but Dallas went to a gym downtown instead of using the dusty, outdated equipment in the workout room.

I'd heard that Mr. Branson had plans to revolutionize the team gym and put assistant coach Huck Hart in charge of training the guys. But the renovations were coming along slowly, one big game of telephone between the contractors up here in Casper and Mr. Branson's secretary in Denver.

So, for the time being, our team was split down the middle. That much was obvious the second they skated into the rink. There was no cohesion, no unity or harmony, between the first line and the rest of the team. In fact, there was outright animosity roiling around, ready to erupt into a shouting match at any given moment, especially when Nate and Reid were on the ice together.

Though Reid hadn't been back for another massage and wouldn't give me the time of day, I still had the sense that he was guarding me like an overprotective dog. Most of all from Nate. And Nate seemed to get off on teasing him by flirting with me, though in reality, we couldn't stand each other.

Despite our shared animosity, he still came in for a massage at least three times a week. He wore his shorts and minded his manners, but there was something molten hot between us that was undeniable, and every time I touched him, it was harder to remember why I shouldn't give into his cocky fuck-boy charms and let him use me.

Will and I hadn't discussed being exclusive. As much as I enjoyed spending time with him, I wasn't in a hurry to tie myself down to any one man. Would it be worth it to fool around with Nate, to make Reid jealous? Or was it a bad idea to poke the bear?

I was always wet by the time I finished massaging the star center, but then he'd make some rude comment on his way out, and I would have to fight off the urge to slam the door behind him.

It was confusing, to say the least.

At least Lars was making significant progress. He smiled and nodded and told me that he was feeling much better, rolling in and out of bed like a young man, logging up to three miles a day on the treadmill. He was proud, I could tell. But his mood also seemed darker every time I saw him. As I was working the knots out of his lower back, more were forming in his neck and shoulders.

Tension and stress.

I wanted to pry, try to find out if something was wrong in his personal life, but I knew it wasn't my place. I wasn't the team shrink.

I told Will everything. We met in his office every night for a debriefing that usually ended in a steamy make-out session and sometimes escalated to sex on his cluttered desk or in his chair. When I knew he'd had a particularly rough day, I would kneel at his feet and suck him slowly, gently. I'd run my hands up and down his thighs as I nursed the tip of his cock, staring into his dark green eyes, holding his gaze as I took him deeper and deeper. I delighted in watching the worry fade from his brow as bliss took over.

It felt good to do my part, even if I could only lift his burden for a few minutes. He would cup my head in his big hand, stroking my hair with his thumb, but I could always feel it when he came back down into his body and started to close himself off. I knew he felt guilty for letting this continue when I could be fired, and he'd told me that he sometimes felt like a dirty old man with a twenty-three-year-old on her knees for him.

He was forty with the chiseled body of a lifelong athlete. He had crow's feet, sure, but an old man he was not. When he called himself that, I laughed, but a cloud passed over his face. He wasn't in the mood for jokes.

I straddled his lap and pressed my palm to his cheek.

"You're not old. And you're not any dirtier than I am," I said with a grin. I braced my knees in the chair on either side of his hips and nestled my pussy against the bulge in his khakis.

Will tightened his jaw and then let out a rush of air, surrendering. He grabbed my hips and pulled me down hard against him.

"I don't know about that. You're pretty fucking dirty."

I leaned in until my lips were brushing his.

"Let's get each other filthy, then," I whispered into his mouth before I covered it with mine.

His cock throbbed through the thin material of his pants, and his grip on my waist tightened as our tongues danced.

After a breathless minute, he broke the kiss and leaned back in his chair, lacing his hands together behind his head and nodding down at his lap.

"Well, then," he said evenly, his face a mask. "You know what to do."

My whole body pulsed as I slipped out of his lap and landed on the floor between his feet.

"This is what makes you feel like a dirty old man?" I asked innocently, widening my eyes and batting my lashes at him. He clenched his jaw and gave me a single nod. Biting my lip, I dropped my eyes to my hands as I worked to free his cock from his pants. As soon as my fingers closed around it, he shuddered and moaned. I felt his restraint snap.

"You want Daddy's cock, baby?" he asked in a rough, raw voice. His dick jumped in my fist. He said that it made him feel like a lech, casually fucking a girl so much younger than him. His employee. But here was the truth, in the palm of my hand.

He liked it.

He wanted to play Daddy.

The thought had me gushing. I nodded, too, an understanding passing between us. Then I flicked my tongue out against the tip. The muscle in his jaw jumped, and his hand came up to grip my ponytail, wrapping it once around his fist, then once more. He had me on a short leash now and could steer my head exactly where he wanted it to go.

"Tell me," he said quietly, his eyes turned to embers as he stared at my mouth.

"I want to suck your cock, Daddy." He squeezed his eyes shut, bending over me like I'd punched him in the stomach. A second later, he straightened up and guided me forward without another word. I opened wide to take him down my throat.

He grunted, applying firm pressure until his big cock squeezed through the barrier and he was in. Fucking my throat. Tears stung my eyes, but I'd already become a pro at pleasing him.

I really enjoyed giving head. I gave so much in college that I could have minored in it. A masseuse with a minor in fellatio. The jokes wrote themselves.

I'd decided to make Will my pet project. I could see in his eyes how defeated he was from the moment we met. He was tired, and he wanted to give up. On these guys, on this team. But I wasn't going to let that happen. I was going to remind him exactly who he was. And if *who he was* was a dirty old man who wanted to be my Daddy dom…well then, we were both winning.

"Lola," he moaned. He used his grip on my ponytail to pull me off of him, tilting my face back so his eyes were boring down into mine. "Tell me you want my come."

"I want your come, Daddy," I said softly, holding his gaze. I wanted him to see on my face just how badly I wanted him.

"You're gonna get it," he said gruffly. "But you're going to sit on my cock first. I need to feel that tight little pussy."

He released me, and I stood up. He rested his hands on my hips as I ran my fingers through his hair. I leaned down and kissed him deeply, my tongue swirling around his.

Then I reached under my skirt, pulled down my panties, and held them out to him.

He stared, stunned, for a second, and then he took them from me, slipping the delicate lace into his pocket. I climbed into his lap again, straddling him, and he reached down between us to guide his cock inside me.

I gasped at the size as usual, my head falling forward onto his shoulder as he settled me down in his lap, filling me with every inch of him. I clenched around him and his fingertips sank into my soft love handles as he held me down on his length. Then his hands skated up, tracing the dramatic curve of my back. He took one of my nipples into his mouth, sucking it firmly for a few seconds before moving to the next one. I bucked against him, already panting.

Will just knew how to take me there.

I could only assume that, like all hockey big shots, he'd been with an unmentionable amount of women. I sent up a silent thank-you to them for everything they'd taught him that he was putting to good use here, now, with me.

I knew that our situation could only be temporary, that the more we did this, the more we put ourselves in danger of not being able to pull away from each other when we needed to. But I also knew that I wouldn't ever be able to bring myself to pull away. I couldn't break his grip on me. He would have to be the one to let go.

And he might, once he'd fully grasped the details of my preferred lifestyle.

I wanted to soak in every second with him while I still had him.

"God, Lola, baby you feel so good," Will groaned, sliding one hand up to cup the back of my head, holding me against his shoulder while his other raised my hips up and drove them back down. Soon I was matching the rhythm on my own, bouncing on his length, taking all of him with every downward stroke. He dropped his head back and closed his eyes, his Adam's apple working in his beautiful throat. I pressed my lips to it, and then to the spot where I could feel his pulse jumping. Both hands drifted down to grip my ass now. They pushed me down harder, harder.

He sat up and captured my lips with his, plunging his tongue into my mouth as he held me in his lap, impaled. When I squirmed against him, he gave my bare ass a sharp slap. I yelped and then bit my lips together.

"Sit still and take it, baby," he whispered teasingly.

"Yes, Daddy," I murmured. At that, his hand closed into a fist around my ass cheek, squeezing until I whimpered and then landing three more slaps in rapid succession. My jaw dropped as my pussy surged and clenched around him.

"Does my dirty girl need a spanking?" he asked just as quietly, moving his lips to my ear as he held my head against his chest. I knew that I wasn't supposed to move, but the answer to his question was a resounding yes. So instead of giving him what he wanted, I wiggled my hips again, bouncing a little, forcing his dick deeper inside me.

"I'm going to take that as a yes," he said dryly, and then he connected another slap with my stinging ass cheek. "Who does your pussy belong to?"

"It's yours, Daddy," I gasped. His hand tightened on my ass again while his other moved between us, his big thumb brushing up and down over my clit.

"Then come for me, Lola."

I opened my mouth to respond, but he'd knocked the air out of my lungs with his entire length buried inside me and his expert thumb thrumming my button, pushing me closer and closer.

He closed his mouth around my nipples again, sucking gently, then harder, and then he used his grip on my ass to rock me slowly back and forth in his lap, rubbing his thick cock against my inner walls, nudging me toward the edge.

"Are you there, baby?" he panted.

"Yes, Daddy," I whimpered.

"That's my good girl. Come all over Daddy's big cock."

His words splintered me. They were somehow both unbelievably sexy and deeply comforting at the same time. I felt the bond between us open wide as he applied a bit more pressure to my clit and sent me hurting straight over the cliff.

"God, yes, there it is," he hissed as I tightened around him and cried out. "Goddamn it, Lola, you feel so fucking incredible. I'm about to pump you full."

"Give me your come, Daddy," I begged. "Please!" Fisting my hands in his hair, I held his face between my breasts as he let out a strangled yell, and warmth spread through me as he gave me what I'd asked for.

When we were finished, we stayed like that for a long time, his cock softening inside me, my head on his chest, cradled in his big, reassuring hands. He dropped soft kisses into my hair, and I wanted to stay right there in his arms for the rest of time.

8.
Nate

"You really think she's ever going to give you the time of day, man?" Dallas asked, shifting the heating pad under his back. He was laid up on the couch, grouchy, speed-flipping through a hundred and forty channels of daytime cable.

Tanker had tried to get back on the ice for a practice skate, and his back had immediately gone into spasm, landing him on his ass on the sofa where he had now been for three days. He smelled stale and had a shitty disposition. But he was my buddy, and I wasn't about to abandon him in his hour of need.

His words might have stung if I didn't have one hundred percent absolute certainty that Lola Rey, sports massage therapist extraordinaire and absolutely scrumptious piece of ass, would give it up to me. And soon. There was simply no other possibility. She was the yummiest snack I'd seen in a while, and I wasn't about to let all that body go to waste sucking the coach's cock and wiping his tears.

She may not realize it yet, but she wanted me, too. I'd been with enough women to be able to feel the heat from a mile away when a woman wanted me. And she did. So what if she also hated me?

That was all right. I could work with that. I didn't need her to fall in love. I didn't *want* her to.

I just needed her to spread her legs for me, beg me for my cock, and then run and tell her friend with the righteous flow and the simmering rage all the gruesome details.

I smirked to myself, imagining how that stupid cowboy's face would turn beet red again like it did when I left the massage room in a towel that first day.

It was obvious to the entire world that he was in love with Lola, which made her a perfect tool to use against him.

She'd been playing hard to get so far, but I knew it was just a matter of time until she gave in to me, the way all women did when I set my sights on them. I didn't mind a challenge.

Quite the contrary.

The door of our condo banged open, and Xander and Eric came stumbling in, carrying three pizzas and cutting up with each other about something. It was the end of the week, cheat day, and these three would be stuffing their gullets all night. But I didn't take many days off. Not anymore.

I'd done what I thought was right, what was best for me, back in Denver. I'm not a quitter. But I'm not one to follow a fool, either. And *fool* was exactly how I would describe the Prospector's head coach.

He didn't like being questioned or called on his bullshit, so he'd banished me. Shipped me up here to Moosefuck, Wyoming, and now I had to make nice with the townies and take chirps from minor-league talent while I buckled down and tried to scrape my way back into my old position. I wanted my old paycheck and the respect that I used to get on the ice.

These guys thought they knew me, thought they had me pegged as some spoiled kid with a snotty attitude, but they were in for a big fucking surprise. I was about to take this team in hand and turn it around myself, drive it right back up out of the ditch. Something Reid Wright had failed to do. How he was ever named captain of the team was a fucking mystery to me. But it didn't matter. He may be captain, but I was the one steering the ship.

I'd leave the Ice Hawks better than I found them, and show everyone exactly why I belonged in the major league.

Getting under Cowboy's skin was just an added bonus.

9.
Will

"I don't want to hear *try*, Will," Branson's crackly voice said over my phone's speaker. I stared at the ceiling, my fingers steepled in front of me, searching for my last shred of patience and coming up empty. "The team's a mess! Six losses already this season, and we're just getting started. I need turn around, and I need it now. I need fans in those stands. Print flyers if you have to, I don't care. Just do whatever needs to be done to make the community and the region give even half a shit about this team because that's the only way it stays viable. Got it?"

"Yeah, I got it," I said, swallowing a string of choice words that would have only put me farther outside the owner's good graces.

He was right that the team was mixing like oil and water, distracting each other on the ice more than the opponents ever could, hogging the puck and refusing to pass it between the old guard and the new. Maybe I'd fucked up when I put all the new guys, even the rookies, on the first line. But Branson had been out for Reid Wright's blood, and I was doing my best to spare him. "We'll do some team building, I'm on it. Anything else?"

"Oh, I'm sorry. Am I keeping you from something important?" His tone was acidic. He could be a major asshole when he wanted to be. And I suppose when you'd dropped a couple million dollars trying to revive a floundering development team, you had the right to be an asshole to the guy who was standing in the way of progress. As I sat there listening to him chew me out, I entertained the thought of quitting for the hundredth time, at least. Maybe I really was the problem. Being a strong player didn't always translate to being a strong coach.

"No," I said, keeping my voice even. But just then, Lola opened the door and stuck her head inside, raising her eyebrows at me. I waved her in, picking the phone's receiver up off the cradle so she wouldn't have to listen in if Branson decided to go for another round reaming me. I got it. I'd failed as a coach. He'd trusted me with the team, and we'd been crashing and burning ever since. "I'm sorry."

Lola's eyes searched my face, and try as I might to keep it straight, I could see in her eyes that she sensed my stress. Of course she did. She was like a human mood ring. I'd never met someone so good at picking up on *vibes*.

"Just make it work, Manners," Branson snapped. "Your ass is on the line."

With a click, the call was over. The prick hung up on me.

I opened my arms as Lola dropped into my lap, catching her easily.

"Everything okay?" she asked. I managed a tight smile.

"Yeah, that was just Branson chewing my ass for the way the season's going so far," I said, and then I shrugged. When she was here, the rest of it wasn't important. Plus, it wasn't like I needed this job. I'd made enough money in the major league to spend the rest of my days lounging in a hammock, except that I knew I would go crazy in about a week and a half with nothing to occupy my time or my mind. I looped my arms around Lola's waist, nestling my chin into the top of her head and holding her tight against me.

She tipped her head back to look up at me, and I pressed my lips to hers.

"What does he want us to do about it?" she said when we came up for air. *Us*. Nobody had lumped themselves in with me in a long time.

"Well, I *could* be doing more team building. Guess I've just been a little distracted lately." I flashed what I hoped was a charming smile and tightened my grip on her. "I'm going to invite the guys out to Copper's tonight, on me, and I know that it would really boost morale if a certain sports massage therapist made an appearance." Her eyes unfocused like she was giving my request serious consideration.

"Can I bring someone?" she asked. I froze, turning to stone beneath her. Bring someone…like a date?

"Sure," I said, instead of any of the many questions that were bouncing off the inside of my skull.

10.
Lola

Copper's was a huge pool hall that had been in operation in Casper at least as long as I'd been alive. It was our version of a nightclub. Twenty tables spread out below the bar, people leaning against the wall, bending over to shoot and mingling with bottles of beer in their hands. Everyone looked to be between my age and Will's, which meant most of Casper's eligible dating pool could be found standing in this room.

My eyes scanned the floor until I saw our people crowded around three tables by the back wall.

I turned to Hope, who had an amused look on her face.

"Thank you for doing this," I shouted over the thumping bass of the stereo. She flashed me a smile.

"Of course," she said. But I knew this wasn't her kind of scene. She was twenty-five, and single, and drop-dead gorgeous, but for some reason, her idea of a killer Saturday night was to curl up in a pair of fuzzy pajamas with a romantic comedy—book or film, she wasn't fussy. We'd joked since high school that we were old biddies trapped in girls' bodies. I'd blossomed in my own right since then and learned to embrace my wild side, but I couldn't say the same for Hope. I didn't know much about her time at culinary school, but it seemed she'd done enough partying for a lifetime during those two years.

Still, she strapped on a pair of high heels and a tight dress and joined me. I knew we made an eye-catching pair, her willowy and slim, me petite and bombshell curvy in my black tube top, shin-length pencil skirt, and chunky boots.

Heads turned to watch us as we made our way across the pool hall. I'd already locked eyes with Will, and he was drawing me right to him like a tractor beam.

"Whoa, you and Coach are about to set the place on fire with those smoldering looks," Hope said in my ear. I forced myself to look away from him, blushing.

No matter how discreet we'd tried to be, our relationship was clearly the talk of the town. We might as well be wearing matching scarlet letters.

I could still feel his eyes on me as I said hello to some of the third and fourth-line guys, several of whom had brought their wives. I saw Lars and waved, and he raised his beer in my direction. A pale woman sat behind him, looking terminally bored. Her eyes slid over me before darting away.

Three games were in progress. Just like on the ice, the division here was obvious. Second-line winger James Larsson, Huck Hart, and Will were playing on the table farthest from us. The career minor-league guys were playing on the table we reached first. And in the middle were the new guys. Nate, Dallas, Xander, and Eric were loud and flashy at the center table.

Well, Dallas was reserved, sitting when it wasn't his turn to shoot. He was nursing yet another back re-injury. He had yet to come in for a massage, though he was undoubtedly the person on the team who was most in need of regular treatments. I suspected that a large part of the reason Mr. Branson had hired me had been to tend to Dallas Cash and nurse him back into fighting shape so he could get back to defending the Prospectors' goal. Maybe I could bend his ear tonight and persuade him to at least let me take a look.

My eyes drifted back over to the far table. The voice in my head was screaming at me to get over there, to just let Will take me in front of everyone right here and now and get it over with. I had nothing to hide, if everyone already knew.

Luckily, the sane part of my brain still held more sway. But I let myself look.

Will was leaning against the wall, dangling a beer bottle between his fingers. He was wearing jeans, scuffed cowboy boots, and a short-sleeved black button-up with the first two undone. Ordinarily, I found cowboy boots obnoxious, but in Wyoming, they were as common as sneakers. Here in the wasteland, cowboy boots were "going-out shoes" for a lot of men.

Will's electric green eyes were pinned on me, hadn't left me since I walked into the bar. I met them again, letting the fire between us rage for just a second.

Then I forced my eyes away. Reid was leaned over, taking his shot at the eight ball while Jamie, a tall, stocky redhead with a thick neck to match his bulging biceps, watched on over his shoulder.

Huck was perched on a bar stool beside Will, swirling ice in a tumbler as he watched Reid take his shot. His face, as usual, was dark and guarded. A closed book. His body language and everything about his energy screamed for the world to fuck right off.

Remembering what I'd read about his accident, how he was in the hospital for weeks just learning to walk again, I felt a twinge of pity that probably would have infuriated him.

And yet here he was, the picture of health. You'd never know anything had happened, except for the fact that he was an assistant coach in the minor league instead of a world-famous goalie.

He was respected enough, known to hockey-heads who had been tuned in for a while. But he seemed content to fade away into obscurity here in America's least populated state. He certainly matched the role of the brooding cowboy.

But apparently that was Reid, his nickname on the team because he was from here. *Cowboy*. My eyes jumped back to him. He was taking forever to line up his shot. Was he just avoiding looking at me? Paranoia crept under my skin, but then he jerked his cue back and shot it forward, rocketing the little black ball into the pocket he'd indicated. He raised the stick over his head, holding it in both fists as Jamie shouted and jumped up and down, grabbing Reid around his waist and lifting his toes off the ground. I couldn't help but smile at their enthusiasm.

Then Reid saw me, and the grin melted off his face. His eyes went dark and cold, lingering on me for a second before they slid to Hope. He raised an eyebrow at her, then shook his head and turned his back on us both.

"Have you guys talked since…?"

"My little surprise gone awry? Yeah, not really except for a few monosyllabic text responses from him. And even those have dried up." She was talking to me but looking at her brother, her gray eyes narrowed. I was about to ask if she wanted to head back up to the bar for a drink, but then she was surging forward, grabbing Reid's elbow and yanking him off to the side, where they put their heads together and spoke in low tones for a second. Then they stepped back from each other, waving their hands, the conversation obviously heating up. I watched them nervously. Should I intervene? If I was the cause of all of this acrimony between them, could I possibly also be the solution?

Or would I just make everything worse?

"You made it." Will's rumbling voice, his lips not quite touching my ear. I'd first heard it less than a month ago, but now I'd know it anywhere. I turned to look up at him, fighting the urge to throw myself into his arms, to seek the comfort I knew only he could give. Instead, I forced a casual smile.

"Yeah, well, I haven't had much of a chance to get out and see the town since I arrived." I'd been working non-stop at the arena, trying to get things set up, and then I'd spend an hour at least in Will's office after I clocked out if I didn't just go home with him.

Part of the reason I wanted to bring Hope along was because we'd barely seen each other since I moved in. All I really wanted was another one of those fuzzy pajama nights on the couch, but Will's pull was too strong to ignore. He wanted me here, so here I was.

Daddy's good girl.

I bit back a smirk.

"Wanna play?" he asked, steering me toward his table. I tensed up as we got closer to Reid and Hope, who were still bickering. I could only catch an odd word here and there, not enough to piece together any real meaning, though I could infer a lot from the way Reid kept flinging his hand in my direction. And I kept hearing the hissing sound of the word *she*. I could only assume that *she* was me.

My stomach gave a sick lurch.

I hadn't come here to cause drama for Hope, or for Reid. I really didn't know why life had led me back here just when I was starting to put some real distance between myself and this town. But now that I was here, I wondered if maybe these men were part of the reason. This team.

Maybe I could teach them something.

Maybe there was something they could teach me.

11.
Will

I wasn't allowed to want her, and I wasn't allowed to be jealous when Nate and Xander roped her into a game on their table. Or when Xander stood behind her, his hips bumping her ass as he showed her how to line up the cue.

Had this girl never played pool before?

When she took her first shot, I realized that, no, she had not played pool before. She was supposed to break, but the triangle of balls had barely moved.

She was giving Nate a wide berth, but not as wide as the one she was giving Reid, who had stolen her friend to play at our table. The friend was hot, leggy with a pretty face. Lola told me she was living with Reid's sister, and seeing the two of them stand side-by-side, they could be twins.

My eyes drifted back to Lola when I couldn't resist any longer. She was laughing and chatting, even flirting, with the guys at the middle table, who were eyeing her and grinning like idiots.

Not like I blamed them. She made me lose control of my senses, too. It was taking everything I had to stand here. All I wanted to do was drag her out of Copper's, throw her in the back seat of my car, and fuck her sexy little brains out.

But I was here to be Coach Will, not a horny teenager all hung up on my team's twenty-something massage therapist.

So I watched her move through the crowd as I took turns playing teams with Huck against Reid and his sister. She wouldn't normally be my type—I didn't usually go for tiny, voluptuous, perky blondes. But Lola had hijacked my brain, and while I could register that Hope was attractive, I felt no attraction toward her.

So, clearly, I was screwed. I was already down bad for Lola, and we both knew this relationship, if you could call it that, was going nowhere.

I sank the last three balls to win the game, and then I racked my cue stick and went to the bar to order a much-needed shot of whiskey. When I turned around, I saw Nate and Reid chest to chest, both red in the face and about to come to blows.

12.
Lola

I'd joined the new guys because I was too nervous to face Reid and Will at the far table. I was not going to be able to keep my cool in close proximity to either of the men who were running through my mind on a constant loop lately.

So when Xander threw his arm around my shoulder and steered me toward his table, I let him. He was still a kid, exuberant and daring. And hot. All four of the men at this table were extremely hot. Dallas limped off to take a seat and rest his back while the other three filled me in on the basic rules. I'd played pool maybe three times in my entire life, and each time, I was way too drunk to remember anything about the game.

Xander stood behind me, not quite touching me but I could feel his heat, his energy like static electricity. He pointed his arm out along the stick, showing me how I should grip it to get the best angle and force behind my shot. I kept expecting him to grind against my ass or make some raunchy joke to his friends, based on the little I'd seen of his usual behavior, but he walked me through it in a soft voice at my ear, each step explained clearly.

I sank my first ball.

I turned to gawk at him and he grinned proudly, clapping me on the shoulder. Nate looked back and forth between us and then stepped up to take his shot. We went around until there were only a few balls left on the table, several stripes for our team. A single solid, plus the eight ball, stood between Nate and Eric and victory.

I walked around, eyeing the remaining stripes. There was no clear shot, and the eight ball balanced on the lip of one of the cups, threatening to plunge in at the slightest disturbance and lose us the game on a technicality.

Finally, I bent over the edge of the table, closing one eye and lining up my shot. I pulled the stick back but before I could plunge it forward, something fell hard against my ass.

Or someone.

Nate's arms closed around my waist. His hot breath was on the back of my neck, and his crotch was pressed tightly against me. I jumped and my stick barely kissed the cue ball, rolling it forward a few useless inches. I whirled around as Nate let go of me, holding his hands up with a droll smile.

"I'm so sorry. Clearly I've had too much already."

I stared up at him, my eyes searching his. He was still close enough to kiss me if he wanted to, our bodies brushing as he pinned me against the table.

"Hey—what the fuck?" I heard a familiar voice over my shoulder. "What the hell do you think you're doing, man?" Reid flew around the corner of the pool table, shoving an arm between us. Eric stepped forward and grabbed Nate's shoulder, yanking him a couple of stumbling steps back from me.

"Whoa, there. It was an accident, Cowboy," Nate said, turning his smug little smirk on Reid, who was standing beside me now, staring him down. "And what business is it of *yours*, anyway?"

Reid curled his hands into fists at his sides, and I was afraid he was actually about to punch his new center. I placed a steadying hand on his bicep, and he huffed out a breath.

"I'm okay," I said, turning toward him, trying to draw him away from Nate, who was pulling against Eric's grip as he dared Reid to take a swing. For a brief moment, Reid's gray eyes were tortured as they searched mine. Then he blinked and they were empty again.

"All right guys, break it up," Will said, appearing on the scene and filling the gap between them. I gazed up at him, comfort wrapping around me like a warm blanket at the deep, soothing sound of his voice.

Reid huffed again and crossed his arms over his chest. Nate was still wearing his trademark pompous grin.

"Sorry, Coach," he said. "Guess I got a little bit hypnotized." He held his hands out in front of him and wiggled them back and forth in time with his hips as he eyed me.

Will glanced at me, his jaw tight. There was more tension on his face than just what he was feeling from the scuffle between Nate and Reid. His eyes didn't quite meet mine.

"Just keep it in your pants, O'Ryan," Will said gruffly. He looked at me again. "Why don't you take Reid out to get some air?"

I swallowed around the lump in my throat and then nodded and did as he said, gripping Reid's hand and pulling him behind me across the floor, through the bar, and outside into the crisp fall air.

As soon as it hit him, he jerked his hand out of mine.

I rounded on him.

"I am perfectly capable of watching out for myself," I snapped. He threw his hands up and shook his head, turning his back on me.

"Yeah, I'm aware," he muttered. I was torn between wanting to yell at him and wanting to grab him and hold on tight.

"What do you want from me, Reid?" I asked quietly, all the fight gone from my voice. He stilled, hand halfway through his hair. He let it drop with a thud against his side and looked back at me, his eyes running up and down my body. Then he turned and took two steps forward, backing me against the rough brick wall of the bar's exterior. We stood there staring into each other's eyes, everything we'd never had a chance to say passing between us without a word spoken. And then his pained eyes dropped to my lips. He just looked for a long beat before he pushed away from the wall, away from me.

"I don't know," he said in a broken voice. He moved like he was going to walk away from me.

I fisted both hands in the front of his shirt and held him in place. He raised his eyebrows, and I jerked him closer.

"Tell me what the fuck you want from me," I said again in a dangerous whisper. He stared at a spot on the wall above my head. Then he was dipping his shaggy blonde head to smash a burning kiss to my lips, pinning me to the wall with his hips and grinding his bulge against me. I groaned into his mouth and arched my back, and his hands went to my waist, pulling me closer. His tongue teased my lips, and when they parted for him, he filled me up, clouding my senses with his clean smell and the feel of his big, solid body. The body that had been the subject of all my girlhood fantasies. The one I still dreamed about when I was lonely.

I melted into him, holding him tight. I could feel how hard he was against my thigh and I responded naturally, the way my body had been conditioned to react to him. I remembered every night we'd spent together, the way he fit me just right, big enough to hurt me but he was so gentle, working himself slowly but surely into me until he was fully sheathed inside my pussy.

For a second or two, I didn't think about Will, or my job, or the way Reid had left me high and dry and disappeared from my life five years ago without so much as a goodbye. I just let myself bask in the rush of endorphins I'd never expected to experience again. The way he made me feel. The way he had always made me feel, those gray eyes seeing my soul and wanting to know more.

He was my dream guy. But he broke my heart, and getting over him had been a nightmare.

My blood pounded in my face as he broke the kiss and pulled back. We stayed there like that, barely breathing, our eyes and bodies locked together. Then reality came crashing down on both of us as the door swung open and Will stepped out.

Reid jumped back, cursing under his breath.

"Feeling better?" Will asked. His tone was light, his face revealing nothing of what was going on inside his head.

"Sure," Reid said, clearing his throat. He ducked past Will and disappeared back inside Copper's, leaving us standing there staring at each other under the glittering spangle of stars.

"I'm sorry," I said, because I wasn't sure what else I should say. We weren't exclusive, and he was the one who sent me out here with Reid. Reid had kissed me.

But I had pulled him closer. I kissed him back.

Will's face split in a placid smile.

"Sorry for what, Lola?" he asked. He was still using that even tone. "I'm only your boss at work." He yanked the door handle, holding it open for me.

So that was it?

I narrowed my eyes, studying him, and then I brushed past him. He made a move like he wanted to reach out and grab me but stopped himself.

Hope was standing at the bar, looking annoyed. Her eyes widened when she saw me. I went to her, so grateful to see her I could cry. She gripped my arm and pulled me hard against her side.

"What happened?" she hissed in my ear. I bit my lip. I wasn't sure how to answer. Had Reid already told her that we kissed? I shook my head.

"Nothing, really," I said, ignoring her questioning stare.

"Well, that Nate guy is a dick," she said as the bartender came up. "Two whiskey sours, please." It was our drink. And I needed something to take the edge off. I had a feeling that I would be sleeping alone in my own bed tonight, so when the bartender passed it to me, I tipped it back and ordered another round.

13.
Lola

Things were not any better on the ice. If anything, as November drew to a close, the team was only getting worse. They couldn't seem to get on the same page about anything, and practice regularly devolved into shouting matches between Reid and Nate, and sometimes Huck.

We'd had a series of away games, so we hadn't repeated the eventful "team bonding" night at Copper's yet. A steady stream of players was starting to come through my massage studio, though Reid and Dallas Cash both still avoided me like the plague.

I'd taken a personal interest in rehabbing Dallas. Patch Olson was our current goaltender, and he was passable, but it was clear he belonged in the backup role. Dallas, on the other hand, was a world-class tender. They didn't call him The Tank for nothing. He defended that goal like a brick wall. I'd watched clips, fan compilations of his shut-outs. From what I'd heard, the Prospectors were suffering big time without him. What if he was the engine that could drag the Ice Hawks to a new level? Kicking and screaming, if need be.

But if he insisted on sitting in his pain and misery instead of seeking treatment, the issue was dead in the water.

So I ambushed him.

He came in early every morning to take a long, slow walk on the treadmill, his headphones in, staring at the blank wall in front of him. Usually, by the time I clocked in, he had showered and was on his way out the door, only coming back to sit on the bench for practice or a game. He could get around well enough, but I'd pulled his file, and it showed that his condition had worsened in recent weeks. I knew that Mr. Branson would pay for any medical care that Dallas needed, so I couldn't figure out why he was doing this, letting an injury fester and taking a chance that it could end his career just as he was starting to lift off.

I set two alarms to make sure I woke up before first light. I pulled on my makeshift uniform of athleisure, and a large hoodie I'd stolen from an ex-boyfriend. I didn't wear it because I still had feelings for him—I was glad to be rid of him. I just really liked the hoodie. There was album art for a band I didn't know, faded past unrecognizable, on the front.

I laced up my tennis shoes and slipped out of the house, locking the door behind me. The sky was starting to lighten to gray at the horizon as I drove through town to the arena. There were only three other cars in the parking lot, and I recognized one as Cash's SUV.

I parked on the other side of the lot and went in, scanning my pass at the front door. I often stayed past the time when most people had gone home, so I'd been in the building when it was this empty, but there was something bright and peaceful about it in the morning that centered me. Usually I wasn't needed on-site until after the guys had had their morning workout, a shower, and some breakfast. Most came to me between eleven and four, but I did my best to stay flexible and available so the ones with the busiest schedules could still slip in at odd hours and catch me.

The morning of the ambush, I walked through the halls toward the workout room. The machines were old, and Dallas was one of the only ones who bothered to exercise here. The rest of the big shots went to a pricey gym downtown, but he showed up every morning without fail to plod out his prescribed miles on the treadmill. Movement was great for an injured back—but so was massage. If I could get my hands on him, maybe I could figure out why his body was locking down.

I stood in the doorway, watching him. He was a giant, and with a hurt back, he appeared…less than agile. But like I said, I'd watched clips of him from last season before he got hurt, and he was like a jungle cat in front of the net. It was as if he could sense where the puck would go before it even reached his end of the ice, and nine times out of ten, he knocked it away with ease.

I know he had to be frustrated by his slow progress. I could see from here just how tight his muscles were, and I knew that all the stress he was feeling over the situation would continue to make things worse.

Despite the fact that he'd been hobbling around like an old man the entire time I'd known him, he was built like Hercules. He had the flow like Reid, but his hair was dark, twisting in curls down his neck when he didn't have it tied back in a bun. He was olive-complected, and I wondered if he was Samoan or maybe Native American.

Wherever his genes came from, they were impeccable. Except for the weak back.

With Lars, I could understand his problems. He was on the other side of thirty, had been on the ice for at least fifteen years, and he was built, but his core muscles were far from defined. Since he'd been doing the exercises I'd assigned, he'd tightened up considerably, and he was already getting around better.

But Dallas was in no need of core strengthening. He was shirtless, wearing only a pair of light jogger pants, and despite his slow speed, his skin was shining with exertion. His waist was narrow, his shoulders chiseled from marble.

"Are you looking for someone?" he asked without looking at me. I jumped, my face flushing.

"Uh—yeah, Cash, I'm looking for you."

Now he glanced over, sizing me up.

"And why is that?" I heard the wariness in his voice. I couldn't understand what the hell he was thinking, not accepting treatment from an appointed professional. Did he not trust me for some reason?

"I want to give you an assessment," I said, aware that I sounded like an actress in a bad porno film. But I didn't care. If bad porno acting was what it took to get The Tank on the table, point me to the casting couch.

He snorted and cut those dark eyes at me again. Tribal tattoos snaked up his arms and over his back. I couldn't help but stare, but my mission was too important to let myself get distracted. "I mean…I read your file, and you're not improving."

"You don't say."

He was as sarcastic as Nate, his equally famous and equally arrogant Prospectors teammate. But Dallas wasn't here for an attitude adjustment. He was here because an injury that should have cleared up months ago was dragging on. Mr. Branson had decided to give one of his backup goalies a shot at the big time instead of putting Dallas on the roster and rolling the dice that he'd recover in time to play this season. But Dallas was one of his biggest stars. I couldn't understand why the franchise owner had just abandoned him here in Wyoming with a pat on the back and a *good luck, bud*.

Mr. Branson may have abandoned him, but I wasn't going to let Dallas Cash fall through the cracks.

"How about you come to my studio after your shower and let me take a look?" I pushed. He didn't answer for so long that I was afraid he would say no or simply ignore me until I went away. But then he nodded his big head. A single nod. I'd take it.

Feeling strangely like I was getting ready for a date, I went to work in the studio, dimming the lights and booting up the stereo. I lit a mild citrus candle that gave the room a fresh scent.

Then I sat around for an hour and a half, until I was sure that he'd blown me off once again and ducked out while I was preoccupied. By the time he did knock on my door, I was annoyed and letting it get the best of me. I opened the door and cocked an eyebrow at him.

"Sorry," he said, his eyes shifting away from mine. "I'm a little slower these days."

His sheepish tone softened me. I stepped back and let him inside.

"Huh," he said. "It's nice in here." I smiled to myself.

"Thank you. You can toss your shirt on the chair over there and then lay facedown on the table.

"Want me to lose the shorts?" he asked, deadpan. When I whipped my head up to look at him, the corner of his lips curled. For Dallas Cash, it was the equivalent of a belly laugh. Clearly, he'd heard some stories from his roommate Nate.

I shook my head, a silly grin spreading across my face. He had me feeling all fuzzy and warm.

"Keep the shorts on," I said, turning my back to hide my amusement. I went to my workbench and chose some essential and carrier oils and to stimulate his circulation. I'd spent most of the previous day in my office poring over his file, learning that he had a severe herniated disc that wasn't responding to physical therapy or chiropractic adjustment. He'd declined surgery so far, out of fear that recovery might bench him for another season. But that was rapidly becoming the only remaining option if he wanted to stay on the ice long-term.

I'd have to go easy, take it slow, and feel out what he was comfortable with. He was skittish, but starting to bend to my will. After seeing everything he'd gone through with no results, I didn't blame him for being skeptical and pessimistic.

I turned around to find him lying, still wearing his shorts, with his face in the hole of the table. I took a second to stare. Just a second. Like I said, he had the body of a god. I was trying not to drool.

But I was also a professional. I warmed the oil between my hands and went to his side.

"So, will you tell me a little bit about your injury?" I asked, because the silence was getting to me. As I waited for him to answer, I stood at his hip and probed his lower back with my hands, just little prods with my fingers to test his sensitivity.

He was all tied up in knots. He grunted, tensing under my touch.

"Oh, you know, just the occupational hazard of carrying an entire professional hockey team on my back," he quipped. He was always so dry, it took me a second to realize that he was making a joke. I let out a loud, surprised *Ha!* "No. Well, maybe partly. But I've always had back pain, I've been minding the net since middle school, and all that crouching and twisting takes its toll." It was the most I'd ever heard him say at once. I pressed both palms flat against his spine and slid them upward toward his neck, and he grunted again. "And then one day I just turned wrong, lunged to block the puck and something broke. I haven't been able to put on a pair of skates without being in total agony since then."

After weeks of his stoic, withdrawn routine, I was amazed at the way he was opening up to me now. How he was letting me touch him, letting me explore his back, when he'd spent the first two months of the season pretending I didn't exist.

"And when was that?"

"Three years ago," he said casually. My hands stuttered to a stop.

"But you've only been benched for a year," I said, frowning. He didn't respond. "Cash, are you telling me you were playing with an injury for two years?"

He grew even tenser under my fingertips. I bit my lips together and focused on the massage, making thoughtful little circles, waking up his circulation. The skin of his back was heating up and turning slightly pink, a sign that my ministrations were doing their job.

"Why do you care?" he asked.

"It's my job to care," I said simply. "Do you understand that keeping your injury a secret all that time likely contributed to your prolonged healing process?" More silence from The Tank. I returned to his lower back and started to work my thumb pads in small circles radiating out from his spinal column. He groaned, and the sound was ridiculously erotic. I clenched my thighs together, forcing my mind to stay on the task at hand.

Rubbing up on Hercules.

No. Massaging an injured, anxious client.

"Plus, you're here for a season. If I can get you back on the ice, going through the motions again, in time to earn us some Ws, that's a win-win."

"Ah, so you just want to put me to work pulling this garbage team out of the dumpster," he said, opening up again now that I'd stopped needling him. "Like that won't strain my back further." I frowned at the back of his head.

"It's not a garbage team," I said. "They just need some guidance."

"God knows they're not getting any from Wild Bill," he said, using Will's nickname from his days as a center in the show. Now I was scowling. My urge to defend Will's coaching was immediate and overwhelming, but I managed to hold my tongue. Will himself had said that he could be doing more to build team unity. But I knew that once Will found his faith again and believed this team could be something, he would become a powerful leader for the Ice Hawks. Having The Tank to guard his net might be just the motivation he needed.

It was my turn to be silent as I applied more pressure to Dallas's back. If you were to map the hot spots on his back, the map would be mostly pins. They were everywhere, little tangles of pain and inflammation. I was honestly impressed that he could manage even five minutes on the treadmill in this condition. It was worse than I'd expected for someone who had been in physical therapy for the better part of a year.

He was working with Huck now that he was here, and that seemed to be the only person on the team whose opinion he cared about. "Physical therapist" was one of many hats Huck wore for the Hawks to keep everything moving smoothly. I'd seen them working together and wondered why Huck didn't insist that Dallas supplement his physical therapy with massage. Then again, I wasn't sure Huck took me seriously any more than Dallas did. That was all right. They would all soon see how effective a massage regimen could be at keeping our players in tip-top shape. Most major league professional hockey teams had at least two sports massage therapists on the payroll, and there was good reason for that.

I wouldn't go full deep-tissue this first time, but I wanted to give him a little taste so he wouldn't be surprised during our next session. So I planted my thumbs and dug in, in the general area of his herniated disc. I avoided applying any amount of pressure directly to the injured area. Still, he bowed his back and swore in the lilt of a language I didn't recognize. I might not know the direct translation of the word, but his delivery made the meaning clear enough.

I immediately backed off, swooping my thumbs up and outward in a soothing motion. He relaxed slightly, but I could tell that I'd spooked him. Earning his trust would be an uphill battle with lots of scree underfoot, and I expected I would set myself back several times trying to challenge his self-imposed limits.

The truth was, there was no guarantee. Massage couldn't heal a herniated disc. But it could increase blood flow to the area and restore the health of the muscular structure around the spinal column, providing a more hospitable environment for healing to occur. And it might just be the important piece that had been missing from Dallas's treatment plan.

When the session was over, I wrote up a schedule for him. I wanted him on my table at least three days a week. He looked it over without comment as he tugged his shirt back on. I could finally take a deep breath again once he was covered up.

"I'll do my best," he said, moving toward the door.

"No," I said, stopping him in his tracks. He turned back to me, raising an eyebrow. "You'll come. Three days a week. At least. Especially right now, we need to keep up consistent therapy to get you turned around and headed in the right direction. We'll reevaluate if, after a few sessions, you feel massage is not helping you. But in the meantime, I want you facedown on this table Mondays, Wednesdays and Fridays for the foreseeable future." He rolled his eyes and looked out the window, his jaw tight with annoyance. I braced my hands on my hips, narrowing my eyes at him.

"You may not respect me, or the work I do," I said, feeling the color rise in my cheeks. "But I'm going to help you whether you like it or not. So you'll come. Three. Days. A week."

He pinned me with a menacing glare, but I held my ground. After a few silent seconds, he walked out, leaving the door hanging open behind him.

14.
Dallas

I'm going to help you, whether you like it or not.

I couldn't stop thinking about her hot fucking mouth, forming words I'd longed to hear but couldn't quite bring myself to believe.

I'd tried massage therapy in Denver, and it didn't do much. Plus, deep tissue made me cry. So I'd avoided her, and Huck hadn't pushed me to go in.

I wanted to wallow. I was sick of being positive, and keeping my eye on the prize. My body was revolting against me, trying to take me down and ruin my life, and now I was stranded in this godforsaken state where I didn't know anyone except for Nate, who was a dick. I'd latched onto him so I wouldn't be completely alone, but watching him paw her at Copper's a few weeks ago had nearly made me snap.

She came and sought me out. She wouldn't let me hide. And I knew my body would betray me with her, too. I'd given myself a hand in the shower before I went in to see her so I would have some hope of maintaining control when she touched me.

It was easy to let her, once she'd cornered me. The truth was, I wanted her to run her hands up and down my body. It was even better than I'd expected when she finally did. But it also hurt like hell the second she applied any kind of real pressure. And now I was in deep, serious shit, because she wanted me to come back three times a week. I would have to sit through the delicious agony of her hands on me, but not how I wanted. Instead, in ways that caused me actual agony. Or I would blow her off again, and make excuses until she gave up on me.

I shoved through the heavy door that led out to the arena's parking lot. A few more cars were filtering in now, which meant it was time for me to get out of there. We had a game later, and I had an extensive stretching routine that I preferred to do in the privacy of my own apartment before I had to report back to the workout room for warm-ups with Huck.

But I sat in my car, staring at the big metal building. The words *Casper Memorial Arena - Home of the Ice Hawks!* were printed on a windblown banner.

Where the fuck was I? How did I end up here? Flotsam and jetsam in the dirty ocean of professional hockey, ready to spit you out the second you stopped being relevant. One season on the bench. That's all it would take for the world to forget about me completely. What if Branson never brought me back, and I wasted away playing goalie for the Ice Hawks like one of the gap-toothed married guys who coasted on their sixty grand a year or whatever pittance Branson was paying them so he could afford to shell out high six-figure salaries to me and my teammates in the major league.

After five years of playing professionally, money wasn't a concern for me. I could retire right now, and maybe I should. Take the fortune I'd earned doing my favorite thing in the world, the only thing I'd ever cared about, and get the fuck out of dodge. I could go anywhere. Somewhere tropical. Or I could go stay with Ma for a while up in Wind River, on the rez. I built her a nice log cabin out there after I was drafted to the Prospectors. It was an upgrade from the leaking, rusty trailer I grew up in.

But I couldn't quite bring myself to tuck my tail between my legs and run. Not yet. I still had fight and a few good years left in me. If I could just get this shit with my back figured out, I'd be back on top in no time.

I had to believe that. My last shred of sanity depended on it.

But still. Aside from truly not believing that she could do anything to help me, I couldn't stand the thought of closing myself up in that tiny room with her warm vanilla scent three times a week for the rest of the season. There was no way I could keep my cool around her in such close quarters.

And fuck, that deep tissue shit *hurt*.

15.
Lola

We were in the locker room after the second period, and tensions were high. Will was pacing, yelling, doling out whatever the opposite of a pep talk was. I was massaging cramps out of Eric "Moose" Bouchard's calves. His face was screwed up in pain as I worked them. On the bench beside me, Huck wrapped Reid's knee. I could feel the defenseman's big bulk and hear his little animal noises of pain. An opposing defenseman had hit him hard and fast, knee on knee, in a dirty play that had prompted a couple of scuffles to break out while Reid rolled around on the ice, clutching his leg and moaning in pain. He was benched for the rest of the game, and I could tell that he was pissed about it.

"Bouchard, you ready?" Will shouted in our direction. Eric's muscles had finally relaxed in my hands, and he was panting with relief. He raised a thumbs-up above his head.

"Ready, Coach!"

"Good. O'Ryan, Bardi, Larsson…"

Nate, Xander, and Jamie jumped to their feet, and Will called up the second line. Erik touched his toes gingerly to the floor, and when his calf didn't immediately twist up again, he stood.

"My thanks to the Tenderizer," he said with a cryptic grin.

"The Tenderizer?" I repeated. But they were already filing back down the tunnel toward the rink. I glanced at Huck, who was focused on putting his tape back in his kit.

"It means you're beating them to death in there," Huck said without looking up. "They've been comparing bruises like badges of honor."

I laughed out loud. My strong hands and pointy elbows were part of what made me such a good sports massage therapist. My diminutive size was deceptive. I could manhandle even big, reluctant professional athletes with my firm grip.

"Your guys are surprisingly soft for hockey players," I teased. Now Huck raised his eyes to mine, matching my smile.

"Maybe you can toughen them up," he said. The words were light, casual, but something shifted in the air between us. His smile dropped. "I heard you pinned my injured goalie down and made him take some of that tender love and care." I raised an eyebrow.

"That a problem?"

"Cash has had deep tissue, hot stones, ice baths. He's getting tired of trying when nothing works for him."

"So he's just going to lay down and quit?" I asked, tilting my head to the side. Huck clenched his jaw.

"I didn't say that. Just...don't get his hopes up. And don't hit him too hard in the beginning. He's softer than he lets on."

I just stared at him, caught off guard by his frankness. The assistant coach gave me a curt nod and then stood, storing his bandage kit before heading after the team back to the rink.

I watched him go with an eye on his slightly hitched gait. At first, I thought he didn't have a limp because it's so subtle. But the more I watched him, the more I saw signs of his injury. I could tell that he was in pain, probably every day. I wondered what it would take to get him to come in for a little after-hours therapy.

I could show him firsthand how I put those bruises on his players.

I bit back a smile at the thought of making Huck Hart squirm and moan. Then my brain dove into the gutter, and I blushed bright pink as I jumped up to follow him out.

16.
Lola

Dallas was back to dodging me despite the fact that I'd gotten Huck's vote of support. I was done playing nice. Finished. My patience was beyond worn thin. It was threadbare, and the last thread was about to break.

He didn't show up for his scheduled appointment on Wednesday, so I made sure to set my alarm extra early on Friday morning so I could catch him during his daily walk. But when I stormed into the gym with a triumphant grin, ready to ambush him, it was empty. The treadmill was collecting cobwebs.

I frowned.

Now he was skipping his daily workout, too?

Maybe there was something more serious going on than him just not taking me seriously. Or maybe he was *that* determined to avoid me. I shook my head and set my jaw.

If The Tank wouldn't come to me, I'd have to go to him. And there was one place where I knew I could always find him.

As predicted, he showed up that afternoon to warm his spot on the bench during practice. I waited until the entire team was gathered in the locker room, changing into their sweaters and hockey pants. Then I went striding in with my chin held high.

"Dallas Cash," I said loudly. Everyone went still and quiet, turning as one to look at me. Dallas raised his head, his dark eyes finding mine, and the color drained from his gorgeous face. "Do you *want* to become incontinent? How about impotent?" His eyes widened. "Because patients with an untreated herniated disc have an extremely high risk of developing both conditions." Reid and Jamie exchanged a look, and Nathan grinned at me like he was a kid on Christmas morning as I propped my hands on my hips and planted my feet. "So unless you want to be carting around a colostomy bag and a limp dick at the ripe old age of forty, you *will* be attending your scheduled massage appointments moving forward. Am I clear?"

Everyone in the locker room, me included, held their breath, waiting to see how the goalie would react. His eyes still trained on mine, he nodded slowly. His mouth was a thin line, his shoulders hunched in defeat.

My own mouth spread into a grin. He could be annoyed with me. He could even hate me. But no matter how much he might want to wave the white flag, there wasn't a snowball's chance in hell that I was giving up on Dallas Cash.

17.

Lola

True to his word, Dallas knocked on my door bright and early Monday morning. He was back to his treadmill routine, too, and honestly, even with the cloud of irritation on his brow, I could tell that he was looser, as if a serious weight had been lifted off his back.

Whether he knew it yet or not, he was safe in my hands. If he would keep his appointments, I would prove it to him.

I gestured to the table. Neither of us smiled. I could feel how much he didn't want to be there. His frustration and trepidation were rolling off of him in waves.

"Don't worry, we'll take it slow," I assured him quietly. Now that I'd nailed him down, the next step was getting him to open up and trust me. Otherwise, the tension between his shoulder blades would chase out all the good I managed to do.

He pulled his shirt off and I averted my eyes, turning to the workbench to get my tools together.

Will was right. I was a dirty girl. My mind was playing a montage of all the inappropriate and unprofessional methods I could use to work out Dallas's…kinks. I'd forced him to come here, and now I was fantasizing about taking advantage of him.

I tried to shake the damning thoughts out of my head, but they were sticky. At least when I turned around again, he was facedown on the table, and I only had to contend with his back. His back needed my attention anyway, so what was the harm in staring at the rippling mountain ranges and valleys of tight muscle that stretched from his neck down to the elastic waistband of his athletic shorts?

Pull them down. Tell him you need access to everything.

I took a deep breath and invited my horny inner voice to go fuck herself.

"How was your pain after our last session?" I asked casually, as if he hadn't spent the rest of last week blatantly dodging me. His response was a non-committal grunt. "Sorry, what was that?"

"Bad, like always," he said loud enough for me to hear.

"I'm sorry about that. Sometimes these types of injuries hurt the most when they're healing." I ran my oiled fingertips lightly down either side of his spine, and his skin erupted in goosebumps. "Are my hands cold?"

"No," he grumbled at the floor.

"Okay, good. Just try to relax, Cash," I said in my best soothing voice. I'd never been the spa type of therapist. My tranquil elevator voice was barely passable. I tried to make the studio inviting, but hospitality wasn't exactly my strong suit. In fact, the vast majority of my strength was in my hands, and that's what made me a stellar sports massage therapist. The guys I worked with usually didn't want that frou-frou stuff anyway, just a good, hard rub-down.

I was glad Dallas couldn't see the stupid grin that spread across my face as *a good, hard rub down* bounced around in my head, sounding dirtier with every pass.

"Give me a number on the pain scale for how you felt the day after your last massage," I prompted him again.

"Six," he muttered.

"And is that about average? Little better, little worse?"

"Better."

Now, my grin was proud. Vindicated. I knew he would benefit from the right regimen. What the hell were the massage therapists in Denver doing to him? From the sound of things, trying to work out the knots too soon after his injury, before he was ready.

I worked for most of the next hour in silence, slowly building pressure, backing off, then applying even more. He muttered a curse every now and then, but otherwise he lay still and took whatever I dished out.

I went to the break room for ice packs when I was done with his massage, but by the time I got back to the studio, Dallas was gone.

18.
Dallas

I had to take my one opportunity to get the hell out of there so she wouldn't see the laughably huge tent I was pitching in my basketball shorts. Her touch made me crazy, the smell of her, the way the feathery end of her ponytail occasionally brushed against my side or the back of my arm.

When she left for the cold packs, I fled. I snatched my workout bag from my chair in the locker room and power-walked all the way to my truck.

As I reached it, I said a little prayer of thanks. I slung my bag into the seat behind me, slammed the door, and dropped my forehead on the steering wheel with a loud groan.

The rod in my pants still hadn't deflated. Not even close. I drove the whole way back to the rental house with blue balls, my cock pounding in time with my accelerated heartbeat.

When I walked in, Nate was reclined on the couch, flipping through channels on the TV. One glance at me had him smirking. I wanted to slug the smug look off of his pretty boy face. I could feel the heat in my face and neck as I left him chuckling in the living room and locked myself in my bedroom. I dropped my bag the second I was inside. Then I marched to the ensuite bathroom, jaw set, to take care of this ridiculous business so I could get my head on straight.

How the hell was I supposed to manage an entire season of *this* three times a week? My balls were going to fall *off* if she kept touching me without wrapping her hand, slick with that sweet-smelling oil she used, around my cock.

I let myself imagine the hypothetical happy ending as I twisted the shower faucet to the right temperature and climbed in. I'd showered before I went to her studio, of course, but now I was a whole other kind of dirty.

The hot water sluiced down my body, washing off the first layer of my anxiety.

As soon as I touched my desperate, throbbing cock, I had to stuff my other fist in my mouth to keep from moaning her name. I closed my eyes and imagined her telling me to roll over on the massage table. Her getting an eyeful of what I had for her, what I wanted so badly to offer her, though I knew I never would.

I was pretty sure she was fucking the coach, and even if she wasn't, I was here to heal up and maintain focus, not to get attached to some fine-ass massage therapist with the hands and body of a goddess.

I was getting close, moving faster, thinking of Lola's little hands sliding up and down my cock, her sweet pink lips pursed in concentration.

Just then, there was a banging on the other side of the wall. My bathroom butted up to Nathan's, and his voice was clear as he crowed out: "Hey, Tanker! The Tenderizer called and wanted me to tell you to save some of that man meat for her!"

I squeezed my eyes shut, my hand clamping down around my cock, my teeth clenching together hard enough to crack. I glared at the shared wall, then leaned my forehead against the cool tile, my dick going soft in my hand as the water plinked all around my feet.

19.
Will

I stared down in awe at the blonde bombshell on her knees in front of me, with my cock lodged firmly in her mouth. She rolled those wide, dark eyes up to stare into mine as she deep-throated me, pushing forward to take as much as she could manage and holding there, her muscles working around my shaft until she had to come up for air.

I ran my hand through her hair, and her lips curled into a coy smile as she sucked on the tip and swallowed it down again.

It had been a hard week. I was pretty sure my best players were going to kill each other before we'd even made it halfway through the season. Reid was a machine, but there was no one working the controls right now. And Nate…

He was just looking for trouble. And he was going to get it from me if he didn't stop bumping into Lola's ass at every opportunity, showing up naked to his massage appointments, and cat-calling her whenever she walked into a room. Reid's fury was obvious, his face flushing stop-sign red and his hands curling into fists at his sides. I had to keep tighter reins on mine. There might be rumors about

Lola and the coach, but I wasn't about to confirm them by pounding in my star center's nose for requesting a happy ending every time he saw her.

She, on the other hand, might rearrange the little dickhead's face soon. If she could beat Reid to the punch. Literally.

She cupped my balls in her palm, rolling them, bringing me right back to the present. My hand tightened in her hair, pushing her down, making her take a little more of me. I swear, it was like this girl could read my mind. She knew when I needed a shoulder massage, and when I needed a blow job. When I needed her to just come home with me and let me hold her all night, let me pretend like this was something real.

Hell, I was pretty sure I was in love with her after she'd straightened Dallas Cash's crooked spine in a week. He'd been walking around like a question mark the entire time he'd been here, but today, for the first time, I saw him striding upright, his shoulders squared, into the barn for practice. I was nowhere near comfortable enough to let him strap on a pair of ice skates yet, but if this was the progress he'd made in a week, Lola might not be crazy after all for suggesting that he could end up guarding the net by the end of the season. Then he'd go right back to the Prospectors. But maybe he'd give us enough of a boost while he was here to get Branson off my ass.

I mean, seriously, what did the guy expect when he used this team like a revolving door and whisked any stand-outs off to the major league the second they showed an ounce of promise?

Between my feet, Lola sat back, gazing up at me with a pout on her perfect mouth as she stroked me with one hand.

"You're even farther away tonight than I thought," she said. I smiled and shrugged, my cock jumping in her hand. I never wanted her to stop sucking me, touching me. Reading my emotions plainly on my face no matter how hard I tried to hide them. Could I just hire her to sit here and do this all day while I took on everybody's bullshit? Probably not legally. Last time I checked, prostitution was still prohibited in the great state of Wyoming.

"I was just thinking about how good Cash looked today," I said, and she beamed. I pressed my palm to her cheek, brushing a thumb over her puffy lips. "You're a miracle worker, baby."

"Just doing my job," she said with a lilt in her voice. I could tell she was as proud of herself as I was.

I'll admit that I had my doubts when we first met, regardless of the fact that my cock was trying to rip its way out of my jeans to get to her. I wasn't sure this tiny young girl had what it took to manhandle eighteen minor league hockey players. But Branson sent her, and who was I to question the great and powerful leader? Now, she had them all drinking out of the palm of her hand just a few weeks into the season, and I was starting to see real changes in the team now that most of them were seeing her at least once a week. For once, I was more than happy to eat crow.

"You're damn good at it," I told her. She gave another shy smile, and then she dropped her head back into my lap.

This time, she had my full attention. I watched her, breathless, as she took more of me into her mouth than I'd have thought was possible.

I shoved both hands through her hair, cupping the back of her head and pulling her forward, pushing her down, making her choke on my cock. She gripped my thighs, but she didn't squeeze or slap, didn't pull away, as I forced myself further down her throat. Her mouth was warm and wet and inviting, but her throat... As it surrendered to me, gave enough to let me work the tip down into that impossibly tight heat, I swear I transcended to another plane of existence.

I pulled her back just an inch and then drove her down harder, putting force behind my cock as I face-fucking her with savage thrusts. She choked again, then gagged, but one of her hands slid between my legs to play with my balls again, stroking and rolling and sucking me until I was about to burst.

"You ready to swallow Daddy's come?" I groaned.

But there was no time for her to answer. I knew what her answer would be. This beautiful girl would give me anything, except the one thing I really wanted.

Her heart.

I held her down, everything inside me drawing up tight like a bowstring, and then I broke.

20.
Reid

"Just make an appointment, dude," Jamie said, watching me with a worried scowl. I was lying on my back with my knees curled up against my chest and my feet in the air, trying desperately to work out the kink that had formed in my back after yesterday's practice.

There was no fucking way—no *fucking* way—I was stepping foot in Lola Rey's studio ever again. I'd called the two masseurs that turned up on the map in Casper, and both were booked solid. We had an away game tomorrow, which meant four hours on the bus to get there and four hours back. I'd be genuinely surprised if I wasn't locked up in a fetal position by the end of it all. If I was ice-ready when we got there, I'd be lucky.

Lola was the one who got me hooked on massage in the first place. She'd always had small but incredibly powerful hands, which had spawned plenty of jokes back in high school when the guys spied her rubbing my back after practice or before a game. It wasn't sexual, at least not at first. She massaged Hope, too.

She was already dreaming about this life back then, just like I was. Our paths were bound to cross. I just never expected it to happen here, where our awkward childhood memories played out on every street corner.

Awkward, and painful.

That kiss I'd seen, the one that ended things between us, lived rent-free in the back of my mind. Lola and Chase, my former best friend and friend-turned-girlfriend, locked together in a dark corner at a party. His hands all over her body, his tongue in her mouth.

I could picture it like it happened yesterday, five years later. My heart was still a raw wound.

"I'm not making an appointment," I grunted at Jamie, who took my bad attitude in stride. He was a true best friend, ride-or-die loyal. He always had my back, on or off the ice. And he was right, of course, that the only logical thing to do was to call the masseuse the team now kept on staff for exactly this reason. But her skin on mine just that one time, that first day, was enough to scare me off for good. I couldn't take it, plain and simple. Every ounce of pain and anger and heartbreak I still felt so strongly rose to the surface like a tsunami the second she touched me. And then, of course, the session had come to an abrupt and disastrous end. I'd decided that it was best not to revisit the issue.

My back had been hurting me for a while, along with my knee, hip, shoulder, and every other part of me. I'd ignored it, as you do. But it would no longer be ignored.

"Huck's going to bench you in a heartbeat if he sees you like this," Jamie said, earning a snarl from me. I felt like shit for lashing out. But I was a coiled snake, ready to strike.

My body was shutting down on me, trying to force me back into her arms. It was fighting a losing battle. I was paying attention. If she wasn't fucking Nate already, she would be soon. He'd wear her down. Plus, there were those highly suspicious early morning sessions she kept having with Dallas Cash. And then there was Will…

I shook my head. It was already killing me to see her give her attention away to anybody else. I couldn't share her with half the hockey team. I'd managed to resist giving into my raging need for her so far. But I knew I would get myself in serious trouble if I let her massage me. Just the thought was getting me both hard and angry.

It was a dizzying combination.

Jamie had a point, though. I couldn't even get up off the floor. Skating in the game tomorrow was a long shot. Every hockey player I knew had back problems, usually nothing a few painkillers couldn't fix. But this was stretching on, and I knew I ran the risk of being benched for the season like Cash if I kept my head in the sand much longer.

I gritted my teeth and snatched my phone up from the floor beside me.

Threw my back out.

The text whooshed off to its intended recipient, my well-meaning, meddling sister. It was a pussy move, a cop-out, no doubt. But I knew she would tell Lola, and then Lola might come here and help me. All my pride flew out the window as I pictured Cash, plodding along on the treadmill, bent over like an old man, wearing a permanent frown because, like me, his major league aspirations had been put on hold and were in danger of evaporating completely. I broke out in a cold sweat, panic pounding a frantic rhythm in my head.

The message chime kept me tethered to reality. I held the phone up to read Hope's short reply.

I know. Jamie texted twenty minutes ago.

I was turning narrowed eyes on my literal wingman, my so-called ride-or-die, when a hammering knock sounded at the door.

21.
Lola

I pounded on the door of Reid's apartment, fully prepared to strap his ass down if that's what it took. I already had Huck's number pulled up in my phone, but I hadn't dialed it yet. If the issue was something I could solve myself, I would. But it was possible Reid would have to sit out the next game and head to the sports injury doctor instead.

I suspected that it was the same old injury flaring up again, just like his bum left knee that had gone out every spring after our sophomore year of high school when another dirty hit on the ice had left him with a ruptured MCL.

I drew my fist back and was flinging it forward with even more force when the door swung open, and I nearly socked the redheaded winger in the jaw instead. He was the one who had called—James Larsson. He was usually unflappably cheerful and upbeat, but now his cold blue eyes swept down my body, sizing me up before he stepped aside to let me in.

Reid was lying on the floor like a turtle flipped over on its shell, clenching his phone in his fist, glaring at Jamie like he hadn't even noticed me yet.

When Jamie ignored him, he turned to me at last, and I was surprised to see his brow smooth a bit. Almost as if the sight of me was a comfort to him. But I knew better.

"Hey," he said resignedly. My irritation dissipated on the spot when I heard his voice. I hurried over to him, dropping down on my knees at his side.

"Same old?" I asked. It was shorthand we'd used back in high school when he was hurting.

"Same old," he confirmed flatly. "I didn't realize Jamie called you."

"Well, he texted Hope. And I'm glad he did. How long has this flare-up been happening?" He winced at my scolding tone, and with that, I knew it had been happening for a while.

I glanced over my shoulder at the door to the kitchen. Jamie had disappeared through it, and I could hear him clanging dishes around in there. I was starting to get the distinct feeling that the guy did not like me. Did he hold the same mysterious grudge against me as his best bud, or was this some fresh hell?

I needed his help flipping Reid over onto his stomach and stretching his limbs out. There was no way I could do it alone without risking further injury.

"Jamie?" I called tentatively. There was no pause in the cacophony that was going on behind the swinging door. "Jamie?" I said a little louder, and there was a big crash followed by heavy footsteps.

When he appeared in the doorway, his face was blank.

"I need help rolling him over."

He crossed to us right away and knelt down, closing his arms around Reid's torso as I guided his hips and eased his legs out straight. Ever so carefully, we moved him until he was lying flat on his stomach.

"Thank you," I said, flashing him a grateful smile. He didn't reciprocate.

This guy is seriously not a fan.

I put him out of my mind as I pushed Reid's shirt up, bunching it under his arms. I could actually see the knot, right where it always was. I'd untangled this son of a bitch more times than I could count when we were kids. But sometimes, management was the best you could do with these soft tissue injuries, especially so with high-performance athletes.

I planted my thumbs right where they needed to be, and Reid relaxed instantly, groaning as I pushed against the muscle spasm, encouraging it to relax as well. His groans morphed into a rumbling peal of laughter as the tension started to loosen, little by little, releasing a flood of emotion and energy and stored-up residual pain into his system. He sucked in a shuddering breath, and when he let it out, I felt the knot ease even more under my gentle kneading.

I massaged not just the trouble spot but his entire back. He begged me to walk on it with my bare feet like I used to, but there was no chance I was going to be reckless with him in this state. I'd since been educated on the dangers of standing with all my body weight on an injured back. Who knows, I may have even caused more damage to him when I'd agreed to it in high school.

Instead, I straddled his hips and put all of my weight behind my elbows, and after a few seconds of hardcore digging with the points, it was as if he had deflated. He gave me everything, going limp as the strain left his body. He let out another soft moan, sounding spent and weak with relief.

Just like that, I realized that touching him was turning me on. I gave the sides of his spine a few more quick passes, and then I stood up.

"Pain level?"

"Nothing. Amazing. So good," he mumbled into the carpet. "Miracle worker." I couldn't help but laugh. For a second, he was the old Reid again, and everything was easy. But then Jamie's frigid voice broke in and chilled me to my core.

"Thanks a lot for coming. Sorry to pull you away from your busy schedule." I could tell by his biting tone that by "busy schedule," he meant more than my regular work hours. He was referencing my… extracurricular activities.

Was that what his attitude was about? I mean, it couldn't explain why Reid had ghosted me all those years ago, but I could see it getting under Jamie's skin that I was sleeping with his coach. Since everyone seemed to know everything around here.

"No problem," I said with what I hoped was an unbothered smirk, turning to leave the way I came in. "Use ice packs, and if it hurts in the morning, you need to tell Huck." I glanced back at him over my shoulder. "That's non-negotiable if you want to stay on the ice this season."

"Wait," Reid said, pushing himself up on his elbows into cobra pose. The amount of mobility was honestly impressive after the shape he'd been in a few minutes ago. I paused, my hand frozen in the act of reaching for the doorknob. "Seriously, I mean it. Thank you. Do you want to…stay for dinner?"

Alarm bells went off in my head. The fact that we'd managed to get this far without a blow-up confrontation was the real miracle. If we spent any more time together, the polite facade was bound to crumble. I had questions I still wanted to ask him, and he clearly had problems with me that he hadn't worked through. Jamie was staring at him like he'd grown two heads.

"You don't have to—," I started.

"I want to," Reid said, pushing himself up until he was sitting with his legs straight out in front of him. "I know I've been less than welcoming." He shot a look at Jamie that suggested the winger had been, too. I shrugged.

"It's okay, really," I said. "I mean, I'd expect as much, given that you excised me from your life with a scalpel five years ago."

Shock flashed across his face before an iron curtain came slamming down.

"Well, that's what happens when you cheat on a guy with his best friend," he quipped snidely. The hair on the back of my neck stood up as I stared at him with wide, searching eyes.

I was dragged back in time to that shitty, awful, fateful night. We were all celebrating the end of the summer at said best friend's lake house. Chase's parents were loaded and couldn't be bothered to watch him or spend time with him, so that was where we went for blowout parties.

Chase had been giving me weird looks for weeks by that point. After a few too many beers, he'd backed me into a corner and smashed his mouth against mine, shoving his stale tongue between my lips.

And *that* had led to a person I'd known my entire life cutting me off like split ends? I glared at him, speechless, trying to form my outraged jumble of thoughts into a cohesive sentence. He watched me smugly, as if he'd dropped the mic instead of just showing what a dumb, ego-driven kid he was back then. In a lot of ways, I suspected that that dumb kid was still behind the wheels of his brain. And there was no reasoning with children.

I rolled my eyes, and then I grabbed the knob, yanked the door open, and slammed it behind me without another word.

22.
Lola

"Why didn't you ever tell me?" Hope asked, her brow knit. I shook my head, staring down into my glass of wine. There was no good answer, except that it had been a gross, embarrassing three seconds I'd just wanted to forget. Reid must have stormed away a moment before I pushed Chase off of me hard enough to send him sprawling backward onto his pompous ass.

But now I'd learned that those three seconds had affected my life in ways I still couldn't fully fathom.

"God, my brother is an idiot." She closed her eyes, pinching the bridge of her nose between her fingertips. "He could teach a college course on how to sabotage your own happiness."

The image of Reid standing up in front of a classroom in a tweed jacket with leather elbow patches hit my funny bone like a hammer. *Ding.* After hours of anger and frustration volleying my brain around like a hockey puck, I let out a belly laugh. Then Hope started laughing, and then we both dissolved into a hapless, helpless giggle fit.

It was fucking ridiculous when you thought about it. The idea that a single honest conversation between Reid and me could have drastically changed the course of the last five years. The way we all thought we were so grown up back then, but we were just kids play-acting at love. The feelings were real, but we had no idea what to do with them.

So Reid had done what he knew best and bailed. Just like Hope said when I first got back. The only thing I'd ever seen him fully commit to was hockey. Knowing him, he probably would have grabbed onto any excuse to take the easy way out at the end of that summer when he was headed off to college in Laramie, and I was stuck in Casper for my senior year.

My broken heart was just collateral damage.

We drained the box of wine in the fridge, flipped through multiple streaming apps without landing on anything good, and tossed buttery pieces of popcorn into each other's mouths from opposite ends of the couch. We did our best to forget all the shit. But it was still there.

Once upon a time, I had loved both of the Wright siblings more than I'd ever loved anything. Back then, I'd imagined a future where we were family. Hope my sister-by-law. Reid and I with a gaggle of sandy-haired babies that would stitch us all even more tightly together. When that illusion was shattered, I spent senior year just trying to survive. Hope kept me together, even though part of me wanted to hate her because she reminded me so much of Reid. And then I left for college, and she went to culinary school. We would go months without speaking and then finally call each other and spend five hours catching up, carrying our phones around to the bathroom, the kitchen, the couch, as we recounted the recent events of our lives. No matter how much time passed between conversations, we always picked right back up where we'd left off. The links in our chain were unbreakable, even as I pushed her away and did my level best to run in the opposite direction of my hometown and all the bad memories there. I never stopped loving Hope. But I had no safety net, no home to go back to, once Reid shut me out.

So I'd become more self-sufficient, more determined.

Stronger.

I'd made a life for myself, and I wasn't about to let some boy from my past up-end everything I'd worked for, everything I'd built. No matter how handsome he was or how much being near him made me feel like a girl again, innocent and optimistic and loved and free.

My memories of Reid might be all warm and fuzzy, even laced as they were with bittersweet pain.

But the reality was this. The real Reid, the flesh-and-bone man that was standing in front of me, just made me feel like shit.

23.
Lola

Dallas's condition had already improved significantly. He stood up straight and walked tall. Will was thrilled at the prospect of getting him on the ice in a silver Hawks jersey, but he agreed with me and Huck that the goalie wasn't quite there yet.

Most mornings, Dallas, Huck, and I met in the gym. I would come in thirty minutes after they were scheduled to begin physical therapy, and we would work together on stretches and discuss his treatment plan. Then Dallas would go with me back to my studio for some deep tissue.

We'd worked our way up to the big boy stuff now. He still cursed, but he did it gleefully as I reduced his pain for the first time in years with sweet, pointy elbow pressure.

The mornings I spent with them were happy, peaceful, quiet times. All three of us working together toward a common goal and seeing real results. My hands braced against Dallas's thighs as I assisted him in a stretch, and Huck watched on.

Because I was…well, *me,* a hopeless romantic and also, as Hope so kindly put it, a "confirmed nympho," I couldn't help but fantasize about how it might feel to be with both of them. Separately, or together…

There was no harm in daydreaming. Luckily, unlike the guys, I could have all the dirty thoughts I wanted without an unwieldy signpost between my legs giving me away.

Now that Dallas wasn't living in constant pain, teetering on the verge of giving up his life's dream, he was a sweet, fluffy teddy bear of a man. He brought me my favorite coffee, sometimes in the middle of a busy day. I knew that Will had noticed the hunky goalie's sudden increased attention toward me, but I also knew that he put his team above all else, even himself. I'd gamble that Will would gladly officiate our wedding if I could get Dallas back on the ice guarding the net for the Hawks.

At the thought, my stomach gave a sad little twist.

It was possible—even likely—that I was falling in love with Wild Bill. But it was also likely that I had never fallen out of love with Reid Wright. Now Dallas Cash was starring in my wet dreams and giving me butterflies with that toothy grin he now wore plastered to his face more often than not.

And then there was Huck Hart, the team's smoldering, complicated assistant coach/physical therapist/mental health counselor/personal trainer. Sometimes, he would lock eyes with me for a second over Dallas's head in the morning, or during a heated moment in a game, and everything would slow way down. In moments like that, the world was just for us.

I didn't know what the fuck to do with that.

But I wasn't the type to run away from a challenge. No, I was the type to square my feet and dig in my heels and face head-on whatever was trying to take me down. So that's what I did.

My physical relationship with Dallas began easily enough. We just slipped right into it. One day, he stripped off his shirt in my studio and as usual, I tried not to stare. But instead of lying on the table, he pulled me against his chest and kissed me deeply, exploring my mouth with his tongue. He didn't stop there, either. His tongue explored a lot more than my mouth that day.

Our sessions started to go long, sometimes two hours. I always insisted that I actually massage him first, but when I was finished, he rolled over and I gave in, let myself get lost in him for a little while. Will brought up the extended appointment time with a twitch of his lips, and when he saw my blush, he nodded. Later, in his office, after bending me over and fucking me hard and fast, he held me in his desk chair.

"Just tell me if you need to let me go," he said softly against the top of my head. He planted a kiss on my crown and sighed. I opened my eyes and looked up at him, frowning.

"I don't ever want to let you go, Will," I said, confused. He gave me a half-hearted smile.

"Whether it's Dallas Cash or Reid Wright or someone else entirely, you're going to find a guy your age who wants you all to himself. Does Cash know about us?"

I shook my head. I didn't like lying by omission, though I was pretty sure rumors about me and the coach had been going around since that first practice game. But I also felt uncomfortable revealing personal information about Will that could get him in trouble.

He didn't want anyone to know about us, and I'd honored that. His arms tightened around me.

"Let's keep it like that, at least for now," he said. "If you decide you want to be exclusive with him…"

I shifted in his lap to straddle him and planted a hand on each side of his face. I made him look at me.

"I don't want to be exclusive with anyone," I said, finally voicing the thoughts that had been bouncing around in my head. He raised an eyebrow. "I have feelings for you, Will. And yes, I have feelings for Dallas, too, and maybe Reid. It's…complicated. I don't expect any of you to be willing to share me. But at least right now, I can't bear the thought of opening one door and closing the rest."

He watched me with those deep green eyes and I held my breath, nervous to see how he would react to my confession that I wanted to keep fucking him and Dallas and maybe add another player or two to the mix. Maybe an assistant coach, too…

I was being selfish. I was still attached enough to reality to know that. But after a long beat, Will's face split into a grin.

"You want to be shared and passed around by a bunch of big, rough hockey players, baby?" he asked, his voice raw. I brushed my thumb over his bottom lip and bit my own.

"Yes, Daddy," I whispered with a devious smile. His eyelids fluttered and he made a small sound at the back of his throat.

"You want Daddy to hand you out like a trophy to his best players?"

I moaned with need, bucking forward to grind my pussy against him. He wasn't as young as Dallas, so he didn't bounce back as fast —to be fair, no one bounced back as fast as Dallas Cash. I'd literally never seen the goalie's dick soft. But Will was already thickening again as he gripped my hips and tugged me down, arching to meet me.

We leaned our foreheads together and closed our eyes, soaking each other in.

It was something of a miracle that we'd found each other, two people who were open to living life on the edge like this, letting their sexual appetites carry them away. I hadn't seen judgment or even hesitation in his eyes when I told him what I wanted. Just jumping green flames of desire.

24.
Huck

Goddamn it. This woman was going to be the last straw that finally sent me to the asylum. It took everything I had to keep my hands off of her. Because we were both working with Dallas—who was very obviously fucking her, by the way—I sometimes had a reason to brush briefly against her back or touch her hand with mine. Right now, that's all I was living on.

Crumbs. But it was better than nothing.

I'd floated the idea to Dallas of adding in a physical therapy session on the mornings he had massage now that his mobility had improved. He would also benefit from it, of course, but the main benefit, as far as I was concerned, was that I could be near her for a little while with no one else around. Well, no one except her fuck buddy.

Predictably, I'd walked right into the trap I'd laid for myself, and now I was committed. I had to pretend to ignore their flirtatious pinches and games of grab-ass.

I wanted to be the one grabbing her ass. That perfect peach of an ass that could stop traffic in the skin-tight leggings she always wore.

I was only ten years older than her, which was ten less than Wild Bill, who was also taking his turn with the new massage therapist. But I still felt like a dirty old man when I fantasized about her sucking me dry at night while I relieved myself of the pressure that had been building in my balls all day.

The rest of the team was similarly horny for her, even some of the married guys, though they were all too decent to ever act on it, even if she would have them. I'd wondered about Lars, since he'd been having some serious marital issues, but their dynamic seemed more like big brother-little sister.

My mind was on paranoid jealousy overdrive, analyzing every word she said, every look she shared with a guy on my team. I was ashamed to admit that I'd been keeping track of who went like clockwork to her studio for appointments.

Not that any of it mattered. I was way too fucked up and broken to have a relationship with anyone, let alone a twenty-three-year-old sexpot that looked like she'd just waltzed right out of my wildest fantasies—blonde hair long enough to tie her up with, innocent eyes that hid the dirty little life she was leading. Add to that a roller-coaster body, all dips and curves that left me breathless, and I was completely fucked.

I met Cash at five-thirty on Monday, Wednesday, and Friday in the player's gym. We had a home game that Friday, and I was considering sending him out onto the ice for a few minutes toward the end. Patch Olson's hip flexor injury was flaring up now that he was getting more ice time than he'd had his entire career, and the team could use a fucking break from having him as the tender, anyway. He was mediocre at best.

I didn't expect Dallas to even be able to block a shot, but I was going to put him on blades for today's warm-up skate and see what he could handle. That might be all we got from him today. But like a baby bird leaving the nest, at some point, we had to just jump. And he'd made such stellar progress over the last couple of weeks that I was starting to think a little time on the ice might be exactly what he needed to supercharge his recovery and his confidence.

He came in a few minutes after me that morning, wearing a baggy hoodie with the hood pulled low enough on his forehead to almost completely cover his eyes. I had no idea where a person even bought clothes so big that they could still be baggy on his enormous frame. He nodded his head in greeting and dropped his bag by the bench, heading directly to the wall of mirrors to do his stretches. He wasn't ever much of a talker, let alone in the morning, but he seemed like he'd hardly gotten any sleep at all.

"How you feeling today?" I asked, bringing over the resistance bands and the large, arched back-stretcher. He nodded and flashed me a tired grin in the mirror.

"I'm feeling fan-fucking-tastic," he said. I eyed him. Then, behind me, I heard the sound of Lola opening up her office.

Earlier than usual.

They spent the night together.

I broke eye contact with his reflection as he moved through his standing lumbar stretches. I arranged the back-stretcher on the floor beside him and looped the resistance bands around one of the weight machine's support posts so that he could do some gentle standing rows. He wasn't able to do a single row when he came here, after a year at the mercy of an entire team of doctors and physical therapists. Now here he was, breezing through standing rows, throwing himself down on the floor easily for cobra pose.

It's not that I hadn't believed in sports massage therapy before Lola. I knew that massage was an important component of overall musculoskeletal health. But I hadn't realized to what extent it could help my players until she came to us. Her work seemed like a miracle, but I knew it was real-world knowledge applied by expert hands that had brought Cash to this level. I liked to think I had a little something to do with it, but I had to admit that his recovery had accelerated tremendously as soon as he gave in and started showing up for his massage appointments.

And she was obviously giving him a hell of a rub down after-hours, too.

Okay, maybe I was bitter. I knew I had no right to be. People want things they can't have all the time. It's a fact of life. Maybe I would want her every single day and night for the rest of mine, and never get a chance to touch her like I wanted to. There were apparently several people in line in front of me. But still, I was drawn to her like a moth to a porch light.

"Be right back," I said to Cash, who didn't bother to respond. I went to her ajar office door and rapped lightly.

"Come in," came her bright voice. Even before dawn, she was a ray of fucking sunshine. You could see her light landing on the guys as she moved through the locker room or the dining hall, the way she reflected, shimmering, in their eyes.

"Hey," I said, clearing my throat when my voice came out hoarse from disuse. Or nerves. I stepped inside and pulled the door closed behind me. Her eyes flicked to it, but then she sat back in her desk chair and crossed her arms over her chest, smiling at me.

"Hey, Huck," she said. My eyes clung to her mouth until I forced them back up.

"Hey." I said that already. "I just wanted to thank you for the work you've done to get Cash back on his feet."

Her eyes sparkled mischievously.

"It's my pleasure."

I honest-to-God blushed. The thought intruded in my mind of my extra-large, injured goalie laying back and letting this tiny blonde bombshell bounce on his undoubtedly massive cock.

It was turning me on.

I cleared my throat.

"Well, anyway," I rushed out, backing toward the door and then just turning around on the spot to hide my rapidly growing bulge as I fumbled with the doorknob. "We'll be done out here in a half-hour or so."

"Huck?" she said, her sweet voice stilling me.

"Yes?" I didn't turn around, just stared at the wood grain in front of my face and tried to think about anything except her plump, gorgeous body jiggling with every stroke.

"Don't sell yourself short," she said, surprising me. I glanced back at her over my shoulder. "Your work with Dallas is making a real difference. I'm just facilitating his progress."

I scoffed.

"That's nice of you," I said, reaching again for the doorknob.

"One more thing."

I winced, waiting.

"If you ever want to come in for a massage or anything, you'd be welcome." I glanced back at her, trying to parse whether her words were innuendo or if she was talking about a literal massage. "I know about the accident." My blood ran cold, and my bulge was no longer a problem. I stood up straight.

"Thanks," I said. "But you're here to work on the players. And I'm not one."

"You could come by after hours—"

"Thanks, anyway!" I called, waving a hand over my shoulder as I jerked the door open and stalked out.

I was inexplicably angry at her for bringing up my accident. I'd put it firmly behind me a long time ago. I had no interest in dredging all that up now.

No matter what she'd done for Cash, my injury was totally different. I was at least five years older than him, and I had no major league hockey career to go back to. I'd been living in chronic, constant pain for so long that I couldn't even bear to imagine a life in which I didn't have to shoulder that burden. I couldn't get my hopes up, not for Lola or her magic hands.

Back in the gym, I gathered the rest of the equipment that Dallas and I would need for today's exercises, doing my best not to slam the cabinets as my blood boiled in my ears.

25.
Lola

I lay on Dallas's bare, burly chest, his cock hard inside me. We were the only two people in the building this early, aside from Huck, who was out there in the locker room somewhere sorting equipment and getting set up for the day. I couldn't stop thinking about him, even in Dallas's gentle arms. The way he had looked at me earlier with so much heat and then was crawling the walls trying to get out of my office a minute later.

It was like he was upset with me for offering him a massage treatment. Did he think I was propositioning him or something? I guess I could understand how he might make that mistake. I was annoyed by how the interaction between us had unfolded, but that hadn't stopped me from fantasizing about him non-stop since it happened.

I imagined him walking in on us like this, and my pussy clenched around Dallas's big dick. He hissed and gripped my hips, pushing me down until another inch of his impressive cock slipped inside me. I braced my hands on his chest and leaned back, putting most of my weight on my hips as I rode him, swirling circles with them and rocking back and forth, just enjoying the feeling of being so full, trying to banish the dark-haired, icy-eyed assistant coach from my mind.

I'd never met someone with walls so thick and high. But that only made me want to scale them even more.

I glanced at Dallas's face. I felt guilty thinking about another man when I had this absolute Adonis under me.

I truly was insatiable.

But I wasn't ashamed. I just wanted to be fully present for Dallas because he deserved at least that. He was so thoughtful, so attentive in bed. We'd been together last night, but we still went at each other as soon as he walked into my studio like we'd been apart for a week. I craved him whenever he wasn't pressed against me. But I didn't just crave *him*.

I wanted them all, like a damn collector. And maybe *that* was something to be ashamed of. Or it would have been, except that I genuinely cared about each of them. I wanted to sleep with more than one of them, sure. But I also wanted intimate relationships with all of them. I wanted to really know them and spend time with them outside the bedroom or the massage studio. I wanted to share myself, not just my body, but my heart, which felt big enough to hold them all.

I wanted them all, but I doubted that any of them except Wild Bill would be on board to share me.

The reminder that Dallas still didn't know I was sleeping with Will made me pause in the act of riding him. I'd told Will I would keep us a secret, but Dallas barely spoke to anyone outside his immediate circle—like, at all. He was the definition of the strong, silent type. I knew, even after only a couple of weeks, that I could trust him. And I couldn't stand the thought of lying to him for another second. So I leaned forward until he slid out of me and stared down into his eyes. He squirmed under me, trying to get back inside.

"Wait," I said, biting my bottom lip. He stared at my mouth and waited. "I need to tell you something."

"Is this about you and Coach?" he asked, wiggling his eyebrows at me. My jaw dropped.

"Does *everyone* know?"

He shrugged his broad shoulders.

"Pretty much," he said. "No one cares. Well, maybe your boyfriend cares. Cowboy."

Reid.

"You don't care that I'm sleeping with someone else?"

Dallas's hands slid from my hips up my sides to circle my waist. He smiled.

"I'm not greedy, Lola," he said. I gazed down at him in amazement, hearing his words but not yet daring to believe them. "I want you, but I don't want to own you. I don't need to own you. I know that you are mine and that you will always come to me. And come for me," he teased, grinning as his hands dropped again to grab my ass. He pushed me down, pulled me forward, holding me against him so my clit slid along the ridge on the underside of his shaft. He pulled me forward a bit more, arched his hips, and slipped back inside of me before driving me down hard onto his cock. I cried out and then bit my lip, but it was too late. I heard the movement outside the door stall briefly. Would Huck come in and scold us?

Or maybe join us?

I held my breath, but after a beat, the sounds of him readying the locker room resumed.

Dallas reached up and clapped a hand over the entire bottom half of my face, covering my mouth and most of my nose, too. With his other hand, he guided me, back and forth, up and down, in a steady rhythm, until the massage table started to creak under us. For the first time, I worried we might break it. Dallas was a big man, after all. But I couldn't have stopped for anything when I was so close to the edge.

His fingertips left half-moon bruises on my skin as he propelled me down onto his pulsing cock with even greater force, using the hand still covering my mouth to drag me down harder, harder, making me take even more of him, more than I'd thought was possible until at last he buried himself to the hilt inside me and growled low in his throat as he came in massive spurts against my inner walls. The tremors of his cock ricocheted through my whole body and sent me off like fireworks. I was grateful for Dallas's hand on my mouth because I could no longer control my whimpers and moans as my body wrung him out until we were both lifeless with satisfaction.

26.
Lola

Nate showed up for his usual Tuesday appointment looking cheerful. Always a dangerous sign.

"Good morning," I said with a nod, changing the sheet out from Lars, who had been in a serious funk. I'd decided to do my best to pry the truth out of him during our next session, because as long as he was this stressed out, a million massages wouldn't root out the knots in his back. He was backsliding, and I was frustrated.

"I need a different kind of stress relief today," Nate said, bringing me back to Earth. He pulled his shirt off over his head.

"What do you mean?" I asked warily, doing my best not to make eye contact with his pecs. This guy was a jerk. So why did my body betray me every time he took his shirt off and gave me that smug, smoldering look?

"I heard it through the grapevine that you give excellent head," he said with a cocky grin. All my thoughts were wiped away, replaced by pounding rage. My face was white-hot. Who had he been talking to? Was Dallas out there giving his friends the run-down every time we had sex?

For a second, I just stared at Nate as my wits gathered back together like a thundercloud.

"What the fuck did you just say to me?" I asked, crossing my arms. His smirk didn't falter.

"If you can manage to get The Tanker's baseball bat down that little throat, mine should be no problem." So it *was* Dallas.

Nate untied the drawstring on his pants.

"Get out of here!" I shouted, pushing him toward the door. He laughed, holding up his hands.

"I'm just playing with you, babe," he sneered. I rolled my eyes.

"Fun game. Please leave."

His face was suddenly serious, and I was afraid he might lash out at me or hold me down and force himself on me. Was that vicious envy I saw in his eyes? Or was he just this much of a fucking creep?

A second later, his brow cleared and he chuckled, snatching his shirt up from the chair. He tugged it on and jerked the door open.

"Your loss," he muttered as he stormed out.

I stared at the empty doorway without seeing beyond it, my thoughts a whirlwind. Then I realized that Reid was standing across the locker room, staring at me, his face twisted up in an unreadable expression.

27.
Reid

I was going to fuck him up. The question wasn't *if*. It was *when*. I couldn't wait to pound his pretty boy face into the gravel of the parking lot. Or maybe he'd let me catch him out back of Copper's one night.

As it turned out, the opportunity presented itself much earlier than I expected.

We had a game Thursday with a team we'd already been trounced by once this season. Wild Bill was tense, and Huck was off the charts, snapping at anyone who breathed a little heavy in his direction.

Nate was sitting across the locker room from me as we traded our cheap suits for our hockey kits. Well, his suit was sharp and crisp, some designer label. He hung it up and wrapped it in a dry cleaning bag. I rolled my eyes and snorted, and he shot me a look, his lip curling. Then he leaned in to say something to his wiry, energetic little buddy—the big shots called him Xaddy. They both laughed, glancing in the direction of Lola's closed studio door. She was in there with Dallas for their little pre-game ritual. She was still trying to hide her relationship with Will, but with Dallas, she didn't bother. I'd like to fight him, too, but I was less certain of a victory when it came to Cash. The guy was a behemoth—six-six, two-eighty, pure muscle. It was no wonder he blocked the goal like a brick wall.

The thought of what they might be doing in there was enough to put me firmly on edge.

A few minutes later, as we were skating out into the rink, Nate sped by me and then turned around, zipping backward across the ice. He gripped his cup through his hockey pants. Underneath his face guard, I saw that trademark smirk. After that, all I saw was red.

28.
Lola

I stared in horror as a fight erupted on the ice, players falling into each other like dominoes as they threw off their gloves and started raining blows.

Fights were common in hockey, even out-and-out brawls. But this was different in one major way—the brawl was one-sided. Every single player slinging punches was wearing a silver jersey.

Huck screamed at his team from the bench as other players flung themselves over the barrier and joined the fray. I saw Xander get punched in the nose by Jamie, and Eric Bouchard swinging his stick into the backs of Reid's knees as Nate tried to get him in a headlock from the front. Reid went down, and a second later, Lars plowed into Eric, sending him flying on his back across the ice.

It was Dallas's first game back, and he stood in front of the net, watching on stoically as his teammates beat the living hell out of each other. He shook his head, glancing at the bench as referees flew in to break up the fight. Huck ran out onto the ice in his shoes, red-faced and shouting as he fought to maintain balance.

If it wasn't a literal fucking nightmare, it would have been hilarious. But I knew exactly what Will was thinking when he tossed a hooded look at me over his shoulder.

This was my fault.

The game was a DQ. Back in the locker room, Huck was livid while Will was defeated. Nate and Reid had to be physically restrained from going to blows again, and another brief scuffle did break out, but Huck sounded his air horn loudly enough to temporarily deafen everyone and they fell apart, both panting.

"Way to go, guys," he said. "Now my entire first line is benched for the next two games. I hope you're happy with yourselves. Whatever the fuck is going on between you two," he said, pointing at Reid and Nate before his eyes flicked to me and away again, "figure it the fuck out. This shit is ridiculous."

With that, he stomped out. Nate and Reid were still glaring at each other. Dallas was standing behind Nate, but he was glowering at both of them.

"What's going on, guys?" Will asked tiredly.

"This piece of shit needs to keep his mouth shut," Reid spat. Nate's lip was split, but that didn't keep the grin off his face.

"It's a free country, Cowboy."

"Shut the fuck up, Nate," Dallas growled, surprising everyone. We all turned to stare at him. His eyes were narrowed and trained on his fellow Prospectors teammate, who looked as taken aback as everyone else. "You've been begging for that ass-kicking for a while. We all know you want Lola so bad you're about to cream your briefs every time she looks at you, but if I hear you say one more foul word about her or to her, you'll be benched for a whole hell of a lot longer than two games while all your broken bones fuse back together."

He didn't stutter, and he didn't blink. Nate blanched, though he kept up his arrogant swagger.

"Et tu, Tanker?" he quipped. I wanted to melt through the floor, just disappear. I'd been so worried about chasing my own bliss that I hadn't paid attention to the fact that the divide in the team was widening, largely because of me.

The two big shots and Reid continued to argue as I backed away. Will's eyes met mine just before I ducked into my office to grab my purse, but he didn't say anything as I reemerged and fled the locker room.

29.

Lola

"Come on, Lols, they're grown-ass men," Hope said, rolling her eyes and swirling her wine glass as if we were drinking something that came with a cork. I chugged my boxed wine and relished the acidic burn at the back of my throat.

I'd been hiding out all day. I'd missed several massage appointments and the game. Dallas had called several times, leaving several increasingly anguished messages, but I hadn't heard a peep from anyone else.

Will was probably glad to be rid of me. I'd caused him way too many headaches since I arrived. And the rest of them were probably pissed that my refusal to just pick one guy had caused them to be DQ'ed.

I shook my head, chewing on my bottom lip and staring into space.

"It's not like you forced anyone. From what I've seen and heard, they're clamoring for it. And Reid and Nate are just mad that they haven't gotten any yet."

I hadn't been ashamed of my sexual appetite until now. Now, I was embarrassed. Even my best friend saw me as little more than the team bicycle. I can admit that that thought had appealed to me. But in reality, it was surrounded by ugliness and in-fighting, and I couldn't deny that despite the small amount I'd done to help the team, I'd ultimately made everything much worse.

"Maybe I should quit and go somewhere else," I said. Hope placed her wine glass on the coffee table with a loud clink.

"No," she said firmly. I looked at her. "I'm sick of everyone bailing when things get tough. You're going to stay here, and you're going to help them turn this ship around. Because that's the right thing to do, and if I can count on you for one thing, it's doing what's right. This isn't your fault, Lola. You're a loving person. A giver. You aren't obligated to sign yourself over to one of them, especially not one of those two pricks."

"Reid is your brother," I said with a weak laugh.

"And? He's a possessive prick who is too scared to make a move but wants to be mad when other people do. He needs to get over himself."

But my guilt, which had been a whisper even just a day before, was now screaming in my ear. I ate my dinner of kale salad with salmon and fresh rolls, Hope's signature garlic-butter recipe I could happily eat with every meal for the rest of my life. Then I sat on the couch with her as she dozed off, my eyes glued to the television screen but my mind far away.

30.
Lola

Around midnight, my phone rang. Dallas again. I stared at the screen until it went dark. Then I heard a light knock at the front door.

Was he here?

I jumped up, raking my fingers through my hair and rubbing at the circles under my eyes. I pulled the curtain back on the window just enough to see the huge goalie standing on Hope's front porch with his hands in his pockets, waiting. What the fuck was he doing here?

I opened the door.

"What the fuck are you doing here?" I asked, waving him inside.

"I missed you, too," he said with a stiff smile. I closed the door but stayed standing beside it. I wasn't in the mood for company. Hope was still sleeping on the couch, and I was busy wallowing in self-pity.

"Dallas, why are you here?" I asked again, gazing up at him. His dark eyes searched my face, and then he cupped it in his big hand and pulled me forward with his other arm around my waist.

"Why aren't you answering my phone calls?"

I felt the tears sticking in my throat, but I refused to let them show. I shook my head.

"I'm allowed to ignore my phone."

"Not when I'm calling," he said, tightening his grip on me. I put both of my palms on his rock-hard chest and pushed him back. He let me, his arms falling at his sides. "I need a massage," he said, changing tack. He smiled again, a real one this time, as he watched my resolve slip. I'd left him hanging on our last appointment of the week, and there was no way I could refuse him what he was asking for, even if he was just using it as an excuse to get upstairs.

I peeked through the doorway to the living room to see Hope still snoring quietly where she was curled up in the corner of the sectional.

"Come on," I whispered, creeping past her to the stairs. Dallas came tip-toeing along behind me, giving me the impression of a massive, top-heavy ballerina. I stifled a laugh, and when he reached me, I stepped up on the bottom stair and grabbed his shirt collar, yanking him down for a kiss. He melted, gathering me up against his chest.

It felt so good to be held by him. Even if it was wrong, even if we'd have to call things off tomorrow, what could one more night hurt?

31.
Dallas

I'd been going out of my mind for the past thirty some-odd hours since she'd disappeared. I had to threaten Reid's life and the headlights on his truck, but he finally relented and gave me his sister's address. Maybe it was pushy. I didn't care. I needed my massage, but I needed a whole lot more than that.

I craved her. I was going through withdrawals. I needed her body against mine.

I followed her quietly up the stairs, my eyes trained on her delicious ass swaying right in front of my face as she climbed ahead of me. The second we were inside her bedroom, I closed the door and pinned her against it, devouring her with my lips on her mouth, on her neck. I bit down on her shoulder until she gave me a throaty groan.

At that, I picked her up and threw her down on the bed, lunging forward to cover her body with mine. She bucked under me, and I let myself dissolve into her. The sweet vanilla smell of her washed over me as I ripped off the old t-shirt she was wearing and tossed it away. She did the same with mine, and then our hot skin was touching, and nothing else mattered. Not the team or the playoffs or the crowd of other dudes literally fighting for her attention.

In that moment, she was mine.

But I'd been hers from the first second I saw her, and I was afraid I'd be in love with her for a lot longer than I was actually going to be allowed to touch her. Major-league Dallas would have run away and hid between the legs of some puck bunny. Any puck bunny who would have him. And there was always a queue.

But that version of myself had been stripped away when my back gave out. And now she was replacing him with a better man, a man who needed her like food and oxygen. I'd do anything, anything, to have her.

But I knew that I was one of many. I wasn't the jealous type. The sharing didn't necessarily bother me. What bothered me was the fact that I would never be able to hide her away from the world just like this, our bodies and spirits intertwined. She would never be completely mine.

"Dallas," she groaned. I pressed my smiling lips to hers. When she spoke to me at all during the first couple of months we knew each other, she'd always called me Cash. It was heaven to hear my real name on her lips, the one my mother gave me, instead of the fittingly cold surname of my rageaholic, alcoholic adoptive father.

I knelt between her legs, peeling off her pajama pants. At the sight of her, I moaned in anticipation. Her skin was so creamy and smooth, and there was plenty of it to enjoy. My cock throbbed in my pants. I shed them in record time, and then I was moving over her again, kissing my way from her ankle to her inner thigh. Gasping, she let her knees fall open, offering herself to me. My lips parted as I lowered them to her clit, my tongue darting out to nudge the sensitive button. Her hands fisted in my hair and tugged lightly. I could feel the pre-come dripping off the tip of my cock, but I didn't touch it yet.

Her taste was even sweeter than her smell. I pushed her knees up and she swung them over my shoulders, crossing her ankles behind my back and clamping my head between her thick, strong thighs. She held me there, bowing up and riding my face as my tongue delved into her. My dick was so hard I was about to drill a hole in the mattress, but an asteroid collision couldn't have dislodged my tongue from her pussy. This was my happy place, where I wanted to live, lapping up her scrumptious nectar and making her scream as she came again and again into my mouth.

I didn't have to wait long for the first one. I felt the trembling start at the place where her thighs locked into her hip sockets. Her fingers tightened reflexively, pulling my hair a little bit harder. I groaned into her incredible cunt and plunged my tongue as deep as it would go. Her ass shot up off the bed, and her thighs were a vice around my head. She let out an amazed laugh that turned into a desperate moan as the climax surged over her body and dragged her away into the abyss. I propped myself up on my elbows, cupping her ass in midair with both of my hands and dragging the tip of my tongue up and down her slit, savoring the taste of her.

I finally relented, lowering her back down onto the mattress when her legs were shaking violently on my shoulders with every kiss and nibble. I blew a hot breath across her swollen clit and she whimpered. Then I covered it with my tongue one last time before levering myself up to cover her body with mine. When she felt how hard my cock was for her, her eyes shot wide open and her lips split in a hungry grin.

"Ready for round two?" I asked. When she nodded, I tipped in.

32.
Lola

"God, yes, please," I panted as Dallas slid inside me. I raised my hips to meet his, taking him deeper with every stroke.

He was like a reassuring mountain moving over me in the dark. I clung to his shoulders and pulled him down against me as he buried himself, rocking his hips, giving me a little bit more than I could comfortably take.

"Is that good, baby/" he murmured, brushing his lips against my brow.

"You feel *so* good, Tanker," I said with a teasing lilt in my voice. He braced himself on his hands and looked down at me quizzically. Then he let out a rumbling laugh and pulled almost all the way out before slamming into me with the brunt of his weight behind his massive cock.

"I'll show you *Tanker*," he grunted, rolling his hips, sliding out of me and then ramming back in, stealing my breath with the power of his thrusts. I gripped his hips, pulling him in even harder, and he swore under his breath as he really put his back into it. That back that had barely been able to bend a few weeks ago. I smiled up at him in the dark, pride swelling in my chest as his cock swelled in my pussy.

He pulled out and straightened up.

"Turn around," he ordered. "Get on your hands and knees." I jumped to obey him, wetter than ever at the firm tone of his voice. I got into table pose in front of him, shooting a sly smirk over my shoulder. He was looking at me with wonder glinting in his eyes, his big mitts covering my ass cheeks, spreading them. I faced forward then, feeling uncharacteristically shy. The color rose in my face as Dallas examined me.

"Fuck, you're so hot," he murmured. A second later, I felt the head of his cock spearing into me again. He slid all the way home with one unrelenting forward stroke. At first he went slow, working me gently back to meet him as he filled me. But then one of his hands skated up my back, along my spine, all the way to the nape of my neck. His fingers pushed farther up, into my hair, until his hand was cupping the back of my head.

Then, he pushed me down.

I face-planted on the mattress. His hand on my hip slid underneath me to keep my ass high in the air, and he slammed into me as he held me down. When I squeezed around him, he hissed a curse, his fingers coiling into a fist in my hair. With a jerk, I was up on my hands and knees again. He was holding me by the hair as if he had me on a short leash, and he jerked me back to take the entire length of his cock with every rough forward thrust. His hips slapped my ample ass as he took what he wanted from me. Blind with need, I forced my body to relax, giving him full control as he steered me forward and back, impaling me and then holding still for a beat before shoving me away again. I could only go to his arm's length because he kept a firm grip on my hair.

I was vaguely aware that the headboard was smacking against the wall loud enough for Hope to definitely hear it if we woke her up. Hell, it was loud enough for our neighbors to hear if they were still out on their front porch nursing their cheap canned beer.

But I didn't care. I didn't hold back, and I would never want Dallas to hold back. He plowed into me, and I knew he was releasing the frustration of a dozen unanswered phone calls, a dozen messages deleted from my voicemail.

I'd needed a break, a chance to clear my head. But then he came and found me, and now I realized just how badly I'd wanted him to.

He moved his hand from my hip around to my chest, planting it between my breasts, and used it to support me as his other hand pulled me upright by my hair. With my back pressed against his chest and his cock deep inside me, he used his grip to turn my head toward him slightly and pressed his lips to my ear.

"Don't you ever disappear on me again," he said, his voice barely audible even in the sudden silence. He let go of my hair and slid his hand around and down until it was cupping my pussy, his two middle fingers curling inside, wedging themselves between my G-spot and his shaft. I was struck by the sensation of being overfilled, but he held himself there, and I adjusted. He had the heel of his hand pressed against my clit and his fingers as deep inside of me as he could get them, crooked forward to massage that sensitive pad of flesh as his cock slid up and down over them, working into me with deep, slow strokes, tip to base, again and again.

I was on a rocket ship headed for the moon. I was floating out of my body.

I was coming.

"Dallas!" I cried out, throwing my head back against his chest.

"That's it, baby. Come for me, because I'm about to unload so fucking deep inside you."

Maybe he kept talking, but I didn't hear anything else except the explosions popping in the core of me, first small but rapidly growing, radiating outward, and then moments later the hot, wet spread of his come as he joined me.

He held me against his chest, tight in his arms, raising me up a bit and then dropping me back down, an inch or two at a time, his palm suctioned over my clit, until the last aftershocks faded away. Then, without ever leaving me, he laid us both down on our sides like spoons, my ass still nestled comfortably against him, his knees curling up under mine, and within minutes we were asleep.

33.
Reid

BBQ @ my house before you all scatter to the wind for the holidays. Mandatory. NO EXCEPTIONS.

I glared resentfully at the text from Will, which sat expectantly on my home screen, demanding a response.

I'd spent the last two days sulking and hiding out in my apartment. I was benched so what the hell was the point of even showing up? Huck had left me several increasingly irate messages, but I'd only listened perfunctorily to each one before slamming my thumb on that trash can icon.

I was completely fucked up, heartbroken, and right on track for yet another season spent in the minor leagues. Lola went AWOL after the friendly-fire brawl during Thursday's game. I had a couple of missed calls from Hope, but I didn't even bother to listen to those messages before deleting them. Jamie was giving me space, but he'd come by a few times to give me an ice pack for my eye and a pack of crackers or a sports drink. He'd doled out more damage than I had, and taken less. But I had the feeling he was just as pissed off at me as everybody else was.

And they all had every right to be. I wouldn't be surprised if they were sharpening their pitchforks right now. Yeah, Nate had baited me, but I was the stupid jackass who gobbled it up. I was the one with the fishhook in my mouth and the black eye, all from fighting over a girl who had cheated on me and acted like I was the problem, the bad guy, when I cut her out of my life.

The truth was, I couldn't look at her, even after all this time, without my heart splitting open all over again. I couldn't keep going like this, hearing about her antics with the big shots…and the goddamn *coach*…until every day had become a reenactment of that nightmare of a party, Chase's body covering hers in a dark corner.

Maybe I should just quit. Or go to Branson and personally request a trade to a different team. Not like I was doing him any favors rotting away on the Ice Hawks, getting worse with every season.

My phone gave another buzz, and I chucked it across the room.

34.
Lola

My hands were shaking. Dallas spent an hour convincing me to come to this stupid, ill-advised barbecue, but I wasn't even in the door yet and I already wanted to turn tail and run. Guilt was a black cloud raining on my head as he herded me to Will's front door with his hand planted in the small of my back.

I'd approached this door many times under different circumstances. I wasn't sure how I would even be able to look at Will without turning bright red, thinking of how he'd fucked me on every surface of this house, even the table where I assumed we would all sit down to eat. After what had happened Thursday, I thought he was crazy to invite the entire team to hang out in a small, enclosed space together.

It wasn't a cheat day, so at least the players would be drinking water instead of beer.

Winter was in full swing now. Fat, wet snowflakes fell around us as Dallas knocked.

"Come in!" I heard Will call from inside. Dallas reached past me and twisted the doorknob, pushing it open and shunting me forward.

It was like he was afraid that if he took his hand off me, I would bolt.

Not a completely unfounded fear.

I didn't understand why it was so important for me to be here, anyway. I'd been stirring up drama and causing trouble since I joined the Ice Hawks. At this point, if Branson fired me, I would totally understand. Maybe I'd helped get Dallas back on the ice, and that was a big get, but the team was no closer to being united. If anything, they were more divided than they'd ever been.

Will glanced up at me from the kitchen island. The one he'd bent me over more than once. A knowing smile flitted across his face as his eyes jumped from me to Dallas and back again. Had he sent the goalie to convince me, the same way he'd sent me outside with Reid that night at Copper's? He was slicing a brisket, and an aluminum roasting pan at his elbow contained stacks of smoked baby back ribs. He'd clearly been out on the deck with his fancy grill equipment despite the inclement weather.

"Hope you brought your appetites," he said, winking at me. The words seemed to have some deeper meaning, but I couldn't put my finger on what that might be.

"You know it, Coach," Dallas said, hanging his coat off the back of a chair and helping me out of mine. Not only had he blossomed as a player since he'd started to recover, but he'd also blossomed as a member of the team. Where he was sullen and withdrawn before, now he spoke up easily. He was blending in. I wished I could claim some responsibility for that, but the entire team had been twisting themselves in knots trying to win him over. He was an unbelievably valuable asset, even if he was only temporarily waylaid out here in no man's land.

"Good to see you, Lola," Will said, his lips twitching. Then he turned his attention back to the large cut of beef in front of him. I glanced nervously around the room. My eyes landed on Nate, who was sitting at the table with a bottle of water, watching me with a smirk. I narrowed my eyes at him and then rolled them and turned away. Somehow, even though I now knew just how much of a dick he really was, the guy still made me all tingly when he stared at me with those burning eyes.

Dallas looped his arm casually around my shoulders, but it felt like it weighed a literal ton as Nathan's smirk widened. I forced myself to look away from him. I saw Lars and waved at him, and he waved back but didn't smile. The same unhappy-looking woman sat in the chair beside him. I looked at her, but she was staring at her phone, ignoring her surroundings. She must be Lars's wife, but I couldn't understand why she was so miserable if that was the case. Lars was a sweetheart.

Maybe she just felt uncomfortable in large group gatherings.

Just then, the door opened behind us, and Dallas and I turned together to see Jamie Larsson stalk inside, followed by the shifty shadow that was Reid Wright. His eyes landed on me and he froze, that tell-tale muscle ticking in his jaw.

35.
Reid

"Just ignore her, dude," Jamie said, turning his back to them and muttering from the side of his mouth as he shrugged out of his coat and hung it on a hook in the front hall. I did the same, for lack of anything better to do. I couldn't just keep standing there staring at her, imagining fun ways to break off Dallas Cash's most important appendages. Starting with the hand dangling so casually over my girl's shoulder.

She's not your girl, I reminded myself forcefully. I followed Jamie into the kitchen, keeping my eyes averted from the goalie and my ex-girlfriend. I spotted Nate sitting at the table and went to the opposite side of the room, near the sliding glass door. I could feel the cold pushing its way in, and suddenly I didn't feel quite so sick.

I leaned back against the cool glass, watching Coach's hands as they worked to carve up some big hunk of meat. Jamie fell into a boisterous conversation with a couple of third-liners, and everyone did me the favor of pretending I wasn't there.

I wished I could do the same. But I was aware of her presence in the room like she was a wormhole that had ripped open the fabric of space and time and was sucking me slowly but surely in.

I pushed away the image of her sucking me in another way, which popped up uninvited. I knew I had to get over her, to finally let go of the wounds I'd been nursing since high school. Sure, she shattered my heart into a million pieces. But we were both adults now, and so what if she wanted to hook up with half the team? It wasn't my business. That just meant she'd be stomping on their hearts instead of mine.

Except she might as well be stabbing you in the eyes every time she lets another man touch her in your presence.

I shook my head. I still hadn't glanced back at her since we walked in and were confronted with her and The Tank all cuddled up right there in front of everyone. Were they officially an item now? Did that mean she was no longer providing sexual favors for Wild Bill?

I raised my eyes to his face. He seemed unbothered by the fact that his little sex kitten was being felt up by his new star goalie. Probably because he was smart and didn't give a fuck about her. Unlike me.

As much as I wanted to stop caring, I couldn't forget her. She'd been imprinted on my heart before I even knew what love was. I'd always felt the urge, the need, to protect her and look out for her.

And, yes, to marry her and pump her full of my babies.

For a while, that was the only way I could see my life turning out. But then we'd gone our separate ways and figured out how to live without each other.

Could I really blame her for having a life after me?

I mean, sure, I wanted to imagine that she'd been pining after me, saving herself, dreaming of the day we would be reunited. But that was just a pipe dream. The reality was, she was getting dicked down by The Tank on the daily.

Bile singed the back of my throat.

I turned on my heel and opened the sliding glass door, stepping out into the snow in my shirt sleeves. The cold was bracing, but it gave me what I needed—something, anything, else to think about.

36.
Will

The barbecue was a hit. The guys cleaned up the meat and sides like a pack of starving locusts. In another life, I would have opened a chain of family BBQ restaurants after my retirement from professional sports. But I wasn't sure I'd ever really be happy with a life away from the rink.

The lifers polished off their third plates as a few of their wives fussed around in the kitchen, cleaning up.

"Hey, no doing dishes!" I called across the room. "You guys are guests!" The truth was, I wanted them to get their little purses and their gigantic husbands and go home. I had plans for the second half of the evening that did not involve them.

Finally, they started to gather their stuff. The third and fourth liners and their wives usually did things as a group. They all showed up at the same time and left at the same time, whether it was a night at Copper's or a team party, or the women coming to an away game.

It honestly warmed my heart to see the community they'd managed to build here.

But I'd designed a team-building exercise that was not married-folks friendly.

I was grateful when Huck took over at the kitchen sink, and the couples started to move as a group toward the front door, hollering goodbyes that I returned with enthusiasm.

Reid and Jamie went to the foyer, taking their coats down off the rack. I cleared my throat.

"Um, first and second lines hang back," I said. "Except you, Kowalski." The second-line left winger had paused in the doorway, his arm around his wife. "Y'all have a good night!" He gave me a cheery wave and guided his pretty blonde wife out the door. With that, the lifers were gone, and it was just us. Me and Huck, Reid and Jamie, Nate, Xander, Eric, Dallas, Patch Olson, and our powerhouse second-line defensemen, Marcus Crane and Sly Moran. And Lola, who looked a little scared but a lot excited. She was watching me with those bright eyes, waiting to see what I would do next.

"All right, boys," I said, bracing my hands on the kitchen island counter and surveying them. Now they were all ten watching me closely. Huck turned off the faucet and wiped down the edge of the sink, and then he slung the damp rag over his shoulder and turned to face them, too, leaning back and crossing his arms. "We've got a lot of raw potential this season, but there's no unity. Agree?" Big heads nodded all around. Lola didn't move, just kept her eyes trained on my face. "So I've come up with an idea for a team-building exercise." I met Lola's stare and raised my eyebrows. "That is, as long as Lola agrees to be our stand-in for the puck." Understanding smacked her in the face. Her eyes went wide, and then glanced to each side, surreptitiously taking in the hulking bodies all around her. Would she be game? I'd taken a risk not touching base with her first, but was it my fault she came with Cash? She very may well punch me and storm out. Or her boyfriend might jump the island and beat me to death. But we'd had a couple of conversations over the past few months that told me she was interested in being shared by several guys at once.

Could she manage eleven?

Dallas looked down at her, a frown creasing his smooth, tan brow. He really was a prime specimen. It was no surprise that she'd been…less available…since they started sleeping together. Maybe she'd decided that she really was a one-man kind of woman after all. But her eyes returned to mine, and a giddy smile split her face. I couldn't hide my own excited grin as I addressed the crowd.

"So, whoever is interested, I'm inviting you now to hang back with us and do some…bonding." I laughed at the shocked looks on several of their faces, especially Marcus, Sly, and Patch. As far as I knew, none of the three of them had even been alone with her yet. No matter the nefarious rumors that were floating around, they couldn't have seen this coming.

I landed on Reid, and my smile slipped. His face was twisted with emotion I couldn't identify. He looked like he could kill, but he was making no moves to walk away. Jamie, on the other hand, was staring openly at his best friend.

"Are you joking?" he asked, turning to me.

"No joke," I said, holding my hands up. As I said, I knew it was a risk. But no risk, no reward, and to be completely fucking honest, I was out of other options. I had no idea how to bring these players together when a few of them were very clearly divided over one thing in particular.

One woman.

That, I could get. They say that Helen of Troy had the face that launched a thousand ships. Lola's ass could launch ten thousand, no sweat. Everywhere she went, I saw men breaking their necks to keep her in view. Even the married guys, though I knew they were all good, loyal guys. I'd seen enough bunnies throw themselves at every member of my team to know who would take the carrot and who wouldn't. The strapping group of guys I'd assembled here were always down for some sexual misadventure.

But they couldn't seem to come to a consensus on whether or not I was pranking them, let alone whether or not they were interested in my proposition. I rolled my eyes, exasperated, but then Lola stepped around the island to stand beside me, facing them. Dallas's eyes darted back and forth between the two of us.

"I'm game if you guys are," she said in a shy voice that got my cock rock hard in an instant. She made me feel like a teenager sometimes, even if I knew for a fact I would still never be able to keep up with her. Hell, I wouldn't have been able to keep up with her when I *was* a teenager. How does one man keep up with a woman who wants all of her holes filled at the same time?

"Come on, man," Jamie said with disgust in his voice. Lola winced, and I wanted to knock his teeth down his throat for making her uncomfortable. He turned back toward the coat rack, but Reid didn't. He was staring at Lola, and she was staring back. All the anger and resistance seemed to slip out of his grasp. His shoulders loosened, and he dragged his hand through his hair.

"I think I'll stay," he said to Jamie over his shoulder without looking away from her.

Jamie whipped around, glaring at Lola and then at me, and lastly, at the back of Reid's head. He opened his mouth, and I expected him to argue, but he just snatched his coat off the hook and stormed out the door, slamming it behind him.

No one took any notice. Lola was now standing in the center of a pack of sharks, and all those bloodthirsty eyes were trained on her. We turned toward her as a group, circling around her, and I swear she gulped as she pressed herself against the edge of the counter, looking small.

37.
Lola

I couldn't blame Jamie—or anyone else—for bowing out of this exceptionally unusual situation. His clear vitriol towards me stung, but the ache was immediately washed away in the rush of adrenaline that followed as the door slammed and every hockey player in the room turned and showed me their teeth. They were going to devour me, and my blood was red hot in my veins.

I was ready.

Will stepped around behind me and wrapped me in his arms, holding me against his chest and sliding his hand down my stomach toward my denim skirt as every eye in the place watched on.

He gripped the hem of the skirt and yanked it up so that it was more like a belt, and my lacy blue panties were exposed to the group. Dallas and Reid both looked conflicted, like they were turned on and also seriously considering homicide. Nate grinned at me from his spot beside Dallas. He was already gripping his dick through his jeans as Will's fingertips slipped under the elastic band of underwear and found my throbbing clit.

I moaned, fully exposed, as he started to move his hand in little circles. He dipped down further and hooked his fingers into me, lifting me up onto my toes with his grip on my pussy.

Nate came around the island toward us. I eyed him warily. He was about to get what he wanted from me because Wild Bill had offered me up to him. I'd denied him before, but I wouldn't now, and he knew it. He reached out and jerked my panties halfway down my thighs, revealing Will's hand between my legs. His touch was electric. It stoked the flame in me. Nate leaned over me, staring into my eyes, and then he lowered his mouth to mine.

I bit his bottom lip. Hard. He swore and recoiled. I smirked at him, raising the back of my hand to my lips to wipe away the smear of his blood.

"Fucking bitch," he said lightly. Then he grabbed the lapels of my shirt and yanked, popping the buttons off all the way down to reveal my bare breasts. I hadn't bothered with a bra.

He smiled hungrily, lowering his lips, the bottom one still bleeding slightly. He closed them around my nipple, and I knew what was coming a second before it happened. I flinched as his teeth clamped down. It hurt, but it also felt incredible. He gave it a gentle tug, and I cried out. Dallas rushed forward but stopped when he realized I was enjoying the pain. I ground myself into Will's hand. I was overcome with the urge to punch Nate in his smug face even though I liked it, as if the two emotions weren't mutually exclusive. But then Will pulled his hand away from between my thighs and gripped my elbows, pinning my arms behind my back and jutting my chest out toward Nate's mouth.

He put his teeth away, and his lips grew more insistent on my nipples. Then he trailed his way down, dropping to his knees at my feet. I gazed at him in awe as his tongue found my clit and went to work. I opened my mouth, but no sound came out between my shock and the rolling waves of pleasure that were once more crashing over me, even more intense after the sharp, swift pain.

Will kissed my neck and continued to hold my arms together behind my back. I tilted my head to the side, closing my eyes. A few moments later, I felt the air beside me shift. I opened them again to see Reid standing there, that conflicted look still on his face. But then his hand was cradling the back of my head, and his mouth was on mine, our tongues clashing, our teeth bumping as the passion of the moment carried us both away. Something snapped inside me then, something that had been building for a long time. I moaned into his mouth as Will bit down on my neck and restrained my hands and Nate absolutely annihilated my pussy and clit with his tongue.

My heart couldn't even feel the full weight of the fact that Reid was kissing me, holding me…forgiving me? Because I was going to come on Nate's face any second. That face I had to stop myself from slapping more often than not. That pouty mouth that said the filthiest shit to me and then just smirked, daring me to react.

I gasped into the mouth of my high school sweetheart as I came into the mouth of the guy I hated. Nate rammed his tongue inside me and pulled my hips forward, knocking me off-balance onto his face as I gushed and thrashed against Will's hold.

When I was finished, Nate sat back and Will loosened his grip. Reid grabbed me and pulled me out from between them, spinning around to back me against the counter. He lifted me up, wrapping my legs around his waist, and then he entered me for the first time in five years.

It felt right. It felt like coming home. It felt like sunshine and frogs splashing into the little pools in the creek where we used to play as kids. It felt like the bed of his pick-up truck, and a whole galaxy of stars.

Reid pressed his forehead to mine. We locked eyes as he buried himself inside of me, holding me hard against his chest. I could feel his cock jumping as his dark gray eyes clouded with emotion. Then he backed away, pulled out of me, and for a brief second, I was terribly empty and cold and alone. Then Huck was stepping forward, helping me down off the counter, and pushing me gently to my knees.

My hands flew to his zipper, eagerly undoing his pants. All the awkwardness and lingering glances between us lifted away, and we were just two people, finally giving in to the heat that had been threatening to burn us both alive. He stroked my hair and then dropped his head back and moaned as I took his thick, hard cock in my mouth. He wasn't as tall or bulky as the other guys, and his dick wasn't as massive. But it was way more than adequate. I licked it like an ice cream cone and then took it down my throat as another bobbing cock appeared in front of me, and then another.

The guys were crowding around, offering themselves, jockeying for a position between my lips or in one of my fisted hands. I was stroking two and sucking another, and I could no longer keep track of who was who. Fingers tangled in my hair, pulling me forward onto another cock, huge and girthy. Its owner rammed himself straight down my throat, bringing tears to my eyes, and I heard someone else make a noise of protest, but I leaned in hard and took even more. Whoever this was was giving me exactly what I needed, using my body the way it wanted to be used. I truly felt like I was designed for this. To take them all. I couldn't think of another way to explain the need that had consumed me from the moment I laid eyes on the gorgeous, green-eyed coach.

The person fucking my throat made a strangled sound, and I raised my eyes to see shy, round-faced Eric Bouchard gazing rapturously down at me as he stuttered, not quite getting his warning out ahead of his come. He spilled in my mouth, and I swallowed every drop, holding his gaze. He pulled away and stumbled backward out of the circle, still not breaking eye contact with me.

But then another torso filled my field of vision, and I was off to the races again. My fists found another pair of eager cocks, their owners pumping into my grip. A chorus of moans and grunts filled the spacious kitchen as they shared my mouth and hands. Then, just as my knees were starting to go numb, someone pulled me to my feet.

It was Reid.

I buried my head in his chest. Someone else closed in behind me, and I could tell from his sheer size that this was Dallas. I tilted my head to look up at him and then back at Reid. There was no jealousy in either man's face, no possessiveness. Just desire and something deeper shining in their eyes as they both smiled down at me.

Then Dallas stepped away, and Reid turned me around, bending me over the counter with his cock pressed into the crack of my ass. I felt him guide his head into my dripping pussy again, and then he was fucking me hard and fast, his fingertips digging into my hips but his knuckles serving as a cushion between my skin and the bruising granite edge. He pulled me back onto his cock, bending down to trace my spine with kisses as he filled me with fast, deep strokes. My cheek was resting on the cool countertop, and I was staring across the room at the kitchen table, where Will and Huck sat, sipping beers from glass bottles and watching me get railed by their team.

They took turns behind me, first Reid and then Dallas and then Nate, a blur of thick cocks until the last of the second-stringers had been inside me. The sensation was strange and exhilarating, all those different shapes and sizes and lengths. Some of the guys had soft bellies that brushed my ass, others had abs of steel. They all had big hands they used to touch me, rub my clit, slide up between me and the countertop to squeeze my breasts as they pumped into me. One of the defenders from the second line—was it Marcus?—couldn't hold his load. He pulled out and sprayed my back. I felt a droplet land on the top of my head. Such was the force of his explosion. His teammates ribbed him about coming after two pumps, though it had really been more like three minutes. Marcus took a seat at the table as Huck returned to the fray. It was his turn, but when he lined up behind me, he grabbed my shoulders and pulled me upright against him. Then his hand went between us, and he inched his cock between my thighs, up into my tight slit, hissing in my ear as he stuffed himself inside me. He kicked my legs apart, one arm circling my chest to hold me upright and the other going between my legs to spread my lips for the audience. The rest of the guys were watching, still stroking their hard cocks, except for Marcus, who dropped into a chair at the table, out of breath.

My eyes bounced around, landing on each of them in turn. When they found Nate, he stepped forward and once again hit his knees, his mouth going to my clit, sucking and licking as Huck eased his shaft in and out of me. His hand no longer needed between my thighs, Huck grabbed my breast and squeezed as he dragged my earlobe between his teeth.

"You like to be watched, Lola?" he asked, his breath hot against my cheek. I nodded. My eyes found Will's. The mastermind. He smiled approvingly and winked at me. "You like to be used and fucked and filled with come?" I whimpered, nodding again. "Answer me."

"Yes, sir," I gasped. His cock gave a violent throb. He dragged his lips from my cheekbone down to my jaw and pistoned his hips, slapping them against my ass, burying himself again and again as Nate's tongue drove me right toward the edge. For the third time tonight, I was close. I gasped, rocking my hips back to take Huck's cock and then forward onto Nate's tongue, my body racked by pleasure as they took me there together. I screamed a few seconds later as another climax ripped through me, leaving me torn with jagged edges.

Nate stood up, wiping his grinning face.

"Let's take her to the sofa where we can really stretch out," he said, wiggling his dark eyebrows at me. Huck picked me up, lifting me off his cock into his arms, and carried me after Will, who led the way to the living room. His sofa was large and plush, built to be comfortable for big men. Not a sectional but still, there was plenty of room. Huck sat down, spreading my thighs around him so I was straddling him. His hands cupped my ass, guiding me back down onto his length. Will stood behind us, a comforting presence.

"Do you want more, Lola?" Will asked. I glanced back at him with wide, curious eyes. He stepped forward, sucking his fingers into his mouth and reaching down to circle my back door. My eyebrows shot up, my eyes even wider, as the tip of his finger nudged its way inside. "I've got plenty of lubrication if you do. But if not, we'll stick to one at a time. For now." I moaned at the exquisite threat he'd implied. That sooner or later, I would have two cocks inside of me. At the thought, my fear dried up and my pussy flooded. I clenched around Huck. He chuckled.

"I think she wants every hole filled now, Coach," he said with a wry smile as he lifted me up and dropped me back down on his cock. My eyes found his, my mouth hanging open, as Will's finger pushed past the tight barrier.

"Have you ever had a man in here, Lola?" Will murmured, bending down so his cheek was brushing mine. I worked myself back onto his finger, and he hissed. "Tell Daddy what you want."

"I want you to fuck my ass, Daddy," I whispered so only he and Huck could hear. At the use of the pet name, Huck's eyes darkened. His cock throbbed and swelled inside me. He looked from me to Will and then back to me.

"You heard her," Huck said, the corner of his lips curling up. Will disappeared from my back, and a moment later, Dallas stepped in. He ran his hand through my hair and kissed my shoulder.

"You okay?" he asked softly. I nodded, turning my head toward him, leaning my forehead against his temple. Then I heard Will's footsteps as he came back into the room, and Dallas straightened up and moved away.

Will was behind me again. I felt something slick and cool sliding up and down the crack of my ass. His fingers, warming me up. He applied pressure at my back door again, and this time, he slipped inside easily. I gasped. The way he was stretching me was incredible, especially with Huck already inside me. The assistant coach pulled me down hard into his lap, his hands on my cheeks, spreading my ass so that Will could force another knuckle into me. I dropped my head onto Huck's shoulder as Will replaced his hand with the tip of his cock.

"Talk to me, baby," he said as he rocked forward. "Tell me if it hurts."

I had had a man back there before. I had a boyfriend in college who loved anal but only wanted to do it when he was drunk. So he'd been too rough, and I was lucky if he came quickly. Usually, he went into a trance back there until I had to call it and push him away.

This was nothing like that. Will had stretched me, primed me. Huck's thumb found my clit and rubbed little circles around it as the head coach's cock popped inside. Then he was filling up my ass, and with Huck spearing into my pussy, I was afraid for a second that I would rip in two. I opened my mouth to tell Will it was too much, but Huck licked his thumb and then returned it to my clit, and the coarse, slick skin thrumming over my pearl caused every muscle in my body to unclench. I sobbed with ecstasy into Huck's chest. Will paused, misinterpreting the sound.

"Don't stop!" I gasped, pushing back against him. "Please, God, don't stop fucking my ass."

Appreciative grunts sounded around the room. Xander, the youngest guy on the team in his early twenties, all wiry muscle and energy, jumped forward and pushed his cock between my lips, fucking my mouth as his two coaches filled my other holes. Xander was gorgeous and hung like a horse, and I found myself wondering why we hadn't spent more time together as he gripped my head in both hands and thrust deeper.

Will and Huck passed me back and forth, from one shaft to the other, neither ever fully leaving me, while Xander abused my throat in the most delicious way.

I slipped away from reality a bit then, letting myself come undone between them, become a series of parts, holes to be stuffed. No longer a girl, no longer Lola, just a body that existed to be at their service. To please them, and get pleasure in return. My desire flowed between my legs as I threw my hips forward and back, forward and back, clenching my core around them.

"I'm about to fill your pretty little ass up with my come, baby," Will panted at my ear. "I know how bad you want it." I moaned affirmation around Xander's cock as best I could. He was still hammering into my mouth, staring down at my tear-streaked face with a manic grin.

Will buried himself inside me, and I felt him unloading. His open mouth groaned against the bare skin of my back as the last drops eked out of him. Then he hugged me tight against his chest, pumped his hips one more time, and pulled out.

Xander took Will's spot in a second, his formidable third leg stabbing into my tight hole. Huck pulled my face down to his, kissing me, as Xander fucked my ass with the same wild abandon he'd shown my throat.

Sly, who I barely recognized out of his kit, stepped up in front of my face. I opened my mouth for him, but instead of his dick, he pushed three fingers down my throat. I gagged around them, surprised, but he held them in place, ramming them even deeper as my teeth dug into his knuckles. I stared up at him with watery eyes. He was a big guy with a large square head and a heavy jaw, and a cock that could stand up to that of any of his teammates except maybe Dallas. I realized I'd had him in my mouth earlier when I saw the small black star tattoo on his right hip bone.

He pulled his wet hand out of my mouth, giving his cock a few strokes with it before gripping the base and aiming it at my open mouth. He pushed it straight down my throat and held it there, grabbing the back of my head and forcing me forward. I kept my mouth wide open, sensing what he wanted. Still gripping the base, he jerked his cock out of my mouth and it quivered in front of me, glistening with my spit and leaking pre-come. He forced it down my throat again and then put both hands on the back of my head and dragged me forward, hard, until my nose was brushing his happy trail. He held my head against his stomach, his dick thick and throbbing in my throat. Then he pulled back again, still holding himself at the hilt, and grabbed a fistful of hair to keep my head in place as he jerked himself off right in front of my face. He blew his load on my cheeks and chin without warning. I closed my eyes just in time, but opened my mouth even wider. I felt the hot drops landing on my tongue as he milked himself into my mouth. Then he gave my cheek a light smack and walked away, and I heard Eric Bouchard, say "All right, Sly!"

Dallas stepped up next. He was holding a washcloth and used it to carefully wipe my face clean. Then he leaned down and kissed me, his tongue between my lips for a brief second before he replaced it with his monster cock.

His was the biggest of the bunch, without a doubt.

Xander reached out from behind me, where he was still fucking steadily into my ass, for a high five from his Prospectors teammate, but Dallas ignored him. He cradled my head, and I wrapped my hand around his shaft, stroking as I sucked on his tip. I knew by now that this was how he liked it. I could choke myself on him, but I would never manage to swallow more than a couple of inches of his dick. It was literally as thick as a Coke can. But he showed me how he liked to be jerked off with lots of suction applied to the head while I squeezed the shaft. I gave him exactly what he wanted as Xander groaned and buried his head in the crook of my neck, gasping as he spilled his come deep in my ass. He bit down on my shoulder hard enough to make me cry out around Dallas's cock, who grabbed him by the arm and threw him halfway across the room without ever taking his eyes off mine.

Huck was still underneath me, his cock inside me, his hands kneading the cheeks of my ass. Dallas stepped away, and I said a little prayer of thanks that he didn't move behind me. I wasn't sure I was ready for him back there yet, though it really was as good a time as there would ever be. I was thoroughly stretched and already dripping with come.

But he was gone, and it was just me and Huck left. The sudden intimacy was jarring. I straightened up, straddling him, bouncing up and down in his lap. His blue eyes searched mine, then dropped to my tits bouncing in front of his face. He watched them with an expression like he was starving. I leaned forward so that his face was between them as they jiggled, and he grunted, pulling me down hard on his shaft.

"God, I'm gonna—"

He didn't get the rest of his sentence out before his cock started to jerk inside of me, firing his come deep into my pussy with the force of a cannon. I pressed my hips against his and squeezed my muscles around him until he was empty.

For several minutes, we were both limp. He held me, and no one else intruded on our bubble. Then, he pressed a kiss to the top of my head and rolled me over so that I was sitting on the sofa. I realized that several of the guys were gone, either to clean up or home for the night. Either way was fine with me. Everything in the world was fine with me at the moment because I was floating in a cloud, ten feet off the ground.

Dallas came back over, tethering me back to reality. He sat beside me, his big cock still hard, jutting up between his legs. He tucked me against his side, just to hold me, but no matter how exhausted I was, I couldn't resist him.

I leaned my head down and licked his tip tentatively. His grip on my shoulder tightened, and he sucked in a sharp breath. I flicked my tongue out again, and then I swallowed him as deep as I could go. He rested a hand on the back of my head, not applying pressure, just encouraging me as I took him down my throat. I gulped, trying to relax the muscles that wanted to slam shut around him. He took his hand off my head, to say I should come up for air, but I just pushed harder. At last, somehow, the back of my throat relaxed and he slipped inside. He jerked forward, swearing, and grabbed my head. I thought he would pull me off of him, but instead, he held me down. He pushed himself deeper.

"Christ, fuck, that's it, Lola."

Someone sat on the sofa behind me and wedged their hand between my legs, parting them and pushing thick fingers inside. I focused on my breathing, and on relaxing around Dallas's fat cock, as the fingers slid in and out of me and then forward to tease my clit. Then they moved away, and a second later I felt hands on my hips, lifting and shifting me from sitting on my butt to balancing on my knees, my head in Dallas's lap, my ass in the air, and my legs spread.

Someone's cock entered me, slamming all the way home with one thrust. I groaned around Dallas's shaft, and he pushed me down harder, growling. He sounded like a wild animal as his control slipped and he forced me to take a little more of him.

The man behind me started to fuck my pussy with punishing strokes, and the room filled with the sounds of our skin slapping together and me choking on Dallas's cock, punctuated by his muttered curses as he fed me every inch I could swallow.

I still didn't have very much of him in my throat, maybe two or three inches, but it was enough. He'd told me that he'd never even gotten close to being deep-throated. I'd been determined then to show him what he was missing out on, even if it took me months to work up to it. But with how turned on and worn out I was right now, I was able to take more of him than I'd previously thought was even possible. Dallas's hand cupped the back of my head, pushing me gently down, and then he shouted out my name.

"Lola!" was the only warning he gave before he swelled and started pumping his load straight down my throat into my stomach. I gulped repeatedly, even as my nose burned and my eyes watered, but some still dribbled down my chin and splashed onto the leather couch cushion. Finished, he pulled me up at last. I sucked air into my lungs, coughing, the slightly bitter taste of him stuck in my throat.

It was divine.

I smiled up at him and he leaned forward to press a kiss to my forehead. Then his eyes flicked up to the person who was behind me, still steadily fucking my pussy.

I glanced back over my shoulder and saw what I should have known from the moment he buried himself inside me. It was Reid, the last one left. He stared down at me with a tortured, blissful look on his face that said he'd been waiting for this, this moment when it would be just the two of us.

I tightened around him and he clenched his jaw, slamming forward into me. Dallas got out of the way as Reid grabbed my shoulder, using the grip to work me back onto his shaft harder, harder, until he was fucking me with the blind intensity of a jackhammer. I dropped my head down, letting it hang in front of me as I took the full brunt of his power, as he gave me every last iota of the frustration he'd been feeling.

I pushed back against him and begged for more, lost in a pink haze, rapidly approaching my fourth orgasm. Sensing this, as he always had, he snaked his hand around from my hip to my clit. I rubbed myself against his fingers in a frenzy as I took his cock.

I was lost, I was losing it, I was going to lose everything, give up everything, hand everything over. I was his, I was theirs, I belonged to this team, these men, and they were free to use me however they wanted to, take whatever they wanted from me, as long as they kept making me come…

My thoughts became an incoherent babble as the cyclone lifted me up and carried me off, beyond the limits of the world, into the ether where my body could become one with Reid, with Huck, with Will, with Nate, with all of them. They had disassembled me and then put me back together in a completely new order, and now they owned every piece of me.

38.
Lola

Not to give myself too much of a pat on the back, but after that night, the team experienced a total turn-around. The chirping stopped between the big shots and the old crew. Sure, Jamie still avoided me like I was the plague, and I'd rebuffed several of Nate's cocky advances since I let him come in my ass. We weren't living in perfect harmony. But as soon as they hit the ice, it was clear that they were finally on the same team, working for the same cause.

I watched anxiously from the stands as Dallas guarded the net like a rabid bulldog. The other team didn't stand a chance. He'd been back on the ice for two weeks now, giving Patches a much-needed break. Most of the glory actually went to him for the team's marked, seemingly overnight improvement. He'd returned with a fire that could not be quenched, and in a matter of days, he had single-handedly dragged the Ice Hawks up out of the gutter, dusted them off, and given them a swift kick in the ass. Add to that our *team-building exercise,* and we all had a new lease on life. Even the married guys seemed more motivated as we climbed up the roster.

Everyone was in a better mood, except for Lars. He kept coming in for our appointments on Tuesdays and Thursdays, but he no longer made little jokes or teased me. He folded his t-shirt, put it in the chair, and climbed up to lay face-down on the table without so much as a hello. I might have been offended under different circumstances, but I couldn't help picturing the pale woman who was always with him but never seemed to be enjoying herself.

After three weeks of Lars looking more and more defeated while the Ice Hawks emerged on the national sports news stage as a minor league Cinderella story, I couldn't take it anymore.

"Is something…wrong, Lars?" I asked in what I hoped was a casual voice as I worked out a nasty new knot in his lumbar column. He tensed up under my hands and I held my breath, hoping he wouldn't jump up and storm out or break down in tears. I'd prefer the tears, but an illuminating conversation was ideal.

"What do you mean?"

"Well, I can keep seeing you, but if you don't reduce the stress in your personal life, massage is not going to make much of a difference in the long run." I slid my hands up to his shoulders and squeezed. The tension there was like a snarl of iron wires. He huffed noncommittally. "I don't mean to pry—"

"It's my wife," he said, his raw voice muffled by the face cushion. "Jeanine. I…I think my marriage is over." My hands stilled on his back. I'd expected as much but knew I was treading on dangerous ground. The wives would have preferred that the team hire a large, burly, and, most importantly, *male* massage therapist. But I was determined to prove to them that they had nothing to worry about, that I wasn't a threat. The thought that news of my antics with the single guys on the team might have rippled out to the other players with negative consequences made my stomach twist.

"I'm sorry," I said, torn between wanting to be respectful and wanting to know what was wrong so I could stick my nose in where it didn't belong and try to fix things. Meddling was just in my nature, especially when it came to people I cared about.

He took a deep breath and then heaved a weighty sigh.

"She never…well…it's nothing. Don't worry about it."

"No, I want to hear! If you want to tell me, that is."

I'd intentionally waited until the end of the massage to bring up the potentially touchy subject. I hadn't made much progress on his knots today, but I was hoping that given his current state, addressing his tension might do more good than a deep-tissue massage.

He sat up, using the towel around his shoulders to wipe his face. There were imprints on his cheeks where they had rested against the cushion for the better part of an hour. He shot me a nervous glance and then sighed again and shrugged his burly shoulders.

"My wife…she doesn't like…" I fought to keep my face impassive. This situation could still spiral off in any direction. There was no way in hell I would be some guy's sidepiece because his wife had a *low libido*. "Forget it."

"No, I won't," I pressed, though I knew I might still regret urging him to continue.

"She doesn't like sex," he said grimly, like he was announcing he'd received a terminal cancer diagnosis. Guard still up, I eyed him. "And I do, so I'm afraid our relationship is not long for the world."

"What do you mean she doesn't like sex?" I asked. "Like, she's never enjoyed it? Did she tell you that?"

"No," he said, staring at the floor. "She used to like it, at least I think so. But we started trying for a baby a couple of years ago…"

"No luck yet?" I asked, frowning sympathetically. He shook his head.

"The first two or three months, she was all over me. When it still hadn't happened by the six-month mark, it was like she stopped caring about making love at all." The way he said *making love* broke my heart. I reached out and squeezed his bicep.

"Have you tried spicing things up?" I asked.

Now he was eying me.

"Like, a threesome?" he asked. I was relieved to hear that, judging by the apprehensive tone of his voice, adding another woman to the mix was not on his to-do list. I laughed and shook my head.

"No, not like a threesome." I took a deep breath and went for broke, knowing he might get pissed off at me for poking at painful subjects. "Look, Lars…asexual people and people with low libido totally exist across both genders and the spectrum in between." He shot a hopeless look in my direction. "But," I continued, and a light sparked behind his eyes. "Often, when a woman seems like she doesn't enjoy sex, it's because the act has become just another chore for her to do. Do you know…is she coming?" The word bounced off the walls, and we both cringed, but he didn't shy away from the question.

"She makes the faces and the noises," he said, scowling. "But I'm not so sure…"

"Well, when's the last time you did something that was just for her?"

"You mean like…cunnilingus?" He sounded like a little boy saying a big word, but I managed to stifle my laugh.

"That's definitely something to include in the rotation. But even, say, breakfast in bed, or a date somewhere nice enough that she feels the need to put on a dress. As in, not Copper's." Now he looked sheepish, as if the thought had never occurred to him to dote on his wife. "If you want, I could teach you a really nice beginner's massage that you could try out on her. To, you know…get the juices flowing."

He blushed beet red at that. He ducked his head again, but I could see the hint of a smile tugging at his mouth.

"Seriously, Lars. So many people get stuck in a rut, even if they aren't married, trying for a baby, *and* working full-time. You have to make sure you're making the time for her, making her feel seen and appreciated. And yes, cunnilingus is always a big plus." I laughed, and he chuckled, shaking his head.

I walked him through the basics of a hot oil massage that should get all of Jeanine's senses tingling and sent him home with a bag of supplies.

39.
Will

I sat in my living room, a can of beer going warm on the coffee table, my eyes glued to the television as the biggest sports news program in the country flashed the Ice Hawks logo across the screen, followed by a short clip of the shut-out Dallas made to win our most recent game. Lola was sitting beside me, her little body practically levitating off the cushion as she, too, stared at the screen.

"Oh, my god, Will!" she squealed, turning those big, liquid-dark eyes on me. Her cheeks were tinged pink with excitement.

This most recent win put us within grabbing distance of a spot in the playoffs, and not just as a wild-card contender. We'd jumped from the low end to the high end of the conference roster in little more than a month. And I knew damn well that I had the girl sitting next to me to thank.

I turned and snatched her up, hauling her into my lap and squeezing her. She squirmed, turning until she could wrap her arms around my neck and hug me back.

"You did this, Lola," I said into her hair as I held her. She tried to look up at me, but I kept her pinned to my chest.

"That's not even kind of true. You've all been working so hard—"

"Yeah, but we were going nowhere fast until you…stepped in."

I flashed back to that night, right here on this sofa. How she'd offered herself to be used completely. She dropped her head onto my shoulder, giggling against my neck as she remembered, too.

"Thank you, baby," I said, brushing my lips over the top of her head. She nudged her hips forward, grinding her hot little pussy against me. My cock was already waking up with the way she was wiggling around, but now it sprang to full attention. She lifted her eyes to mine and I gazed down at her, grateful that she'd given me an entire night, just us. Since she and Dallas had started up something serious, she still came to visit me in my office, but she hadn't been back to spend the night here very often. I made it clear I wanted her tonight, and she'd shown up with bells—and sexy, strappy lingerie—on.

She sat back, balancing on my knees, and reached between us to free my cock from my boxers. She gripped it with both hands and pumped it a few times, biting her lip and batting her eyelashes at me.

"You want my cock again?"

I'd carried her to bed and fucked her senseless as soon as the front door closed behind her. But we'd eaten dinner and done some mindless petting and channel-flipping since then, and I was hard enough to engrave steel. She nodded sweetly, gripping me tighter.

I grabbed her ass in both hands and pulled her down into my lap. She tilted me toward her opening, guiding me inside, and then she settled, laying against my chest, her ear pressed over my heart, as she moved her hips in tight little circles.

"That's my good girl. I love watching you take all of me, Lola." I brushed a lock of hair behind her ear and she tilted her head back, pressing a kiss to the hollow of my throat. I closed my eyes and gritted my teeth to keep from telling her what else I loved. Namely, her.

She leaned back in the saddle of my lap and started to ride me in earnest. I opened my eyes to see her stripping off my old t-shirt she'd been wearing as a dress with nothing on underneath. I stared openly at her unbelievable body, those big, heavy, bouncing tits, that cinched waist, the sexy swell of her stomach. And that ass. I gave it a light slap with my left hand as my right tightened and pulled her harder against me. She arched her hips forward and leaned her shoulders back, looking like a cowgirl breaking a bucking bronco as she slid up and down on my length, taking me to the hilt every time in her impossibly tight, impossibly wet pussy.

My balls were already drawing up between my legs, ready to pump her full again. My hands on her ass clamped down, slowing her. She rolled her head on her shoulders, dropping down in my lap until our hips were flush together, clenching around my shaft until I thought my whole body, not just my cock, was about to explode.

"Do you know how incredible you are?" I asked her. She looked at me from underneath her eyelashes, her lips glistening and pink. "You're the most amazing woman I've ever met, Lola." She wasn't a girl at all, even if we liked to play like she was sometimes. She was bold, confident, and fearless. She knew what she wanted and exactly how to get it. But she didn't use her sexual power for evil. Since coming into our lives, she'd lifted each and every one of us up.

I traced the curve of her waist with my hands, sliding them up and down, pulsing inside her. Our heartbeats aligned as we stayed like that for minutes, not moving, just staring at each other, into each other, locked together. I never wanted to let her go, though I knew I would have to eventually. What we had now couldn't last forever. Even the most insatiable nymphomaniac couldn't maintain a relationship with half a professional hockey team. And I wasn't optimistic or stupid enough to think that I was the body that she would choose to pull out of this whole mess.

So I would keep her with me as long as I could, and I would bask in every second I had with her because I never knew when she might walk away for good. Whenever that time came, I knew that there would be nothing else for me to do but let her go.

40.
Lola

Lars floated into the studio the next Tuesday, looking ten years younger.

"Jeanine enjoyed the massage?" I asked

He surprised me by catching me in a hard, smothering bear hug. When he let me go, he was grinning and smiling happy tears.

"I'll say she enjoyed it," he said, his misty eyes glistening. "Five times."

"Five times!" I crowed, giving him a light punch on the arm. "You animal!"

He bowed his head shyly, but in the next second, he was requesting that we end his massage a few minutes early for another lesson. I laughed, and then I realized he was serious.

So, that became our new routine. Now that he had some semblance of a sex life back, a lot of his knots were working themselves out, and he didn't need a full hour of deep-tissue twice a week. So we devoted half of that time to kink class.

I taught him about silk restraints, toys, and sensory deprivation. He ordered the remote-control vibrator I recommended, asked Jeanine on a date to the fanciest restaurant in Casper, and then instructed her to wear it for the evening.

The following Monday, he brought me a huge bouquet of lilies.

Word spread that I was giving Lars sex lessons, and so he started sharing my tips with the other married guys. I even caught him drawing a diagram on the locker room whiteboard for a rapt audience one day. When they noticed me watching, they broke into a round of applause.

And just like that, their playing improved, too. If we'd been a force to be reckoned with a couple of weeks before, now we were a freight train barreling right for the playoffs. Mr. Branson visited the arena, ordered a sinful amount of pizza and ice cream, and declared it team cheat day. When he asked what the hell had happened to turn the team around so dramatically, we all pointed at Will and gave him a standing ovation. We heaped all of the credit on him and then some. No one even glanced in my direction. But later that night, Will took me home and made me come so many times I lost count. With his mouth, his hands, his cock, and, to my surprise, a vibrating pleasure wand.

"Where did you get that?!" I shrieked, giggling as he brought it down on my engorged, over-sensitive clit. But in seconds, I was panting and moaning and begging for more.

"The married guys aren't the only ones picking up tips," he said with a wink as he circled the wand around and around until he wrenched yet another screaming climax out of me.

Afterward, he cradled me in his arms, spooning me in his big bed as the big, bright January moon shone through the window on our faces.

"I don't think I'll ever be able to truly thank you for what you've given us," he murmured, on the edge of sleep. But by now, he'd done more than enough. I felt his gratitude.

"You don't have to thank me for anything," I whispered in the silvery dark. "I'm part of this team." He nestled his face into the crook of my neck at that, and soon enough, he was snoring. But I stayed awake for a while, listening to his sounds, reflecting on the whirlwind that had been the past three months. We still had four more to go, longer if we made the playoffs. Which was looking more likely by the minute.

Everyone was getting along so well right now, but we lived in a clumsy house of cards. It could collapse at any moment. And there was at least one rogue element.

As close as I felt to Reid that night when we were all together at Will's house, when he finally touched me and kissed me and fucked me like he used to, he was back to giving me the cold shoulder and dodging me when he could. I'd tried to lure him into the studio for a massage, seeing how stiff he was on the ice, but he brushed me off.

He might still be freezing me out, but every day, he and Nate the Great seemed more able to read each other's minds. They moved together on the ice like two well-oiled parts of the same machine. The rest of the team was falling in line, but there was nothing quite like when Dallas, Reid and Nate were all out on the ice together. That was when the magic happened.

I hadn't pushed Reid to talk to me for fear of disturbing the peace. But could we keep up this awkward, avoidant dance for months? Or would we reach a boiling point long before then?

41.
Huck

These days, they came in together more often than not. Dallas in his workout clothes and Lola drowning in one of his hoodies tugged on over her athleisure. Arms linked, giggling. I choked back the jealous rage that swelled in my throat when I saw them together—or saw her with anyone.

I knew she went home with Will some nights, and of course, I'd outright watched her get fucked by multiple men. I'd taken a piece of the action without complaint. But the gang-bang was as far as things had gone with Lola and me, and I wanted more. Way more. I had to admit that, at least to myself. When she was close to me, my brain went to its happy place—her straddling my lap on Will's couch, her pussy tighter than a rubber glove around my cock as a parade of my guys used her. I was there the whole time, feeling her, absorbing her, and now she was haunting me.

"Morning, Huck," she said brightly with a wave as she peeled herself from Dallas's side and ducked into her office. Dallas didn't greet me, which was typical. Still, I couldn't deny that he was in a much better mood lately. Maybe it was all the Lola time he was getting, or the fact that he was back on the ice. Probably a combination of both.

Things were looking up for him. Unlike me, he would head back to the show next season and have a full career. I hadn't been so sure when he arrived in Casper, but his recovery between then and now had been just short of miraculous. He would head off, pick up the mantle of stardom as if he'd never laid it down, and I would stay here, wasting away as an assistant coach and glorified equipment manager in a promising but ultimately middle-of-the-pack development team. A repetitive stress injury was a far sight different from a broken back, and logically, I knew that. But I was still stuck in self-pitying mode as Dallas stretched in front of the mirrors and I readied the gym for our PT session.

I kept glancing at her office door, which she had left open slightly. I was glad no one else was there to see me snapping my neck every few seconds, whipping my head around at every little noise she made. Hoping she would come and hang out with us.

Some days, she stayed at her desk, running through her schedule, studying treatment plans, or returning emails. Who knew? But some days, she came out and sat on one of the spare benches or a large medicine ball and chatted with us while we worked. She'd said she wanted to be involved in all aspects of Dallas's recovery so that she would know where he was at, not just on the table but in the gym and on the ice. Once they'd started riding in together, she was on-site a lot earlier than she needed to be, and there really wasn't much else to do but talk to pass the time.

Lucky me.

To be honest, those were the best days of the week. Hell, they were the best days of the last six years, with the very best day being the one when I felt her skin on my skin, her body wrapped around mine.

Finally, the door swung open, and this time I wrenched my neck for a good reason. She came out in her trademark crop top and the leggings that showed every last goddamn lick-able inch of her from her hip dips to the bones in her ankles. I had dreams of her smothering me with her thighs. At least then, I could die happy.

She flashed me a smile and a little wave as she crossed the room to join Dallas on the mat, stretching beside him. I watched out of the corner of my eye, feeling like a creep but unable to stop myself, as she raised her arms over her head, circling her hips one way and then the other. Unlike Dallas and I, she could bend over and touch her toes. When she did that, I dropped the bands I was untangling. I ducked to pick them up, my face burning, but they paid me no mind.

Maybe I was just being paranoid, but she seemed damned and determined to ignore me. Unlike with some of the others, she hadn't split off somewhere private with me to "explore our connection." She seemed to be perfectly content with what had happened between us that night at Will's house and didn't seem at all interested in trying to take things further. Which I guess made sense, given that she was already juggling the head coach and our MVP. To be honest, I had no idea how she managed both of their towering egos. But, like me, she seemed able to take a backseat and be an important background player.

I might curse God daily for what he had done to me, but I'd fit well enough into my new role as team support. I still got to experience the rush, the atmosphere of professional hockey—sure, it was minor leagues, but I made enough money to live comfortably doing something I loved, which made me infinitely blessed even if all my biggest, wildest dreams hadn't come true.

"Huck?"

Her sweet, soft voice calling me sliced across my sad-sack train of thought like a machete. I raised my eyes to find her facing me with her hands on her hips, a light sheen of sweat glistening on her chest and forehead. I let myself stare. She'd asked for my attention, after all.

"I think Dallas might be ready to step back into weightlifting."

I frowned.

"I don't know, Cash," I hedged, glancing at him. "We don't want to push you too hard, too fast."

He turned to look at me, and I saw real fear in his eyes.

"That's all right with me," he said, holding up his hands and shaking his head. I cocked an eyebrow and looked back at Lola.

"Are you pressuring him to take on more than he's ready for?" I asked. She shifted on her feet, looking appropriately chastened. Something about it made me red hot for her.

As if I wasn't already.

"I just think that sometimes we have to jump, and if the baby bird won't jump, doesn't the mama usually push him out?" The sentiment was familiar to me.

Dallas looked sidelong at her.

"You calling yourself my mama?" he asked in that old, grumpy, grumbling voice, but I saw the hint of a smile cross his lips. He enjoyed her worrying over him. It was probably nice, comforting, after dealing with this shit on his own for so long. His mom had been there for him to an extent, but no one on the outside truly understood what a player went through when he was benched. Especially for a season or longer. A single game was bad enough.

I understood, which had led him to open up to me more than he might have otherwise. But there was still an impenetrable fortress around Dallas's heart and mind, at least where I was concerned. Maybe she had figured out how to tunnel through.

"I mean, he's back on the ice, and he's killing it," she pressed, ignoring the brooding giant beside her.

"Exactly. So why mess with a good thing when it's working so well?" I countered.

"Because that's how *growth* happens."

"Right now, we're building a foundation. We'll worry about growth next season."

"He's not going to be here next season!" she said, and then the room was silent as the words echoed around. I looked at him, and then my eyes found hers again.

"Then he can grow in Denver."

She made a frustrated noise in her throat and threw her hands up, but she didn't challenge me.

Too bad. I'd have welcomed an excuse to spank her.

I turned my back on her so she wouldn't see my self-satisfied smile. I could appreciate the fact that she'd pretty much single-handedly brought Dallas Cash back from the dead—because if I was being honest with myself, I knew that he wasn't making any kind of significant progress with my therapy until she got involved. The difference between then and now was undeniable.

But the very last thing I wanted to do was shove Dallas off the boat without a life preserver. Plus, it felt good to exert a little influence and make her bend to my will. The fire in her was melting the ice around my heart, and I wondered if she hadn't done the same for him. If she hadn't allowed him the space and safety to *feel* again.

The problem was, I didn't want my heart to feel what was coming when she moved on and I was left alone here, trying to glue the pieces of my life back together.

42.
Lola

I turned back to the mirror, watching Huck's reflection over my shoulder.

I'd seen what Dallas could do, how much he'd improved already. If he didn't return to his regular exercise regimen soon, he would lose even more muscle tone and strength in his abdomen and back, which was the only thing that had kept him from becoming completely disabled in the first place.

He was still ripped. No argument there. I was pretty well acquainted with the human muscular system, but I swear I'd discovered some new ones running my hands over his naked body. It wasn't enough, though. If he would be on the ice full-time again, he should already be building his core back up.

But I could concede that Huck might know a little more than me on this particular subject, if the three degrees on his wall were to be believed. Apparently, he'd received a biology degree while he was playing hockey in undergrad, and when he had his accident and got knocked out of the major league, he'd channeled all of his pent-up energy and frustration into tearing through two different graduate programs. That's what qualified him to wear so many hats on the team. He wasn't just some back-alley "physical therapist." He was licensed and certified. He knew what he was talking about.

My natural instinct was to argue, but I bit my tongue. Dallas's eyes found mine in the mirror, and I could see that he was less than enthusiastic about the idea of pushing himself more than he already was. I reached up and squeezed his bicep, flashing him a reassuring smile. I wouldn't press the issue, especially if he was worried. Maybe a slow build-up was the best approach after all.

"Hey, Lola, do you mind helping me spot him on this exercise?" Huck asked as he arranged work-out equipment in the center of the room.

"Sure," I said, letting the tension between us dissipate. Well, some of the tension. There was the Other Thing. Would we or wouldn't we have a relationship beyond the group dynamic?

He watched me with dark eyes as we crossed the room to him.

"Lay flat on your stomach," Huck instructed, pointing to the mat. Dallas dropped, stretching his large frame out. His toes dangled off the end, but it was a pretty good fit. I looked up at Huck to find him watching me again. "He'll stay like this for a couple of minutes. After that, I'll lift his right ankle up, bending his leg at the knee, and then I'll cross it over his left leg and pass it to you. You'll push it as close to his left hip and the ground as possible without using *any* force, okay? Then we'll reverse it all and cross his left leg over his right. It's called a scorpion stretch. Dallas, you'll work up to doing this one unassisted, but I want every move to be controlled the first time we do it." The goalie made a muffled sound of assent. A month ago, he had panted with exertion simply while lying flat like he was now. These days, he was much sturdier. Lying down was hardly a high-intensity exercise, but I was still thrilled to see how he managed it with ease.

I understood scorpion pose, at least well enough to assist Huck. I hit my knees on Dallas's left side, and Huck mirrored me on his right.

"Okay, here we go. Breathe through it, let me guide you, and tell me the second you hit your limit. If we can't get your legs all the way across today, that's fine. We're just feeling this one out for now." Dallas nodded his head on the mat. Huck reached down, gripping the large man's right ankle in both hands. He lifted the right foot straight up, bending the goalie's knee at a ninety-degree angle. Dallas puffed out a sharp breath and then sucked in a deep one. "You doing okay?"

"Yeah," he grunted.

"Are you really?" I asked, knowing how likely he was to hide his pain.

"Yep," he huffed as Huck started slowly pushing the right foot over the left leg, toward me. I reached out to take it, but he shook his head.

"Not yet. How's that?"

"Tight," Dallas said with a strained laugh. I placed my hand on the small of his back, the location of his herniated disc, without applying any pressure. I could feel his muscles flexing, like a winding ball of snakes. But they were still smooth. No knots.

"Can you go a little further or should we back off?" Huck asked in that gentle, clinical voice. I watched him with admiration. Out in the world, or behind the bench, he was all sharp edges and shouts and scowls. He seemed out of place at Copper's, like he didn't know how to have fun. But this was clearly his element. He knew exactly what to do and was in total control.

It was fucking hot.

"Okay, Lola," he said. My name was like honey on his tongue. I stared at his mouth for a beat, and then I blinked, blushing and focusing in on Dallas's enormous foot, which was hovering in the air in front of my face. "Ready?" I nodded. "Now, you're literally just providing enough resistance to keep his leg from flopping back over onto the right side. Don't pull at all. No pushing anyone out of any nests." He smirked at me when I glanced back up at his face with narrowed eyes.

"Got it, Coach," I snarked. He nodded, seemingly satisfied, and let me take the goalie's ankle. Just the act of me providing the resistance in place of Huck naturally intensified the stretch. Dallas swore and made a little gasping sound, but in seconds, he was relaxed again.

"Talk to me, Cash," Huck ordered. He wasn't looking at the goalie. His bright blue eyes were trained on my face.

"It's okay. It's good, actually." Dallas exhaled, inhaled, every breath deep and deliberate.

"Can you go a little further?"

"Mmpff."

"I'm going to need that in English," Huck said.

"Yes," Dallas hissed. I nudged his foot toward me, just barely. "Ah!" he shouted. "No. Nope. Let me go." Huck jumped to his feet, taking Dallas's ankle carefully out of my hands. I knew better than to make any sudden movements. I just waited for Huck to come to me. He took over, slowly and steadily straightening Dallas's leg and lowering it back to the mat. He arched that sarcastic eyebrow at me again.

"And you think he's ready for deadlifts?"

"I didn't say deadlifts," I countered indignantly. "You know as well as I do that exercise is key to recovery. And you're the one who already has him back out on the ice."

The superior look slid off Huck's face.

"Let's switch sides," he said flatly.

The left leg gave Dallas a bit less pain. I was able to pull the ankle down until it was almost touching the back of the right thigh, like a number 4. As Huck lowered Dallas's left leg back to the mat, our eyes met again, and this time both of us lingered.

"Are there any other exercises involving three people that might help him feel better?" I asked in a moment of boldness that I immediately regretted. My face flushed bright red. Huck was staring at me, and Dallas propped himself up on his elbows, his eyes scanning me.

"Is my little nympho craving two cocks at once?" he asked with a smirk. He already knew me so well. I pressed my cool fingertips to my hot cheeks, glancing at Huck to gauge his reaction. He looked a bit like he was choking, his eyes wide and his face as red as mine.

Dallas rolled over onto his back between us, and I could see he was excited at even the mention of sex, as usual. He may call me a nympho, but he was ready as often as I was.

Huck made a strangled noise, and then he jumped up and went to the heavy metal doors that separated the gym from the rest of the locker room. They usually remained propped open all the time, but now he kicked them shut and flipped the deadbolt.

I reached down and rubbed Dallas's growing erection through his sweatpants. He closed his eyes, raising his hips toward my hand and groaning. Huck came back over and knelt behind me, running his hands up my sides to cup my breasts as I freed Dallas's cock from his pants and started stroking it.

Huck kissed his way across my shoulder, up my neck, biting the shell of my ear before exhaling hot air into it. Grinding his rock-hard bulge against my ass, he squeezed my tits in his hands, thrusting forward. I pushed back against him, lowering myself as I did so to wrap my lips around Dallas's shaft. He groaned, his hands weaving themselves through my hair.

"Want me to fuck your sweet little pussy from behind while you suck that big dick, Lola?" Huck asked huskily, one hand planted in the center of my back, holding my shoulders down while his other kept my hips raised high. He thrust against me again, pushing Dallas to the back of my throat. I rocked back and lifted my head enough that I could answer him.

"Yes, sir," I said, breaking into a grin as Dallas palmed my head and guided his cock back down my throat.

In seconds, Huck had my leggings down to my knees and was tracing my pussy lips with the slick tip of his cock. I moaned around Dallas, triggering an even louder moan from him when my throat muscles contracted.

Huck fell forward, slicing into me. He was at least eight inches, but I took him in one hard stroke with how wet I was for them and because Dallas had stretched my pussy in the shower first thing this morning. Huck hissed as he bottomed out inside me, his hands curling into fists around the soft flesh of my ass.

"She feels so fucking good, doesn't she?" Dallas asked, holding me down with his dick in my mouth as Huck pulled out and buried himself again, again, rutting into me. With these two working me out, I was soaked and already getting close. I could come all over Huck's cock just from the way he was taking me, rough and fast like he was staking his claim. Establishing dominance over my pussy.

"She's incredible," Huck agreed. I glowed with their praise. I flexed my inner walls around him, and he bent over, panting against my shoulder blade. "She's goddamn…," he pulled out and slammed in again, "…perfect." Now, he was drilling me in a furious rhythm, and I could no longer control the speed or depth at which I took Dallas down my throat. He raised his hips, forcing himself even deeper, his fingers tightening their grip on my hair. I was powerless to do anything but be used by them.

After several minutes of ruthless railing, Huck stood and lifted me off Dallas. He half-carried me to the weight bench, laying me on my back. Then he walked around, crouched between my legs, and closed his tongue over my clit before shoving it deep inside my pussy. My head tipped off the other end of the bench and I opened my mouth wide, moaning and bucking toward Huck's hungry lips.

Suddenly, Dallas's cock was filling my throat. With how I was dangling upside down, he slid straight in. I still couldn't take him all the way—not even close—but he was pounding in and out of me, cutting off my air supply, and I was loving every second of it.

Dallas pulled his cock out of my mouth and bent down, wrapping his fingers lightly around my neck and kissing me with rough lips. At the same time, Huck's tongue left my pussy and was quickly replaced by his cock pushing all the way in. I cried out, the sound muffled when Dallas shoved his tongue into my mouth. He straightened up and stood in front of my upside-down face, stroking himself, watching as Huck fucked my pussy.

After a few pumps of his massive shaft, he guided it toward my mouth again, burying it in my throat as he leaned over me to watch Huck's dick fucking into me up close. Dallas covered my clit with his fingertips and rubbed gently, firmly, edging me toward oblivion with Huck's every thrust.

I couldn't make a sound, couldn't announce my orgasm as it came. It crashed over me like a tidal wave, raw and sudden. My whole body went stiff and tight, clenching around Huck. Dallas kept fucking into my mouth with short, sharp thrusts while Huck plowed away between my legs, carrying me over that edge, and then we lifted off. We both soared. I felt him jerking inside me, his fingernails digging into the skin of my hips. He groaned, burying himself as he emptied his last few drops deep inside my pussy.

Dallas straightened up, gripped my head in both hands, and slammed into my throat three, four, five times, and then he was pumping his come directly into my stomach. I swallowed around him again and again until he gave a weak cry and stepped back, his softening cock slipping from between my lips.

I was gazing up at him happily, so I saw his face change the second he realized that the custodian had unlocked the door to let Will and some second-line players in for an early workout. But I didn't realize that that was what had happened until I heard the slow clapping. I jerked my head up to see where it was coming from and felt like someone had just dumped a bucket of ice water over my head—but there was no camera and no charity cause. Just the stark, cold consequences of my reckless actions.

They were gathered in the doorway—Will, Jamie, Marcus, Patch, and Reid. Reid was smirking at us with a cold look in his eyes, swinging his arms wide and then bringing them together in sardonic, exaggerated applause.

"Damn, that was a hell of a show, you guys," he quipped. Will's face was blank as he stared at me. Patch and Marcus were grinning. Jamie narrowed his eyes and then turned away, shaking his head. And the custodian, still standing there with his heavy keyring dangling at his side, was watching us with his jaw on the floor.

The message of what I was seeing finally made it from my eyes to my brain. I shrieked, rolling away from them and falling off the bench onto my shoulder on the rubber floor. It was padded, but I still felt a zing of pain radiate from my glenohumeral joint down to my elbow.

"Lola!" Dallas cried, crouching down beside me. Footsteps rushed over, and then I was staring up at Huck, Will and Reid, with Patch and Marcus hanging back. Marcus was craning his head to get a better look at me.

"Oh, my god, oh, my god," I moaned as I flipped onto my stomach and crawled toward my clothes, which had been abandoned on the stretching mat. These guys had all seen me naked before—well, not the janitor, but everyone else. And I liked to be watched. But to be *caught,* so vulnerable and exposed, was humiliating. I jerked my shirt over my head and then struggled with my leggings, which kept getting hung up on my feet. "Fuck!"

"Here, let me help," Dallas said, his hands on mine stilling me. Huck was on my other side, probing my shoulder with his fingers. He glanced at our audience.

"Can you guys give us some space?" he snapped. Patch and Marcus backpedaled. Will and Reid each took a hesitant step back but continued to linger nearby. Jamie had disappeared. "Does this hurt?" Huck asked, turning his attention back to me.

"A bit," I muttered. The injury to my shoulder was minor, and nothing compared to my wounded pride.

I covered my burning face with my hands while Dallas pulled my pants up as if I were a toddler. Then I braved a glance at Will between my fingers, expecting him to be angry. But instead, there was a look on his face like he'd just had a brilliant idea.

43.
Lola

"You know, I'm getting jealous having to hear about all your daring adventures with other guys," Nate said. He was sitting on the edge of the table after his massage, his toes brushing the ground, his shirt still off but his pants thankfully on. I shot him a look and then rolled my eyes. I'd been doing my best to put the mortifying events of the morning behind me, but everyone I ran into kept bringing it up, making it impossible to move forward.

I turned from the workbench to face him, crossing my arms.

"Don't you have, like, six puck bunnies waiting for you back at your apartment right now?" I asked. I was only kind of joking. Nate the Great had a hell of a reputation. Someone online had suggested that they heard his body count was in the triple digits. Not that things like that mattered to me, necessarily. If anything, I hoped to match him one day. So we were both sluts. So what?

The fact was, he was an entitled shit, and I wasn't too keen on the idea of giving in to his relentless demands. He could have any girl he wanted, and he could have me in a group setting when I was open to being used. But one-on-one? That wasn't about to happen any time soon.

"You mean the apartment where I have to hear you get dicked down by my monster of a roommate every morning?" he asked sulkily. I narrowed my eyes at him, trying to read his tone. I'd done my best to skirt around him, Eric, and Xander when I stayed the night with Dallas. We usually left for his AM workout before the rest of them were awake, so it wasn't too hard. But apparently, we'd made more noise than I realized. Still, I wasn't sure why he cared.

"Sorry if we've been too loud," I countered with a smirk. Barbed banter was the only way I knew how to communicate with Nate, so that's what I stuck to. He raised his eyebrows and sucked his teeth, then dropped his eyes and nodded.

"Don't worry about it," he said, jumping down from the table and going to the chair where he'd left his shirt in a pile. He tugged it on, heading for the door. Then he looked back and fixed me with his dark eyes. I was surprised to see that they were burning with a strange intensity. "If you ever get a wild hair, come on down the hall to my room. Bet I can make you scream twice as loud as he can." I opened my mouth, though I had no idea how to respond to that. It didn't matter because he was gone in an instant, snapping the door shut behind him. I blinked, staring blankly at the wood grain, feeling shaken up.

Nate made uninvited sexual remarks toward me often. Usually, he did it in the form of a crude joke, light and mocking. But this time, things felt different.

I was still mulling over the odd conversation when the door swung wide and Will marched in, holding Reid by the elbow, who was struggling to escape.

"What—?" I started, frowning at the scene unfolding in front of me. Will pushed Reid forward and blocked the doorway so he couldn't storm out.

"Let. Me. Go," Reid ordered the coach through gritted teeth.

"You're going to let her massage your back if I have to hold you down on that table myself."

My heart sank. I knew Reid needed regular massages, but I'd been secretly glad that he was avoiding them as a means of avoiding me. If he was stubborn and childish enough to share me with his friends and then continue to freeze me out while his spine exploded, that was his prerogative. I didn't want to touch him, didn't want to be trapped alone in a room with him, forced to tolerate the disdain and revulsion that rolled off of him whenever he was around me.

Except when he was fucking you up against that kitchen counter…

Not the time to reminisce about that.

Reid finally stopped trying to push his way past Will and fell back, panting. Then he glared at me over his shoulder.

"Twenty minutes," he growled. I held my hands up, palms out.

"Don't do me any favors," I said. He rolled his eyes and rounded on Will again.

"See?!" he shouted, flinging his hand in my direction.

"What's going on?" I asked, growing wary. Neither of them looked at me.

"I'll pay for my own massages at that place in town."

"That place in town doesn't have a sports massage therapist."

"I don't need—"

"You absolutely need—"

"Fine!" Reid roared, spinning on his heel, marching over to the table, and throwing himself facedown onto it. I looked at Will and raised my eyebrows.

"He's about to be benched. See if you can make him see reason. Twice a week, *Cowboy*," he said loudly, narrowing his eyes at Reid's bare, impassive back. Then he left and closed the door hard behind him. I squeezed my eyes shut and just stood there for a second, gathering myself. I was afraid of what might happen when I pressed my skin to his. But I knew I couldn't exactly refuse him. So I took a deep breath and went to the workbench, turning the music up a couple of notches and mixing essential oils into a carrier. Juniper and ginger to warm his muscles and encourage them to relax.

"Where does it—"

"Same old," he answered shortly. I nodded, pursing my lips. Then I dipped my fingertips in the oil, rubbed my hands together, and stepped up beside him.

"How long—?"

"We don't need to talk," he said. My hands froze in midair as I fought down the swell of indignation that threatened to spew out of my mouth in the form of yelling and insults. Swallowing it, I ran my hands up and down his back and zeroed in on that old injury, rubbing out the tension. I could feel him going to pieces under me, but I didn't let up, and he didn't ask me to stop. I gave him the twenty minutes he'd asked for, and when I was done, he stood up and walked out without a word or a glance in my direction.

Exasperated by how unthinkably shitty my day had been so far, I stormed into my office, snatched up my purse, and then marched out to my car.

If nothing else, I could take an off-site lunch. A *long* off-site lunch.

44.
Reid

Hope swore up and down to me that Lola wouldn't be home tonight. Probably out with one of her numerous fuck buddies. No surprise. Hope had told me that she didn't actually spend much time in the room she was paying rent for.

I tried not to think about Lola—correction, *obsess* about her—constantly. The team was improving on the ice every day, even though we still had a lot of wrinkles to iron out. I'd thrown myself wholeheartedly into the game, into every practice, until my back was so bad I could barely get out of bed. So Wild Bill *forced* me to go to her studio for a massage. Twenty of the most tense, agonizing, *un*relaxing minutes of my life.

And every night since then, I had dreamed of her hands on me. How her skin felt against mine. I woke up every morning rock hard, but that was nothing new. That old teenager's curse had come back in full force the first day I said eyes on her, all grown up, both of us back in Casper as if we'd never left.

I shook my head, scowling out the cracked windshield as Jamie drove us through a snowstorm to have dinner at my sister's house.

I knew I was asking for trouble, even though she wouldn't be there. I'd be fighting all evening not to slip away upstairs, let myself into her room, to smell her sweet, soft scent. To touch things she'd touched. I wouldn't let myself be near her any longer than was absolutely necessary—okay, except for that night at Wild Bill's house, but we were all a bit out of our heads then. Caught up in the moment. That was it. And it had been a mistake. Now my dreams had texture. I knew exactly what she tasted like, what she felt like, all over again. I'd finally gotten to the point where my memories of her and our time together were vague and fuzzy, mostly just impressions I'd done my best to forget except during weak moments in the dark before bed when I would sometimes let myself drift in them for a little while.

But it was too late to change course now. My sister could royally piss me off, but Hope and I were so close in age that we'd grown up practically inseparable, and that included her best friend Lola, the tiny blonde girl with the curling pigtails and the wide brown eyes. I'd seen her as another little sister, another innocent to protect. But that last year of high school, everything had changed. The fact that I'd ever thought of her in platonic terms was hard to believe now.

Jamie parked and pulled the emergency brake, and then we both jerked up our hoods and hoofed it to the front door.

I rang the doorbell, and a few seconds later, Hope opened the door with a grin. Mouth-watering smells crept out of the house and into my nose, and I closed my eyes, savoring them and this moment that was always so perfect, the moment of anticipation just before a God-tier meal. I knew this meal would be divine because Hope had prepared it, and she was a literal wizard in the kitchen. Since we were kids, she could conjure up something out of nothing. She started making bread when she was ten, for Christ's sake.

Who does that?

With her notable skills, it was honestly a surprise that none of us ever got fat. I'd skipped my usual Sunday cheat day knowing I was coming here. I wanted to leave enough room in my weekly caloric bank to eat until I was sick, and let Hope's food soothe the wound deep down inside of me that only had one other balm. A blonde-haired, dark-eyed girl.

Exactly like the one who was frozen halfway down the stairs, those brown eyes fixed on me. Hope slammed the door behind us, jolting me out of my momentary state of shock.

"You said you were making dinner for some of your friends from the restaurant!" Lola shouted at Hope, who turned to look up at her with that same big smile.

"I know," Hope said. "I lied."

"Hope—," I started warily. I could feel Jamie seething at my shoulder. He was like a rabid guard dog, and Lola was his prime target. He was just waiting for me to give the command so he could rip her to shreds. But if I wasn't going to get the satisfaction of screaming obscenities at the girl who broke my heart, neither was he.

"You are my brother," she said, her eyes searching my face. She looked back to Lola. "And you are my best friend. You guys don't have to get married, though I've been wishing you would since we were kids." I blinked at her, stunned. Had she inadvertently put a spell on me all those years ago, to make me so infatuated with her best friend that I would never be able to love another woman or even look at one with more than a passing interest? A silly thought, but that would have been easier to accept than the fact that I was just plain in love with Lola and always had been. And maybe I always would be. "But you can't hate each other. You can't run in the opposite direction every time you see each other. I have wanted this dinner to happen since you moved in, Lola. This is how I pictured our life—all of us friends, all of us spending time together. Can't you at least try? I think if you guys talked about what happened…"

"Hope," I bit out. She rounded on me.

"Don't *Hope* me, you dumb jackass. You ghosted the love of your life over a stupid misunderstanding. Chase basically assaulted her that night, and you just happened to see the moment when it happened and not the next moment when she shoved him away."

"Hope," Lola said, echoing me as she hurried down the rest of the stairs.

"I'm sorry, Lols," Hope said, and I could tell by the look on her face that she was. My universe was expanding and crashing down around me. I stared at Lola, hoping that what my sister had said wasn't true. I didn't want to think about anything like that happening to her, and I sure as hell didn't want to think about the fact that I'd iced her out when she needed me the most instead of being there for her like I promised I would be. "I've kept the truth to myself because it's your business and your story to tell. But I can't do it anymore. It's only hurting everyone involved. It was one awful, unwanted kiss a million years ago. Are you going to let it keep doing damage forever?"

Lola opened her mouth, her eyes bouncing from Hope, to me, to Jamie, who had softened at my back a bit after hearing what Hope had to say. I stared at Lola's face, my brain a jumble, wanting to apologize but unable to form any of my thoughts into words before she turned on her heel and darted back up the stairs. She ran down the hall into her room and slammed the door loudly behind her.

45.
Lola

I landed facedown on my bed and let out a sob. I couldn't stand to cry in front of Reid and Jamie, who had both been looking at me moments before Hope's big speech like I was some sewer rat. And then Hope made the unilateral decision to share my trauma with the class, and both of their faces collapsed into caricatures of pity. I heard one of them, maybe Reid, call after me as I locked myself in my room, but there was no way I was going back down there.

I was crying hot, angry tears into my bedspread when a loud knock sounded at my door. I sat up and rubbed my cheeks roughly.

"Lola."

It was Reid. I hurled the closest pillow at the door, where it hit with a soft thud and slid to the floor.

"Go away." I knew I was being dramatic and irrational, but in a way, I was embarrassed that he had shut me out for so many years over something that was ultimately so insignificant. Hope was right. That kiss had been a blip on the radar of my life, or would have been if not for the fallout. It was gross, but people had lived through much worse. Losing Reid was the true pain of all of it, and the fact that he had no problem walking away from me, cutting the cord without so much as a follow-up question.

"Can we please talk? I'm sorry. Lola, I'm so fucking sorry." He wasn't yelling. He was speaking in low tones, but I could hear him perfectly, even through the closed door. I sat there staring at the portal, knowing that all I had to do was open it and we might actually be able to turn back time, to go back to the way things were before.

But I wasn't that girl anymore. She was long gone. Was I willing to give up everything else going on in my life right now, throw away all the good, and hand myself over to the guy who ghosted me so easily five years ago? Sure, he had shared me with his teammates that night at Will's, but I had a feeling things would be different if we let ourselves be in love again. I was sure that he would want all of me to himself like had before.

I heard something soft hit the door on his side, and then a slow sliding sound. Like he was dropping down to sit on the floor in the hall. For a second, I just continued to stare at the door. Then I crept quietly off the bed and padded across the room, picking up the pillow and hugging it to my chest. I stood there, holding my breath, waiting to see if he would say anything else or go away like I told him to. I wasn't sure which outcome I preferred. My heart was pounding in my chest. Suddenly, on the other side of this thin wood, there was a boy I hadn't seen in years. A boy I'd missed like a drowning girl misses land.

When he spoke again, his voice was almost a whisper. I knelt down on my side of the door so that I could hear him better.

"I was such an idiot. I still am. I should have tried to sort this out with you the first day I saw that you were back here, or way back then at the party, in the moment. But instead, I threw a tantrum and pushed you away. Fuck, I might end this season on the bench when we're playing the best we ever have because my pride won't let me book you for a massage. I don't… Maybe you can never forgive me for how I hurt you. I don't expect you to. I really don't. I guess I just want to tell you how much I will always regret, for the rest of my life, just letting you go like that."

I sat cross-legged on the floor, staring at the door, trying to make sense of what he was saying. It was everything I'd wanted to hear for five years. I'd been convinced that he wasn't capable of something like this, owning up to his mistakes. But clearly, I'd been wrong, too. I'd wanted to believe the worst of him. Hell, I could have told him the truth about that night weeks ago when he confronted me at his apartment. But I'd let the hurt linger. Not like I'd known for sure that he would believe me, or forgive me even if he did. But I couldn't deny that I'd been just as prideful as him.

Could I really blame Hope for finally doing what we both should have done a long time ago?

"Okay," he said defeatedly. "We don't have to talk tonight. But if you ever want to, just know my door is open. I would do anything to make up for my stupidity, Lola. I want you in my life."

Still, I couldn't make myself speak. I couldn't make myself open the door and let him inside. I believed that he was sorry, just like I was. But I still felt an uncertainty, an anxiety, that wouldn't allow me to give in to the want that was coursing through me. I lay down on my side of the door and propped my head on the pillow, trying to decide which of the words banging around in my head I should say to Reid here, now, at last, in the conversation I'd been needing—and dreading—for so long.

The house was silent. Crying always made me tired, and I'd had a long day that had started at five o'clock this morning in the player's gym with Dallas and Huck. So, as I lay there trying to decide what to say, what to do, I drifted off into a restless sleep.

When I woke again, it was full dark outside and in my room. I sat up with a start, my mind jumping immediately to Reid. His face had plagued my scattershot dreams. I'd never given him an answer or a clue as to how I was feeling. I scrambled to my feet and gripped the doorknob, yanking it open.

Reid tumbled backward onto my feet. He blinked those charcoal gray eyes up at me, and then his lips parted in a surprised smile.

"I'm sorry," I said softly, stepping back. I meant *for everything*.

The rest of the house was dark, too. Where the hell did Hope and Jamie go?

He pushed himself up to standing and stared down at me with a furrowed brow. And then, just like that, we were grabbing each other. He was lifting me up, I was wrapping my legs around his waist. We tore at each other's clothes, our tongues clashing, his bulge growing between my thighs. He walked forward, kicked the door shut behind us, and carried me to my bed. There, he dropped me on my back and covered my body with his, rolling forward and pressing his cock firmly against my wet, throbbing pussy through my yoga pants.

I needed him right fucking now.

I shed the rest of my clothes as he did the same, and then we fell together again like two magnets that could no longer fight the pull. He was inside me, just like that, and it was the homecoming I'd been waiting for all along.

As Reid moved into me, over me, I felt tears leaking down my face again, and this time I didn't try to wipe them away. I buried my head in his chest, pulling even more of his weight down on top of me, wrapping my legs around his waist and driving him deeper, harder inside. He kissed the top of my head, clutching me to his chest, grounding himself to the base in my pussy again and again in a ruthless, driving beat that struck like a hammer at the hottest part of me. I dug my fingernails in and dragged them down his back as my body drew up tight around him, and he swelled inside me, and we came together like twin rocket ships exploding in orbit. Violent, bright, hot fury rained down on both of us as we held onto each other with teeth and claws, like the world was really ending.

Afterward, we lay together, our legs entwined, the bedclothes balled up at our feet. Just gazing into each other's eyes. The hurt was still there, but like a healing cut now, it almost felt good to put my finger on it and press down. I nibbled at his neck and collarbone. Despite five years of words unsaid and secrets kept, and resentments left unaddressed, I found that there was nothing else to say. Nothing to explain, no questions I felt I needed the answers to.

The silence in the room was complete but comfortable, and we languished in it together, the rest of the world forgotten.

At least for now.

46.
Reid

I sat on a stool in the dark, quiet kitchen, staring with amazement at the girl I knew long ago, with the open-mouthed laugh she kept trying and failing to hide with her tiny hand. We ate the leftovers from Hope's incredible dinner cold from the fridge, picking pieces of chicken off the bone with our fingers. My sister had gone to bed at some point much earlier in the evening, and we were doing our best not to disturb her, but it was hard when I wanted to shout and run around and bang on every wall in the house.

She wanted me, and I wanted her, and I didn't give a damn if every other player on the team wanted her. I assumed that every man everywhere she went wanted her. And she could have as many of them as she wanted, as long as she found herself in my bed at least a couple of days a week. I would take what I could get and know I was lucky to get it after what I'd put us both through. I'd be atoning for the rest of my life, which I would devote to her. I never wanted to let her out of my sight, but I knew that I would, and often. I would give her the freedom to spread her wings instead of deluding myself into thinking I could control her or had any right to.

Shame burned like a bonfire in my chest for what I'd done. I'd kicked her while she was down. I'd hurt her far more than that sack of shit Chase ever could.

I knew something she didn't about Chase. He had also stalled out in minor league hockey, just like me, and we'd played his team several times already this season.

We would play them again in the lead-up to the playoffs. I'd hated him since that night, even more than I'd hated her—if you could call what I'd felt for Lola hate and not bitter, jealous love. I cut him off, just like her. I hadn't even given in to the temptation to pick a fight with him during a game because I was afraid that if I started hitting him, I wouldn't be able to stop.

But now…let's just say me and the boys were going to make sure he had an unforgettable night the next time we caught him on the ice.

47.
Lola

I missed Dallas's workout the next morning. I woke up to the bright sunlight, still wrapped up tight in Reid's arms. His deep, steady breaths ruffled my hair. I peeked over my shoulder at him, and my heart leapt into my throat like it always did, always had. He was right there, the boy of my dreams. I'd worried for a second that last night was just that, a dream. But here he was. Here we were. We both laid down our swords and our egos, and we found a way back to each other.

The time we'd spent apart now felt laughable, but back then… It's hard to explain. The grief was all-consuming and exacerbated by the lack of closure. What Chase did to me was wrong, and then Reid had rubbed salt in the wound by disappearing on me.

Here one second, gone the next. After he blocked me, I couldn't bear the thought of asking Hope to relay a message to him, begging him to talk to me so that I could tell him what really happened, which I could hardly admit to myself. I knew it was assault, even back then, and that the way Chase had been treating me in the weeks leading up to the party was harassment. It was like one day, he just decided that he was going to steal me away from Reid no matter what it took. He was going to claim me. I still didn't know why. But he'd managed to blow up both of our lives in pursuit of his selfish goal.

And yes, we let him. Just like all emotional decisions, mine seemed like the right ones when I was making them. Ghosting him right back had seemed like the only option available to me. Now, all my justifications seemed like excuses and bullshit, shields I'd been using to protect myself.

I snuggled back against Reid as he snorted and his breathing shallowed out. He woke up, and a second later, his arms tightened around me as he buried his face in my hair. He'd already been sporting a semi against the small of my back, but now it grew quickly to its full potential. He rolled me over in his arms and pulled me on top of him, staring up at me in wonder as he grabbed my ass and showed me how he wanted me to ride him. He raised me all the way up and then brought me down hard and fast and held me there, thrusting up to push himself even deeper inside me. Then he picked me up again, brought me down again, spearing into me and gritting his teeth. I let out a little scream. He was filling me up, not just body but soul.

He dragged me down into his lap harder, harder, with the same urgency he'd had last night, like he wanted to be as deep inside of me as possible. We were rattling the bed frame against the wall, but I didn't care. Right then, I didn't care about anything but him. Us.

I was a bit more self-conscious when we made it downstairs to find Hope sitting demurely at the kitchen table with her coffee steaming in front of her, smirking down at the newspaper.

"Guess you guys made up," she said without looking at us. We exchanged a sheepish look. "Which apparently means I need to invest in some noise-cancelling headphones if I ever want to sleep again."

"Sorry, sis," Reid said, walking over to hug her shoulders and planting a loud kiss on top of her head. "Be careful what you wish for."

Now Hope folded her newspaper and leveled me with a self-satisfied smile, looking like the cat that ate the canary. I sighed and gave her what she wanted.

"You were right and I was wrong. Thank you for helping me see the error of my ways, bestie." She laughed out loud.

"Now, was that so hard?" she asked as she lifted her mug triumphantly to her lips.

48.
Will

"You want me to do what?!" Lola cried. I grinned. I knew she would do it. I wasn't worried about that. Her pussy was probably already wet just thinking about it. I pointed at my lap and she moved across my cramped office to drop obediently onto my knee. I circled her waist loosely with my arms.

"I want you to sit in the penalty box wearing nothing but a pair of ear muffs and fur-lined boots, and I want you to perform sexual favors for the guys when they nail a drill or a sick slap shot or, you know, what have you." I pressed a light kiss to her shoulder, my hand drifting down between her thighs to cup her warm pussy. The heat told me I was right. She was into the idea.

She looked over her shoulder at me, studying my face.

"And this would be a *closed* practice?" she asked. My grip on her pussy tightened.

"Very closed."

"Like, the married guys wouldn't be there? No spectators?"

"Would you like me to invite some spectators?" I asked.

"No!" she shrieked. I leaned forward, grinning into her fragrant hair.

"We'll lock the doors and have the practice after hours." I tucked a lock behind her ear and watched her profile closely, looking for any little tells of discomfort. I knew it was a big ask, and under any other circumstances, it would be an insane thing to do. But Branson still hadn't gotten around to replacing the security cameras with ones that worked. If I made sure to warn the custodian away, a vital step that Huck had missed when he decided to fuck her in the gym, we should have complete privacy. Just the eleven of us. Some of the guys who could really use special training would miss out on *this* practice, but all our MVPs would be present, and those were the players most likely to make the difference as we vied for the championship. "We're ramping up for playoffs, and the next games are crucial to secure our spot on the roster. A few extra drills for our most aggressive players, with an irresistible carrot to motivate them, might just do the trick. We're so close." She stiffened against me, and I could tell she was thinking it over. Then she glanced back at me again, and this time, she wore a devilish smile.

"I'm game," she said throatily, already short of breath just thinking about what we were going to do to her in the barn tonight. I ran my hand over the front of her damp panties and she whimpered.

"That's my good girl," I whispered in her ear as I pulled my hand back, wedged it between us and unbuttoned my slacks. Then I jerked her panties to the side and rammed my cock inside her. She threw her head back against my chest as I fucked up into her, gripping her cunt, my fingers curling over her clit. I lifted her up and down, up and down on my shaft. I was going to pump her full of my come first, so they knew exactly whose orders she was obeying when she spread her legs for them.

And I was going to do it soon, because the thought of her pert little nipples hard enough to cut glass, right there rink-side…

I grunted, pressing two fingers to her switch and flicking it as I drilled her. She started writhing around in my lap like a bobcat, and I knew from how she clamped down around me that she was coming all over my cock. I went careening after her, not bothering to muffle my yell as I made her mine.

49.
Nate

This had to be some high schooler's fake letter to Penthouse.

I stared at Lola, sitting bare-ass naked on a cushion in the penalty box across the ice from our bench. Wild Bill told us that all we had to do was get one past The Tank to earn five minutes in there. Given how often I'd been jerking off to fantasies of her lately, it wouldn't take me anywhere near that long to stuff her sweet little pussy full of my come.

But The Tank was especially motivated now to protect the goal and, by extension, his girlfriend's holes. I chuckled behind my visor.

I respected my friend and teammate. He was one of the best in the business. But I was about to score on his ass and then make him listen to Lola moan and beg for more as I fucked her brains out while he tried to keep his head in the game and stop the others from lining up behind me.

"Nate, you're up," Will shouted from behind me. I couldn't help but grin as I jumped to my feet and pushed onto the ice for a shootout. Huck tossed a biscuit, and I scooped it with my stick, arcing wide away from the net before looping back around and building speed. I zagged from the right to the left and back again, with Tanker's eyes tracking my every move. He may be the Tank, but I was the fucking great. Everybody said so. And I wasn't about to let such a sweet prize slip through my fingers yet again. I'd heard the word *no* from her one too many times.

I faked right and then curved hard to the left and snapped the puck over Cash's shoulder with a quick wrist shot, lighting the lamp. He swore loudly and threw his stick down, snatching his water bottle from the top of the goal and shoving his helmet up to chug from it.

"Show me another before you hit the sin bin," Will called from the bench. I glared at him as Tanker knocked the puck out to center ice. I took off in pursuit, picking it up easily and coasting back around toward the goal. Now my teeth were clenched, and my eyes were slits, and I wouldn't be surprised if they could see steam curling out from under my helmet. Cash thought he would block me easily this time, but I reared back and sent a hard slap shot straight between his legs before he could even move to react. He threw his hands up, shaking his head, but no one stopped me this time as I coasted to the penalty box.

Lola watched me approach. Her curvaceous legs were crossed at the knee, and her blonde hair was tied in pigtails beneath her ears, which were covered with fuzzy pink earmuffs. Shearling boots kept her toes warm, and the rest was up for grabs. I stepped inside, dropping my stick and gloves and ripping off my bucket. Then I shoved my pants down to mid-thigh and dropped onto the freezing bench.

"Fuck!" I shouted as the cold bit my warm, sensitive skin, but I pushed past it. "Come here," I said, reaching over and pulling Lola into my lap. She straddled me and stared down at me with her jaw set. Like she'd accepted a challenge. Like she was holding her nose, only fucking me because her *Daddy* had ordered her to. I smiled coldly, locking eyes with her as I reached down and grabbed my cock, driving it home inside her tight, slick pussy.

Goddamn. I missed being right here.

She rode me dutifully, bouncing up and down on my dick, her tits jiggling in my face. But that wasn't good enough. I wanted more from her. I gave her ass a light slap and her eyes jumped to mine.

"Come on, cowgirl. Ride me like you mean it. Reward me for all my hard work." I winked at her, and she glared at me but started pounding herself into my lap more forcefully. I squeezed her tits in my hands and then gripped her ass and dragged her forward, hard and fast, as I buried my face between them.

She was heaven. Everything I'd ever wanted. I wanted to lose myself in her. But I wasn't a fool. I knew exactly what this relationship was. Transactional. She didn't like me. Couldn't stand me, in fact. I might not be able to have what I really wanted with her, but I would have her. She could hate-fuck me if she had to. The joke was on her. I was into that shit.

"That's it, baby. Put your back into it." I was close, and taunting her got me closer.

"Shut up," she said under her breath as she squeezed around my shaft, raising herself all the way up so just the tip was inside and then dropping with all her weight onto my cock. Again and again, milking me with her elastic pussy. No matter how much cock stretched it out, that shit snapped right back. She was unbelievably fucking tight.

"You know you want my dick, Lola." I was whispering roughly in her ear as I put bruises on her ass, forcing her down harder into my lap with every stroke. "You want my come. You know it, and I know it. Hate me all you want. Just let me fuck that sweet little cunt every once in a while. I'll make you come and scream and beg for more, and then you can go right back to hating me."

She tilted her head back, exposing her long, graceful neck.

"Shut up," she moaned desperately, but she pulsed and trembled, and I could feel just how hot she was for me.

"You love being used, especially by an asshole like me." I closed my mouth around her nipple and sucked roughly until I made her cry out with a mix of pain and pleasure. She bucked her hips forward against mine, digging her nails into my shoulders. The five minutes were almost up, but I was right there, and so was she. "Give it to me, dirty girl," I whispered against her skin. She screamed and came like a gunshot, locking down around my shaft as I jerked and groaned and fired off inside her.

I expected her to jump up as quickly as she had hopped onto my lap, so imagine my surprise when her head rolled forward, landing on my shoulder, and then she turned her face in toward my neck and pressed a kiss against my flushed skin. I gasped with surprise and need, throbbing inside her, still hard even though I'd just blown what felt like my soul all over her walls.

I slid my hand up her back and into her hair, holding her, breathing her in. We stayed like that for a few more seconds until Huck blew his whistle and Will called me back to the bench.

50.
Lola

I'll admit I had some reservations about Will's "sin bin drill session," as he so charmingly put it, but then Nate left me in a puddle, and after him, Eric Bouchard came in and pushed me unceremoniously against the plexiglass partition, his hand on the back of my head smashing my breasts and cheek against it as he fucked me from behind. The sight and the sounds I was making as he railed me distracted Xander Bardi enough that he missed his shot and went tearing back to the bench, cussing Eric all the way.

Eric deposited his come inside me along with Nate's and Will's as Reid skated out onto the ice. He was a defenseman these days, but I knew well enough from watching him all through school that he could play any position with precision and skill. Still, Dallas wasn't called The Tank for nothing. I held my breath as I watched Reid circle the net like a bird of prey, lining up a shot. When he took it, it bounced off Dallas's glove. I frowned, disappointed, but he'd get another chance.

I wasn't surprised that Dallas was guarding the net, and me, with everything he had. But I also wasn't surprised that some of his more dedicated teammates were still managing to get around him to get what they wanted.

Still, it obviously wasn't easy for them. I was starting to get cold, sitting alone, dripping come onto the cushion as shot after shot bounced off Dallas's gloves and shin pads.

Sly Moran missed, and so did Marcus Crane. On his second go-round, Reid sank the punk and skated over to me, still stewing from his miss the first time. I made him feel better with a quick, sloppy blow job. I knew what he liked, and he was shooting into my mouth before the whistle blew.

He left and I sat back on the bench, enjoying the burn in my throat. I closed my eyes and laughed at the ridiculous, unlikely, insane situation I found myself in. I would have never dreamed that something like this was possible. For some women, this might be their literal nightmare. But Will was giving me a gift he knew I craved. He was pushing me to my limits, and then blowing right past them. He wanted to know how much dick it would take before I stopped reaching for more. He wanted to find the bottom of my sexual well.

So far, no luck. My pussy tingled with excitement as Xander "Xaddy" Bardi hit the ice again. Dallas was starting to get tired, but he also knew how much I loved, needed, craved being used. Even if it made him jealous to watch a succession of his teammates use me like a toy and unload inside me, he wanted me to be happy. He would be well-rewarded for his own performance on the ice today. He could be sure of that, at least.

Again, I felt the twinge of guilt, the thought that maybe I was being selfish, asking too much. I was greedy, that was an undisputed fact. I wanted all they had to give and more. But what was I supposed to do with these big feelings I had for Dallas, and Reid, and Will, and even Huck? Things might be casual with the rest, but narrowing my choices down to one man, when they all fulfilled different needs and desires…felt impossible.

Xander lit up the goal light and zoomed over to me, wearing a grin that could only be described as ecstatic. I welcomed him with open arms, and helped him push down his hockey pants. I couldn't quite put my finger on what I liked about this guy, but there was something about him I'd found instantly endearing.

Maybe it's the fact that he's an amazing kisser, I thought as he tossed his helmet aside and captured my lips with his. *Or maybe it's his giant horse cock*, added the filthy part of my mind.

His hands were attentive to my body, seeking out and petting my erogenous zones until I was squirming for another release. He stood up straight and rubbed his leaking tip against my lips before pushing past them. I did my best to swallow him. He was not quite as thick as Dallas but he was maybe, possibly, a little bit longer.

I relaxed my muscles as best I could, and he fucked my throat hard and fast. Then he pulled out of my mouth and dropped to his knees between my legs. With his pads on, his cock was even with my pussy. He grabbed my hips and pulled me to the edge of the bench, notching himself inside me. My eyes rolled back in my head as he filled me up. He felt so good. His dick crooked slightly inward toward his navel, which put it in the perfect position to stimulate my G-spot as he fucked me. He kissed me again, our tongues battling as he bottomed out inside me. There was a scorching, undeniable passion between us, a chemistry that had me clinging to his shoulders. I scooted forward until my ass slid off the edge of the bench, taking even more of him. His skin slapped mine as he held me up and jackhammered into me. He pulled back and then rammed in, again and again, supporting my ass with his hands as he rocked on his knees. The sounds of the arena faded away. I had no idea if Huck had blown the whistle yet, and I didn't care.

I clung to Xander's neck, my face in the hollow of his throat, my pussy clenching around him as he impaled me over and over again until, just as I was approaching a crescendo, he let out a ragged groan and sagged against me. He dropped his thumb to my clit, strumming it as he pulled me down with him. We fell together, free and clear, totally open in that moment of ecstasy.

Then I heard the shrill chirp of the whistle. Xander pressed another kiss to my lips and lumbered back to his feet, balancing on the blades of his skates as he shook out his numb legs and pulled up his pants. He flashed me a boyish grin and then snatched up his helmet and coasted away from me. I went limp against the wall, snaking my hand down between my thighs and dipping my fingers into my pussy to feel what he had left behind.

51.
Reid

Today was the day. The most important game we'd had so far. The Golden Eagles, the team out of Bozeman. The team on which Chase played as a center.

Today was the day he would pay for what he did to my girl.

I spotted him instantly. Tensions were high. This game would also determine who went on to the playoffs, which was why everyone else was on edge. But I was raring to go, ready to get my hands on that slimy motherfucker. He'd never know what hit him.

I glanced down the bench and locked eyes with Jamie, who gave me a short nod. Then I looked at Nate, whose lips were already curling in that trademark manic grin that said he was ready to fuck shit up. I'd pulled him aside after *that* closed practice as Lola rode off into the sunset with Wild Bill. I told him what Chase had done to her, and Nate was out for blood. His reaction made me respect him more than any play he could make on the ice. He hadn't known Lola a fraction of the time I had, but he was just as ready as I was to beat the ever-loving shit out of the guy who had caused her so much pain.

And sure, it would make me feel better to take out my fury over all those wasted years on Chase's head and knees and face. If I could place the blame on him for hurting Lola, I could avoid acknowledging that what I'd done had been much worse. The scars I left on her would be much slower to heal. But I would do everything in my power to expedite the process.

We were on the ice together immediately, but this game was important for reasons other than my vengeance, and my teammates would never forgive me if I got us DQ'd to settle an old score, even one as righteous as this. But when Nate had the puck and Chase was coming in hot to steal it, I saw my chance. I crouched in front of him right as he reached me, and he went sprawling, ass over elbows. He landed hard on his back on the ice and stared up at me, bewildered until he saw my face. Then, he paled.

I skated away from him, already planning my next attack. But I didn't have to do much planning. He sidled up to me.

"Let's go, then, Wright," he tossed over at me. "I spotted Lola in the stands last game. Maybe I'll chat her up after I wipe the ice with you, *Cowboy*. It's been a while." Jamie was circling us, close enough to hear. He shot me a dark look. I returned it, and then my eyes slid back to Chase just as he was throwing down his gloves.

We were both on him in an instant. I jerked his bucket off and started wailing on his face, bouncing his head against the ice with every punch, as Jamie planted a skate in his side.

"Fuck you, you fucking roughneck," Chase spat as he fought to get the upper hand. But he never stood a chance, and none of his teammates were rushing over to help him out. Big surprise. They were probably enjoying watching him get his ass beat.

The official's whistle didn't slow me down. I didn't stop until they dragged me off of him, and then I took my seat in the penalty box with a satisfied smile on my face.

52.
Lola

I had one arm looped through Dallas's and one through Reid's. Nate and Xander trailed behind us. We were headed back to their swanky downtown apartment for some post-game celebration. The Ice Hawks had scored in the final minute of the third period, pushing ahead and securing a spot in the playoffs. I was walking on air.

There were even more fights on the ice than usual tonight, but I didn't really think anything of it until someone stepped out from between two cars in the parking lot.

"Hey, Wright," called a familiar voice I couldn't place. Reid froze, and Dallas slowed to a stop with a wary glance at the shadowy figure. Just then, two larger shadows stepped out to join him.

"You ready for another lesson already, Chase?" Reid called in a falsely bright voice. Chase… All the air left my lungs. Reid pushed me gently behind him as he and Dallas moved forward and closed ranks. Xander caught me as Nate joined the other two. He pulled me away from the group, and they lunged.

"No!" I shouted, but they didn't pay me any attention. Bodies were rolling and fists were flying. Spat curses were cut short by the meaty sound of punches landing. I heard footsteps pound up behind us, and then Will and Huck were pushing past us into the fray. They grabbed our guys and yanked them to their feet. Chase and his goons pursued, not ready to give up just yet.

"Whoa, whoa, chill the fuck out," Will shouted, holding Reid by the scruff of his jacket and shoving Chase away with his other hand. He might as well have been breaking up a dogfight. "What's going on?"

"This piece of shit assaulted Lola," Reid growled. My eyes went as wide as saucers. Huck frowned back at me. Will paused for a second, considering Reid's words. Then he released him.

"Well, then, by all means. Carry on," he said. Reid and Dallas jumped forward together and knocked Chase to the ground, and he let out a strangled yell as they pounced on top of him. Nate and Huck fended off the other two while Will looked around, located me, and came my way. Entrusting me to the coach, Xander gave a gleeful hoot and joined his teammates.

"Are you okay?" Will asked, grabbing my shoulders and examining my face. "Reid said you were assaulted."

I rolled my eyes.

"Five years ago," I clarified.

"What?" Will blinked at me.

"It was one kiss, and it happened five years ago. Make them stop!" I shouted shrilly, waving my hand at the snarl of bodies still tangling on the ground. Will glanced over and shrugged.

"Sounds like he deserves it."

"They're going to go to jail if they kill him, and then how are we supposed to win the playoffs?" I demanded. He raised his eyebrows and nodded.

"All right, all right, let's break it up," Will said as he turned to survey the brawl. "I think you've made your point, guys." Dallas stood up at his coach's order, but Reid didn't. He kept hitting Chase, though Chase had long since stopped fighting back.

"Reid!" I shouted, a sob escaping my throat. If he wasn't careful, he was going to let this asshole ruin his entire life. Chase definitely wasn't worth his future. And for the love of God, it was one kiss! Five! Years! Ago! "Please!"

He finally went still as the sound of me begging got through to him. He jumped up and reared his leg like he was about to plant another kick in Chase's ribs. Then he paused, shook his head, and took a big step back. Chase was curling up into a fetal ball when Reid spat on the side of his face.

Dallas grabbed his teammate's elbow and pulled him away from the sniveling prick that was still cowering on the ground. His friends let us go.

"What were you thinking?" I hissed as we hurried across the parking lot toward Dallas's SUV. Reid was bleeding from his lip and a cut above his eyebrow, and from every single one of his knuckles. It looked like he'd missed Chase's face a few times and punched concrete instead.

He didn't answer, just picked up his pace, putting distance between us with every pass of his long legs.

53.
Lola

I'd been in a shitty mood since the whole thing with Chase happened on Monday. I was ducking everyone, hiding out at home with Hope. I couldn't figure out if I was grateful to Reid for giving Chase what he desperately deserved, or anxious and freaked out by the scary way he lost control. I was afraid that we had all lost control over the situation, not just with Chase but with our relationship, if that's even what you called it when one girl was hooking up with half the hockey team, falling in love with anyone who could make her come.

I still went to work and had to see, touch, and talk to all of them. But Reid and Nate seemed to have decided to give me space for now. It was surprising, especially from Nate. I didn't realize he understood the concept of personal space.

It was Friday, and we had an away game Saturday night. The whole team was buzzing around the arena. Will was running defense drills—this time, everyone was clothed. Huck was checking minor injuries, wrapping knees and elbows, stretching hip flexors. And I was in my studio, working out the kinks.

I looked up at the sound of a knock to see Xander standing in the doorway with that big, goofy grin. He had the kind of face and body you'd expect to see on some moody, narcissistic male model. Just absolutely perfect in every way. But I'd never seen him in anything less than a giddy mood. His positivity was infectious. He was the definition of Big Dick Energy, insanely talented but more than happy to create space for other players to shine. He lifted his teammates up and cheered them on.

He didn't come in for massages often. He was our youngest player, after all, and had many years of abusing that perfect body ahead of him before he started to have any serious trouble. Plus, the young guys never value preventative care as they should, which was why I ended up massaging the older ones multiple times a week and still wasn't able to get most of them below a pain level of three.

But here he was now, *Xaddy*, standing in front of me. The sight of him scrambled my brain.

"Hi!" I said and cringed inwardly at how vapid I had managed to sound with one word.

"Hey, there," Xander said with a slow, easy smile. His dark eyes drank me in.

"What's up?" I asked.

"I've had a crick in my neck for four days. Huck sent me in here to you. And I didn't argue, mami," he said, smirking. I blushed the second his words hit me.

"Okay, no problem," I said, finding it difficult to hold his fiery gaze. "Take off your shirt and lie on your back on the table. I'll have a look."

"Yes, ma'am," he said in that deep, throaty voice like velvet. At the sight of his bare chest, my self-control was slipping. I turned away, opening and closing drawers but unable to think clearly enough to figure out what I needed.

This was silly. We'd already slept together, after all. More than once. He'd had his tongue firmly lodged in my most private places. My mind was playing over that practice on a loop, how he made me come so hard in the penalty box. But I forced myself to focus on the task at hand, swirling a few drops of cedar-wood essence into jojoba. Mixing the oils together was like a meditation. I closed my eyes as my heart rate came back down to normal.

I carried the bowl to the top of the table. His hair brushed against my thighs as I slid my hands under his shoulders and felt his neck, probing, searching for the problem.

"Where does it hurt?" I asked.

"Right side. I got in a wreck my junior year of high school and kind of fucked it up. 'Scuse my language."

"And what happened this time to trigger it?"

I was gliding my fingertips over his skin, from his shoulders up his neck to his hairline and back down again. I could feel the tension in the right side, the twisted, angry muscle. I applied light pressure, and he nearly came off the table. At that, I withdrew my hands and crossed my arms over my chest, frowning down at him. He glanced up guiltily.

"We were playing two-on-two pick-up and…Nate shoulder-checked me. I flipped over him and landed on my head," he grumbled all in one breath. I stared down at him in disbelief.

"You're telling me we're headed for the hockey championship playoffs, and you've given yourself a *football* injury?" His eyes darted away from mine. "Did you tell Huck what happened? I assume not, since you're still alive."

"I told him I slept on it funny," he admitted.

I barked out a laugh. "Can you turn it at all?"

"Sure," he said, looking to the left.

"Mmhm, and what about the right side?"

He straightened his head and then tried to turn toward the right. But nothing happened. He stopped cold, and then looked the rest of the way with his eyes.

"You can't play like this," I said. He bolted up into a sitting position and spun his entire body around to stare at me. Because he couldn't just turn his head.

"I have to play, Lola," he said vehemently. My name was like music on his lips. I blinked, feeling stupid. Being so close to him in this tiny room made it hard for me to think straight.

"You have to tell Huck the truth about how bad it is," I insisted. "Let him make the call. If you hurt yourself worse, you could be out for the rest of the season. And then we're really fucked."

He met my eyes again, and I could see the regret in his. But there was something else sparking there, too, as he stared at me.

"I'll go with you if that will make it easier," I said, even as my conviction was slipping. He glanced down at my mouth. "But you have to tell him. Now."

At that word—*Now*—he shuddered. His eyes darkened. I glanced down to see that he was sporting a monstrous erection.

"Sorry," he said with that same lazy smile. "I just love it when a gorgeous woman bosses me around." I was throbbing from my center outward, surprised and strangely excited that my sternness had had this effect on him.

"Does that mean you're going to do as I say?"

"Yes," he said, biting his bottom lip around a smile.

"Well," I relented, staring openly at his mouth. "I guess we don't have to go tell him *right* now." I stepped closer to the table.

"Yeah," he agreed with a solemn nod. "It would be a shame if you were to march me out there to the principal's office in front of everyone with this raging hard-on. So embarrassing." His lips twitched, and so did his cock. At that moment, I recognized something in Xander that also lived in me. He got off on being dominated.

I'd always been submissive to my partners, had never considered myself a dominant or domineering personality. But as I realized how turned on he was by a gentle scolding, how readily and willingly he yielded to my authority, I understood what my partners had been getting out of the arrangement all along. A sense of power flowed through me, hot and metallic.

He didn't wait for a response. At least for the moment, he seized control as my whole body tingled. His arm snaked out, and his fingers locked around my wrist. Then he jerked me down over him, cupping the back of my neck in his strong hand and crushing my mouth with his. I moaned into it as he parted my lips with his tongue. He swung his legs over on my side of the table without breaking the kiss, and his hands slid down my body, cupping my ass, pulling me forward between his knees. He held me there, grinding me against his steely bulge.

"I'll go fess up to Huck," he murmured without taking his lips away from mine. "But I really want to eat your pussy first." Together, our mouths smiled. Then I peeled his arms off of me and stepped back again, eyeing him. I'd have to be careful of his injury. Now was definitely not the time to sit on his face.

"You want to taste me, Xaddy?" I teased, taking another step back. He watched me with those black eyes. He nodded, not smiling now. This was the most serious I'd ever seen him.

I snapped my fingers and then pointed at the floor in front of me. The moment stretched out between us. I waited. A second later, he was melting off the edge of the table. As I pushed my leggings down and kicked them aside, he closed the distance between us on his knees. Then he leaned back on his heels and looked up at me, the blissful grin back on his face.

He was waiting for permission. A thrill shot up my spine.

Holding his burning gaze, I spread my feet slightly. He licked his lips like I'd just placed a whole frosted cake in front of him.

I reached out, ran my fingers through his thick black hair, and his eyelids drooped at my touch. Then I curled my hand around the back of his head and drew him gently, firmly, forward.

54.
Xander

I finally had her all to myself, and I was dying to be inside of her. Any part of me, I wasn't fussy. After our encounter during practice the other night, I knew I had to get her alone so that we could experiment with this explosive chemistry that sparked between us.

Her hand on the back of my head told me exactly what she wanted. I gladly buried my face between her legs, reaching down to grip my painfully hard cock. I didn't stroke it yet, just squeezed the base as I flicked my tongue against her clit and then plunged it between her pussy lips, lapping her up like candy. She was so fucking sweet.

Her head fell back and she groaned, bucking her hips forward. But when I leaned in harder, she put a hand on my shoulder, panting.

"Take it slow," she said in a forceful voice that shot straight to my core, soothing me, assuring me that I could take my time with her. "Don't put any strain on that neck." My dick swelled in my fist at her gentle instruction and correction.

She'd fallen so easily into this role. I'd been with lots of women who were submissive and very, very few who were dominant or even able to play both parts. But I'd had a feeling that Lola would be that mythical unicorn, the switch. I'd seen her kneel at Will's feet and submit to him completely. But now I saw that she could take the reins, too, and that set me on fire for her.

I was fucking in love with the way she had taken a strong hand with me so naturally. We couldn't be very far apart in age—she might have been a couple of years older than I was. But I still felt like a dumb kid who didn't have his shit together. She, on the other hand, had no loose ends. She ran a tight ship. I wanted to let her take over my life.

I licked her clit reverently, like I was accepting the holy sacrament. I worshipped her pussy with my tongue, exploring every inch of her I could reach, all with a firm but feather-light touch. I did exactly as she said, didn't put any undue pressure on my neck. It was a challenge, but one that my tongue quickly rose to meet. She was gasping and moaning in no time, and her hands kept itching toward my head like she wanted to grab my hair with both hands and ride my face. And fuck did I want her to do exactly that. But instead, she braced them ever-so-lightly on my shoulders and stepped away from me again.

I fell back with a frustrated groan. She had to stop doing that. I only ever wanted her to be stepping closer. She smiled down at me, and my heart settled even as my cock throbbed and ached for her.

"I don't want to lose control of myself and hurt you," she said. "Go lay back down."

I jumped to my feet, licking the lingering taste of her from my lips as I obeyed her order. I stretched out on the massage table, my cock standing at full, drooling attention.

"You don't have to—," I started. I'd wanted to taste her, to make her come, not to make her feel like she had to take care of my boner.

At the thought of her taking care of it, my cock gave a violent jerk.

She pushed a button to lower the massage table until it was at knee height for her, and then she swung her leg over me and eased her delicious, soaking-wet pussy down.

When I entered her, her inner muscles clamped around me so hard I nearly rocketed off the table. Her skin, her body, was made of white-hot electricity and she was lighting me up. My neck sent a warning jolt of pain to my brain and I settled back down, letting her take control like I so badly wanted her to.

She planted her palms on my chest and rocked forward, backward, taking more of me with every pass until I was buried balls-deep inside her.

"Fuck," I moaned, staring up at her tits as she freed them from her sports bra. As she pulled up the hem, I could see the underside of each pale globe smashed flat by the elastic material. Then, the heavy weight of them was too much to be contained, and they dropped back down against her chest, bouncing and jiggling right above my face. Something about it was so erotic that I nearly blew my load before we'd even gotten started.

She tossed the sports bra away over her shoulder and then braced herself on the table on either side of my head and leaned over me.

"I want you to come in my pussy," she whispered, lowering herself further to brush her lips over mine. I nodded my head, whimpering.

"You're going to get what you want any second now if you keep that up," I choked out. She leveled me with her rich brown eyes as she sank all of her weight down onto my hips, impaling herself on every last inch of my hard dick.

"No," she said, surprising me. "I'm going to get it when I give you *permission* to come. And not a second before." I gasped, going crazy, wanting to force her to ride me, but way more turned on by the fact that I had to just lie here. I couldn't take control even if I wanted to because my body wouldn't let me without risking further injury. I wanted to fuck my rock-hard cock up into her drenched pussy until she screamed, but I had to keep my back pressed flat to the table as she rode me closer and closer to the edge. And now she was telling me to wait for permission…where had this woman been all my life? How did she know exactly what I needed and exactly how to give it to me?

I sucked in a deep breath, approaching the point of no return. I reached between us, squeezing the base of my cock. She didn't slow down, didn't show any mercy as she took me to the hilt.

"Lola," I groaned. "I'm gonna…"

"No, you're not," she said matter-of-factly. Now the rhythm of her hips did slow, just for a beat or two, letting me get a finger-hold of control over myself before she picked up the pace once more, slamming herself down again and again on my cock. I was *so fucking deep* when I bottomed out inside her.

Oh, fuck.

There was no way I could hold it much longer, no matter how badly I wanted to please her. I shut my eyes because one more second of her tits bouncing in my face and it would be a moot point.

"Look at me," she demanded. Reluctantly, I opened them again to find her staring at me. Her mouth opened as she took my entire length inside her pussy, grinding her hips against mine with every downward stroke.

Her fingers flew to her clit, and she rubbed it frenetically as she threw her hips forward and back, forward and back.

"Now!" she moaned, throwing her head back. "I want your come right now!"

That was all it took to completely wreck me.

My cock went off like a bottle rocket, coating her insides as she strangled my shaft in a ribbed, rippling vice-grip.

If you'd asked me right then, I couldn't have told you my own name.

55.
Huck

Here we were, the first game of the playoffs. Word had gotten around sports media about our dark-horse season, and the stands were packed. Xander Bardi was benched with a neck injury, and to say I was pissed off about that would be a drastic understatement. The last thing I wanted or needed was to be down a star player headed into the highest-stakes part of the season. But when Lola marched him over to me and made him confess, aside from having to fight the urge to find Nate and throttle him—no good, then we'd be down two star players—I knew she was right. Xaddy would have to sit this one out.

At least we had Dallas on the ice. Everyone was getting along for the most part, and our warm-up could not have gone better. Really, ever since Lola had offered herself up as incentive during practice, the guys were playing on a whole new level.

I was riding high those first three minutes.

Then our star goalie lunged for the puck and went down hard, his strangled cry of pain reverberating off the rink's domed ceiling.

Everything was in slow motion as I ran out to him. The rest of the team skated up, surrounding him to protect him from prying eyes in the stands. I heard the shrill whistles of the officials as they joined us on the ice. I could still hear the way Lola screamed when his back went out. I knew she was thinking exactly the same thing that was rattling around my skull as I crouched over the big man.

We did this. We pushed him too hard, too fast, and now his career is over, and we did this to him. We should have let him sit on the bench and wait out the year getting better. Instead, we pushed him out onto the ice to serve our own selfish interests—my own selfish interest...

"Bring a stretcher!" I heard one of the officials shout to someone in the stands. I could hear the senseless chatter of my team all around me, but I was focused on Dallas's face. It was twisted up in agony like every breath was a knife to his spine. I gripped his hand, and he opened his eyes, pinning me with a pained stare. Then, to my shock, his lips curled into a smile that was more like a grimace before his face crumpled once more.

They took him off the ice and straight to the local hospital, where they gave him muscle relaxers and discharged him. Lola and I had followed the ambulance there, and Will arrived as soon as the game was over. I could tell by the look on his face that we'd lost.

He threw himself down into the chair on the other side of Lola and reached across her to pat my knee. He knew I was beating myself up for clearing Dallas to play. We sat in silence for a minute or two, and then I heard sniffling near my elbow. I glanced down and froze when I saw the fat tears streaking Lola's cheeks.

"Hey," I said, sliding an arm around her shoulders. Will turned to her, shielding her from the room with his body, and smoothed his hand over her hair.

"You two both know good and well that you couldn't have kept Cash off that ice tonight without a restraining order. Lola, look at me." She forced herself to raise her head and meet his stern gaze. "This is not. Your. Fault. Same goes for you, Hart," he tossed at me. I clenched my jaw, swallowing a retort. I wanted to argue. I wanted to rage. I wanted to take all the blame and whip myself in the hopes that it might make me feel better. I kept seeing Dallas go down, that big body landing hard on the ice, over and over, until I felt like I was going to be sick.

A few minutes after Will, more people trickled into the waiting room. First Nate, Xander and Eric, the three of them looking frantic. Then Reid and Jamie. Then Patch Olson, Marcus Crane, and Sly Moran. As they wheeled Dallas back out into the waiting room, Lars was leading the remainder of the third and fourth lines through the sliding glass doors, bringing in a cold rush of night air with them.

We all gathered around him. The doctor's eyes jumped around the group and finally landed on Will, who was still wearing his suit from the game and was the oldest guy here by at least a few years.

"He'll be all right," the doctor said. "Just exacerbated his previous injury. He tells me he's been making a rock-star recovery lately with the help of his team. Which I can only assume includes you all. So just keep up what you're doing once the pain lessens enough that he feels comfortable. But I want him to get clearance from a bone and joint doctor before he steps foot on the ice again."

I scowled at those words, a storm cloud of self-pity rolling over me. *This is all my fault, and it will be my fault if The Tank can never skate again.*

56.
Lola

Dallas was sinking into a serious depression with his hands tied behind his back as playoffs ramped up. The guys were actually managing surprisingly well without him, after the first disastrous game. We were eking out enough wins to advance with Patch tending the net but losing Dallas was a serious blow to morale for the entire team. He still went to every game, but he wore a dark sweatshirt and kept the hood pulled up, hiding his face from the spectators who had come to gawk at the star goalie with the bum back.

Late at night, which was the only time we really got to see each other these days, he would whisper his fears to me under the cover of darkness when we were both spent and exhausted and ebbing toward the sweet release of sleep. The other guys seemed to have handed me totally over to him as a consolation prize for the fact that he was having to watch yet another playoff season from the sidelines. Everyone was running on fumes, and opportunities for sexy time had been thin on the ground. But there was a different kind of energy running through the team now. I'd done my small but arguably important part to deliver them here, and now the momentum and excitement of the playoffs were taking over, and even without Dallas, they were coalescing into a fairly unstoppable force.

That was one of the fears Dallas shared with me when he couldn't get to sleep. That they—*they* being the team, Will and Huck, Mr. Branson, the fans, and I sensed maybe he meant me, too—would realize once he was gone long enough that they didn't need him after all. Like anyone in a high-performing, competitive field, he knew that he would keep getting older and younger, faster, better goalies would come up to replace him. But he wasn't ready to be done yet. If he had to stop playing to avoid spending the rest of his life in a wheelchair or something, he was willing. But he couldn't just give up, this close to all of his dreams coming true. He couldn't accept the same fate that Huck had been left with, slogging away as an assistant coach in the minor league just because it was better than nothing. Watching other people live his dream. He needed to be where the action was. He needed to be on the ice. But had he abused his body so much that it would shut down on him whether he was ready or not?

I did my best to stay awake and listen to the stream of his anxieties, but sometimes, I couldn't help drifting off when my eyelids weighed a hundred pounds. I would close my eyes just to rest them while I listened to him talk. That's what I told myself. But then I would startle awake in the early hours of the morning, sometimes to see his wide, muscled back and hear his gentle snoring. Sometimes, to an empty bed. I'd find him in the kitchen, doom-scrolling on his phone, reading horror stories about career-ending injuries. Sometimes, one of his roommates would be up with him, eating a bowl of cereal or just doing the same thing, neck bent, eyes glued on the shiny rectangle that held endless hours of entertainment curated especially for them. They would glance up at me when I came in. If it was Xander, he would flash me that easy smile and invite me to sit in his lap. Eric would blush and duck his head or mumble an excuse and run out of the room. Sexual tension sparked between us, but he was shy and unsure, and I knew better than to push the issue. It was more than understandable that a person might have reservations about getting close to the girl with half a dozen boyfriends.

If Nate was the one who was sitting up with Dallas, I had to tread carefully. He might ignore me, or he might try to drag me back to his bedroom. Both possibilities were equally likely, depending on his mood.

If his mood was especially sour, he might snap at me or make some crude remark intended to humiliate me. Those occasions were rare, but they happened, and then I had to worry about Dallas slamming the center's head through the kitchen table. I still hadn't quite sussed out their dynamic, but *frenemies* was the most fitting word I'd come up with. They seemed to rely on each other in certain ways and to compete constantly in others.

Dallas was bitter about his bad luck and less willing to put up with Nate's mood swings now. He was benched while Nate was out there rebuilding his reputation, starting to get some attention from the media again.

Now that Nate and Reid were truly on the same team, in more ways than one, they had transformed into a power couple on the ice. Reid protected Nate ruthlessly while the center raced down the ice to score goal after goal. The rest of the team was much improved, there was no doubt about it, but Reid and Nate's on-ice chemistry was the reason we were advancing to round two of the playoffs.

Nate caught me alone in the kitchen one afternoon.

I'd wrapped up my business at the arena early so I could check on Dallas. When I found him napping in his room. I'd retreated to get a glass of water and reply to some emails on my phone while I waited for him to wake up.

A few minutes later, Nate came in and slung his gym bag down. We had a home game that night, and I could smell his testosterone raging from across the room.

Before I could even straighten up, he was behind me. His hands skated up my arms, curling around my shoulders and clamping down. Too hard. I winced away from him. He leaned back against the counter and crossed his arms over his chest.

"You know, if you get tired of sucking Tanker's sad dick, I'm just a door away. I'd be more than happy to give your pussy that workout I know it sorely needs."

I gaped at him, trying to decide whether to storm off or strip naked. My pussy was soaked in a second, but my heart pounded a furious beat in my ears.

He had no right to talk about Dallas like that, who was supposed to be his closest friend here.

"What the fuck did you say?" I asked in a low voice, choosing violence. He cocked an eyebrow and smirked.

"Oh, good. We're feisty today."

"Fuck off, Nate." I picked up my water glass and walked away from him.

He followed hot on my heels.

"Come on, Lola," said. "Choke on my cock while Wittle Tankie takes a nap." I spun on my heel and smacked him hard right across the face.

It didn't slow him down at all. He caught hold of my wrist, yanking me against him.

"I deserve it," he continued in a mock whine. "I did really good at practice today." I tried to wrench my arm free, but his fingers locked down. He lowered his face toward mine until his breath was hot on my cheek. He was opening his mouth to say something else when a cold, cheerful voice cut across him.

"What the fuck are you doing, bud?" We both turned to see Xander and Eric standing in the kitchen, fresh from practice, bags swinging at their sides. Xander was wearing a grin that didn't reach his eyes. They bored into Nate, who released my wrist like it was a hot potato.

"Just having a little fun with the team toy," he said snidely, shooting me a dark smile. "Like I told her, it's my turn. She's been coddling Tanker's balls long enough."

Xander was across the room in a flash, slamming his fist into Nate's jaw. The center sprawled backward, and in another instant, the winger was on top of him, landing another two or three hits before Eric dragged him off. Spending so much time around hockey players had made me less sensitive to the fighting, but it still made my stomach twist with fear to watch them pummel each other. I couldn't understand the urge to settle every disagreement with their fists.

"Why don't you watch your fucking mouth?" Xander spat at Nate as Eric hauled him back into the kitchen area. Nate laughed.

"Don't get your panties in a bunch, *Xaddy*," he sneered, climbing to his feet and rubbing his chin. He turned to me, raking his teeth over his bottom lip and pinning me with his eyes. "My door's always open," he repeated for what felt like the tenth time. "In case you get lonely in the middle of the night." He winked, and then he headed down the hall toward his room. Xander was still flailing, struggling to get to Nate as Eric body-blocked him against the island. I went to Eric's side, laying a hand on Xander's forearm. He stilled immediately, his chest heaving with exertion.

"I'm okay," I murmured. He turned and wrapped his arms around me, gathering me up into a bear hug and burying his face in the crook of my neck. He held onto me like we hadn't seen each other in weeks.

Nate's delivery was definitely off, but I knew that what he was saying was true. I'd been devoting all of my time to Dallas since he re-injured himself. Of course, everyone was so busy with traveling and drills and workouts that I hardly even saw any of them right now. And I didn't exactly want to get in the way of a good thing when they were still rising despite all the odds.

Maybe I was being neglectful. It was great, obviously, to have all of these guys focusing on me and fulfilling my needs. But now I had to be there for all of them the way they were all there for me, and that was one hell of a tall order. Not for the first time, I wondered if I'd bitten off way more than I could chew.

57.
Lola

Dallas's pain level was severe initially, and he was barely mobile. But unlike before, we treated him the right way from the start this time, and he rebounded quickly. He'd confided in me that he'd all but resigned himself to sitting on the bench for the rest of the season, but his bone-and-joint doctor cleared him for duty as we surged through round two of the playoffs.

When Dallas skated back out onto the ice for the first time, it was a home game. The arena filled with thunderous applause as soon as they spotted his number. Everyone on our side of the stands and most of the people on the opposite side, too. They leapt to their feet, stomping and clapping and screaming to welcome The Tank back to the barn.

At first, he didn't realize that all the noise was for him. He glanced around, scowling. But then he saw the handwritten signs, and all the people wearing his sweater, and all the smiling, screaming faces turned toward him.

He coasted limply across the ice, his eyes scanning the crowd until they landed on me. I saw what no one else did.

A sparkle. The hint of emotion.

His fears of being forgotten, of being easily replaced, had been baseless. He was beloved, a star, especially here in Casper. None of us were about to forget him anytime soon after the way he'd saved the Ice Hawks in half a season.

With Dallas tending again and Xander back on the ice, our extraordinary first line was back together again for the first time since the start of the playoff season.

And just like that, it all clicked into place.

The Hawks worked together like choreographed dancers. It was as if they could read each other's minds. Each role was perfectly filled, and I could even see an improvement in the third and fourth-line defense. The entire team had elevated over the last few weeks.

Hell, they'd elevated over the last few minutes as they watched what was unfolding on the ice.

By the third period, the crowd was in a frenzy. The noise inside the arena was deafening. Will gave a stirring speech in the locker room after the second period as Hart and I moved around, addressing various ills. Nate jerked me down into his lap, saying he had something I could address, but Huck threatened to bench him and he shut his mouth.

I knew by this point that he was basically just the mean boy on the playground, pulling my pigtails to get my attention. I still wanted to punch him like Xander had, just for the satisfaction of wiping that smirk off his face. He may be childish, but we were grown. So why was I drawn to him regardless of his shitty behavior? There was something about that cocky grin that left me hot and bothered.

The fact that I almost leaned in when he pinned me down on top of him was irrelevant. Also irrelevant was the fact that I had spent days fantasizing about what he might have done to me in the living room if Xander and Eric hadn't walked in. If I was being honest, I wanted to find out. I wanted him to get me alone and have his way with me. The thought sent shivers down my spine as I moved on to check in with Reid, who was glaring at Nate.

"Hey," I breathed. All of a sudden, a wall of emotion hit me. Instead of days, I felt like I hadn't seen Reid in months. I'd been giving all of myself to support Dallas, and I'd helped him through. Now, I needed a shoulder to lean on, but there was no time to collapse into a heap and beg someone else to take care of me. The guys had to keep their heads in the game, now more than ever. We were so close. We could actually win the whole round if we kept pushing. This game was already a gong-show.

"Hey," Reid said, reaching for me. This time, I let myself be pulled down. I rested my forehead on his padded shoulder and breathed in the clean, fresh smell of his sweat.

"How's your back?" I asked. I could feel eyes on us—Will, Huck, Dallas, maybe others—but I didn't care. I was tired of playing politics. I was too tired right now to do anything else except seek comfort in Reid's arms.

They won the game. Dallas blocked a final shot just as the buzzer went off, and the stands erupted in pandemonium. If he were any smaller, I think his teammates would have carried him off the ice.

We were headed to the conference finals.

58.
Will

I pulled my coat collar up around my ears, trying not to feel like a creep as Huck rang the doorbell. There was a moment's silence, and then a drumroll of footsteps. The door swung open to reveal Eric Bouchard, who blanched at the sight of his two coaches standing expectantly on his front porch.

"We're here for Lola," I said. Bouchard's eyes widened.

"She's…"

"With Cash, we know," Huck snapped. "We've been patient while he was healing up. But he's healed. So send her out. She can come right back over here when we're done with her if that's what she wants."

Now Bouchard's pale face flushed red and he backed away, leaving the door hanging open as he spun around and ran upstairs, shouting for Dallas. Huck and I exchanged a glance, and then we stepped inside. I pushed the door closed, cutting off the arctic chill from the snowstorm outside.

A moment later, Lola appeared at the top of the stairs, followed by her hulking goalie boyfriend. Bouchard was nowhere to be seen.

"Just have her back by curfew," Cash said wryly, not cracking a smile. Lola crossed her arms and glared down at us.

"You couldn't have given me a call?" she asked, raising an eyebrow. "You had to come and collect me?"

I stepped forward, holding her gaze with a hard stare, and she fell quiet.

"Let's go," I said. She turned and leaned up to kiss Cash, who squeezed her and then released her. He narrowed his eyes at me as she came down the stairs, but I never looked away from her. When she reached the ground floor, I tucked her under my arm and walked out.

59.
Lola

Huck drove and Will sat in the back with me, guiding my hand to the crotch of his pants, where I could feel his cock growing.

"I'm still not exactly thrilled that you extracted me from their house," I said, but my voice sounded weak even to me as I rubbed him through his slacks, eliciting a groan. He leaned his head back and closed his eyes.

"You'll get over it," he said, his hand covering mine and holding it firmly between his legs. Much like how I immediately shifted into a more dominant persona when I was with Xander, with Will, I became instantly submissive. It was an instinct. I wanted to follow his orders.

I wanted to be his good girl.

I didn't bother arguing the point any further. I squeezed his bulge and then stroked him through the pants, feeling his heat and his hardness as he arched up into my grip.

"Get Daddy's cock out," he murmured. Huck glanced up, and our eyes locked in the rearview mirror. My face burned as I obeyed Will. I lowered my head into his lap and swallowed his length, taking him down my throat as Huck drove us up the highway to Will's house. I'd know the way blindfolded by now.

The coach ran his hand through my hair, pushing me down.

"God, I missed your hot little mouth," he groaned as I collapsed my cheeks around his shaft.

After a few more minutes, the car rolled to a stop. Will slid out of my mouth and buttoned up, but there was no hiding the tentpole he was sporting in his pants.

"Inside," he instructed, getting out and walking around to open my door. Huck led us into the dark house. I thought we would go upstairs to the bedroom, but they didn't even bother to turn on the lights. Will lifted me off my feet and carried me to the sofa, tossing me down and laying himself between my legs. He tugged Dallas's T-shirt off over my head and captured my bare breasts in his mouth, one after the other.

When Huck stripped and sat down on the couch next to us, Will picked me up and flipped me over, placing me on my hands and knees and then palming my head and shoving it down into the assistant coach's lap. I opened, taking him to the back of my throat. Will held me there, choking me on Huck's cock as he filled my pussy with his own.

"Christ, Lola," Will grunted as he bottomed out. "I've seen some of the dicks you take. How is it possible that you're still this. Fucking. Tight?" He punctuated every word with a hard thrust. I closed my eyes and focused on taking as much of Huck in my mouth as I could while Will covered my body with his, spearing into me. He fisted his hand in my hair, pulling my head back and then shoving it into Huck's lap again, pressing me forward until I choked and gagged.

"That's it, baby, take that big dick," he hissed in my ear as he plowed into me. He had total control of my body. He was fucking my pussy and fucking Huck's cock with my mouth. He set the rhythm for all three of us.

Will pushed me down onto Huck's shaft with the same force and speed that he was using to rail me from behind.

"I never want to have to wait four days again to feel this cunt clenching around my cock," he growled in my ear. "Do you understand?" I couldn't respond with Huck lodged in my throat. "I can be generous with my baby, but don't test my limits, Lola."

My eyes rolled back in my head as my body surrendered to him, as I gave in and let them both use me however they wanted to.

Will tangled his hand in my hair and jerked me up against his chest as he pulled out of my pussy and buried himself in my ass. I screamed and sobbed but pushed back hard, taking all of him and needing more.

"Tell me you're mine," he said, levering out and then back into me.

"I'm yours, Daddy," I moaned loudly, proudly. I felt Will's cock throb somewhere deep in my core, and then he snapped and started fucking me like he was trying his level best to break me.

I pushed back to meet every thrust.

60.
Reid

I waited patiently in Lola's office with a latte and a bouquet of lilies. Her favorite flower, ever since she was a little girl. The sun was barely cracking over the horizon, but my body buzzed with energy. I hadn't seen her in a couple of days, and between missing her and the good news I'd received last night, I was about to levitate right off the chair.

When she walked in and saw me, she jumped, slapping her hand over her heart. She'd been in the massage studio with Dallas for his daily rub-down, and for once, I didn't even care whether that rub-down had included his unmentionables.

"Reid?" she asked, looking from me to the flowers and back again. I stood up, handing them over with a flourish, and then I locked my arm around her waist and pulled her tight against my body.

"I'm kidnapping you," I said plainly. She frowned. Not the reaction I was hoping for, but I didn't let it deter me. "Come on. You need a break, and so do I." She disengaged herself from my arms and went around to sit in her desk chair.

"Reid, it's the conference final," she said, looking at me like I'd lost my mind.

"And? We don't have a game today. Come on, let's play hooky. What I need more than anything right now is to blow off some steam."

Her eyes jumped to the door, which was still hanging ajar. I pushed it closed, never looking away from her face.

"Huck would kill us both," she whispered. "Literally." I shrugged. I didn't care about anyone but her. Maybe I was a poor team player. Oh, well. Sue me. "Don't just shrug at me, Reid. You want to move on to the show. That's never going to happen if you skip practice during the finals."

I threw myself down in the chair across from her, my mood temporarily dampened by her reality check. I wanted to get mad and go off on her for rubbing my minor-league status in my face. That's what I would have done before, maybe even as recently as yesterday. But I let it roll off my back. My lips twitched as I geared up to tell her my big news. She watched me suspiciously.

"Now that you mention it," I said in a low voice. "I got a call from Mr. Branson last night."

She bolted forward in her chair, her eyes wide.

"And?!" she shrieked in a stage whisper when I paused to let the anticipation build.

"He says that if I keep playing like I have been, he's going to move me up to the Prospectors next season and give me a real shot at the big time."

She leapt to her feet, all traces of annoyance gone from her face. She pumped her fists in the air, and I felt a surge of pleasure at her pride in me. Then she ran around the desk and jumped on me. I stood at the same time, catching her and holding her against my chest as I captured her lips with mine. We stayed locked together like that, tasting each other, until all the air had left my body and gone into her lungs. Finally, I pulled away gasping.

"So, come on," I urged her. "Let's go celebrate." Her brow creased, and I knew that I was in for more trouble. She slid slowly down my body until her feet hit the floor.

"Mr. Branson said you'd go to the Prospectors next season *if* you keep playing like you have been. And you want to *play hooky?*" Her logic was wearing me down to a nub. I raked my hand through my hair and glared at her.

"Fuck! Okay, fine." As I spoke, an idea was dawning on me. I nodded. "What if we go on a little field trip to somewhere *nearby*, and we'll be back in time for drills?" She pursed her lips and cocked a brow like she was trying to decide whether she could trust me not to abscond with her into the Wyoming wilderness. I rolled my eyes and raised two fingers. "Scout's honor."

Her face split in a grin.

"Okay!" she said, relenting. "I'll have to tell Will I'm ducking out and hang a sign on my door, but I don't have any appointments today except you and Dallas. Does this mean you're blowing off your massage, too?"

"Oh, don't worry. I'll get my massage," I said, smiling triumphantly as I slid my arm around her shoulders and steered her toward the door.

61.
Lola

Reid was getting his shot at the major league. I both could and couldn't believe it. I'd started to worry that he would spin out here and never make it beyond, and I had the distinct feeling that he'd been nursing a similar concern. But now he was walking on air as he escorted me through the locker room, past Will's office, and out the door to the parking lot in spite of Will and Huck's shouted objections. I cast an apologetic look over my shoulder as Reid herded me through the double doors into the sun.

It was a cold, clear day with a bright blue sky. Not a cloud around for miles. I sipped the latte he brought me as he drove up the highway north of town, toward our old stomping grounds. I relaxed, feeling like a girl again in his passenger seat with his hand on my knee, lifting up every now and again to shift and then dropping its reassuring warmth back onto my leg.

"Does Hope know?" I asked in what I hoped was a casual voice. I was almost certain he hadn't told her because she would have called me the second she found out. Or at the very least, she'd have shot off a text. We'd always been close friends and kept in contact, but now that we were roommates, we were on the same wavelength again, sharing everything like sisters.

I understood why she wanted me to end up with Reid, so that sisterhood bond would be complete. There was a time when that was my greatest fantasy, too. But Reid and I didn't have to get married for Hope to be my sister. She already was, and always had been. Maybe her brother would be the guy I ended up settling down with, but the longer I lived in the world, the less sure I was that I would ever get married. Unless bigamy suddenly became legal.

"You're the only person I've told," he said. His gray eyes were trained on the road. I studied his handsome profile, chewing on my lip. "Everyone else is just going to project their own shit onto me. Including my sister."

"I'm not sure that's fair," I said, jumping in to defend my best friend. "Hope loves having you in the same city, but she would much rather see you achieve your dreams. She will support you in whatever you choose to do, Reid." A muscle ticked in his jaw.

"I know that's true, but it's still hard to break the news to her."

"So I guess you haven't told Jamie, either?" That one was even harder to believe. They were as close as Hope and I. They lived right next door to each other and were inseparable most of the time. As far as I knew, they told each other everything.

Reid shook his head, shifting hard and leaving his hand on the knob instead of returning it to my lap. So I went to him. I closed my small hand over his big one, nesting my fingers between his deep knuckles, all scarred up from fighting on and off the ice.

"They're going to be so happy for you when you're ready to tell them," I said. With that, I dropped it. This was Reid's news, and he was the only one who could decide how to deliver it.

And he'd chosen to tell me before anyone else...

I flashed back to the excited puppy-dog look he was wearing when I found him in my office. He shared this moment with me because he had trusted me not to make it about myself. But in the quiet hum of the truck's cab, my brain started mulling over the information. He was leaving at the end of the season. I probably wouldn't be going with him.

I'd hardly even figured out how I felt about all these men in my life. Now, the group would be fractured before we'd even had a chance to really come together to see what this could be. For the rest of the ride, I made it all about me in my head but managed to hide that fact from him. I realized all at once, like a bomb was going off in my brain, just how much I would miss him.

I spent the next several minutes staring at my hands in my lap, struggling to get myself together. When I looked up again, I knew exactly where we were.

He flicked on his blinker and slowed down as we approached the driveway to his parents' house.

62.
Lola

I sat in the truck, staring at the weathered facade of the house that had been more of a home to me than my own when I was a kid. The tears came flooding out. There was nothing I could do to stop them.

"Hey," Reid said quietly, gathering me against his side. He pressed a kiss to the top of my head.

"I'm sorry," I gasped, wiping at my face. "I'm being dumb."

"You're not dumb," he said. "Are you okay?" I nodded, my chin trembling with a fresh wave of emotion. After the way things ended between Reid and me, I'd never felt comfortable coming back here when I was in town for Christmas. I hadn't been here once since moving back. It took a lot of work, a lot of pain and suffering, to cauterize the part of my heart where my surrogate family had lived before Reid cut me out and I, in turn, was forced to excise them.

Somehow, it hadn't even occurred to me that a fifteen-minute drive could deliver me to the doorstep of my happiest childhood memories.

"Come on," he said, popping the handle beside him. The truck cab filled with a faint dinging sound. "They'll be over the moon to see you." He stepped down and slammed the door behind him. In the silence, my mind continued to race. His parents had never reached out to add me as a friend on social media. I assumed they had blocked me because I never even saw them in my recommended friends. They had gone silent along with Reid. Was it just a show of support for their only son, or did they hate me as much as he had?

He opened my door and reached out a hand to help me down. I took it, still shaking and sniffling but determined now to march forth and meet my fate.

I jumped down into the dirt, sending up a cloud of dust. Even after a rainstorm, the dirt in Wyoming was bone dry. This was the dirt I'd gone home covered in every night, that my grandmother had scrubbed roughly from my ears and the grooves of my neck, cursing under her breath the whole time. My grandparents' house, where I actually grew up, was just another minute down the highway. I'd sold it off to a family with kids after Grandpa died. I had no desire to go back there. But I was clammy, my stomach bursting with butterflies, at the thought of seeing the Wrights again.

Reid led me up the path to the modest ranch house. It was built out on the edge of Casper, jutting up from the rolling plains. A ways behind the house, there grew a thick copse of trees, most of them leafless for the winter. I knew that an all-weather creek, knee-deep, ran through those trees. My brain flashed back—Reid's round, little boy face with the spray of freckles that faded to almost nothing as he aged.

In a blink, we were standing on the porch. My heart was in my throat as he rang the doorbell. We waited for a tense second—I was tense, at least. Then I heard footsteps inside and the tired clack of dog nails on the hardwood. The door swung open to reveal Tamara

Wright, the plump, vivacious live wire whom Hope and Reid called Mom. She threw her head back when she saw us and let out her trademark booming laugh. Then she was wrapping me up in a sweet, soft, fragrant hug that dashed all my fears away in an instant. I clutched her to me, squeezing my eyes shut tight, as the old family dog Runner danced at our feet.

This. This was what it meant to come home again. Hope and Reid felt like home to me, but this house was truly it.

Tamara led us into the kitchen, which had been remodeled since the last time I was here, for mine and Hope's graduation party. I remembered leaning drunkenly against the old avocado-green countertop, sloshing beer from a red solo cup and glancing at the door every few seconds, hoping Reid would walk in. He never did.

"Bob!" Tamara shouted in her deep, throaty voice. I stood awkwardly beside Reid, unsure how much they knew about our situation-ship. "Come see who's here."

I was staring at her. I couldn't help myself. I'd missed her full face, her bright, sparkling eyes. Five years didn't seem like a very long time while it was happening, but I could see the subtle differences. Her dark hair was dusted with salt now. Otherwise, she looked the same, give or take a laugh line. Again, my mind flashed back, trying its best to retreat to the past. Stopping myself, I looked around at the renovated space instead. The dim, cramped, eighties-style kitchen had been replaced with everything sleek, clean, and modern. The stainless steel fridge displayed the weather on its touchscreen. The counters were white granite streaked with a subtle glisten of gold. Everything was shiny and fresh, but my mind overlaid the old kitchen on top of the new. I saw Tamara with her hair still pitch black, beaming like she did, while a young, lanky teenaged Reid skulked by, rolling his eyes and begging her to stop going on about some show or book, whatever her obsession was that week.

I loved Hope and Reid, but I could sit at the island and listen to Tamara talk for hours, just basking in the comfort of her loving, joyful presence. She'd never said a sharp word to me or raised her voice the whole time I'd known her. I'd only seen her be firm with her kids a couple of times, and only when it was well-deserved. She was always the most enthusiastic parent in the bleachers, and that was saying something.

I realized then that I should have seen her at a game this season. Especially once the guys had started to pick up steam. Had they come, and I'd just missed them?

A huffing sound came from the living room, and then Reid's dad appeared in the kitchen doorway. When he saw me, he grinned and spread his arms wide. I stepped forward into his bear hug, weak-kneed with relief that, like his wife, he didn't seem to hold a grudge. Bob's hair was a lighter shade of blond, and his nose was a bit redder, but he was pretty much the same, too.

Reid cleared his throat. I turned to look at him. That's when I realized that he told me I was the first person who knew his good news. Which meant his parents didn't yet. I walked back over to stand by his side with a proud smile.

"I've got some news," he started. This close, I could hear the slight tremor in his voice. Both of his parents looked from him to me, and my eyes went wide. "No! I mean, Lola and I have patched things up, and I was a complete jackass, and I've realized the grievous error of my ways. But I've got even bigger news." I snorted, looking up at him. He'd always been one to downplay his achievements. "Branson told me that I'm all but guaranteed a spot on the Prospectors next season."

Tamara and Bob glanced at each other and then back at Reid. For a second, the house was still and silent. Then they exclaimed at the same time, throwing their hands up and talking over each other, surging forward to wrap him up in their arms. They cheered him and toasted him, and they welcomed me back into the fold in earnest. But I'd started to pick up on the tension. The way Bob didn't look directly at his son, even when they were talking. How Tamara had hugged me but not her son when we arrived. The fact that, as far as I knew, they hadn't attended a single game this season.

After a light lunch of cold-cut sandwiches and juice, Reid and I walked across the backyard toward the creek. We still had an hour before we had to be back, and the sun was warm for the first time in months. He tugged me playfully by the hand. As we drew closer, I could hear the babbling of the water rushing off toward whatever ocean it was after.

We broke into the tree line, and the temperature dropped. The air was cool and damp here, even with the leaves long gone. We walked straight to the big overhanging rock we'd used as a camp spot, clubhouse, and home base for years. Though I'd been climbing it most of my life, Reid boosted me before he scrambled up behind me. We made our way to the very tip, which jutted out over the water, and then we sat down on the sun-warmed stone, our legs dangling over the edge, our fingers intertwined.

For a while, we just sat there together, soaking in the filtered sunlight and the stolen moment. Things had been like this between us, so easy, for so long. And then the thing with Chase had happened, that stupid little kiss that wrecked everything. It was difficult, if not impossible, to be around Reid after that. But still, somehow, we'd found our way back to this. And I understood now why he had brought me here.

"Is everything okay?" I asked. "Between you and your parents, I mean."

He froze, staring down at the rushing water until I wasn't sure that he'd heard me. But as I was opening my mouth to repeat myself, he spoke.

"Things weren't, for a while," he said, choosing his words carefully. "I was a real mess when I found out I wasn't headed to the show this season. I went off the rails for a little while. And the people around me suffered for it. Especially my parents. I really lashed out at them." He looked back at the house, just visible through the trees behind us. "Pushed them away, told them never to come to an Ice Hawks game as long as I was playing there. So they gave me space, and I don't blame them."

He exhaled, long and slow, his eyes fluttering closed before they popped open again and found mine.

"Thank you for coming here with me," he said solemnly. "I think you're the only reason they didn't kick me off the porch right away." I shook my head.

"I figured they hated me after what happened between us. They never reached out."

Reid sucked his teeth.

"They're loyal, and they'll always take my side in public. But Mom told me on the regular just how stupid I was to let you get away." He chuckled. "When she found out I'd gone ghost on you like a coward, I thought she would throttle me. I was glad to be six hundred miles away at college. If she could have, she would have come busting through the telephone line and whooped my ass in front of all my dorm mates."

We were both laughing now. I could picture it clearly, Tamara ballooning out of his phone screen and chewing his ass until it bled.

He squeezed my hand.

"You'll never know how sorry I am for being such an unforgivable jackass, Lola," he said, serious again. "I don't deserve a second of your time. I sure as hell don't deserve a second chance."

I smoothed my hand over his hair and then leaned in and pressed a kiss to his temple.

"Mistakes were made," I murmured, trailing a hand down his chest. His breath hitched as his heart thumped. "We should let the past be the past."

There was a time I thought I would never forgive the man I was currently groping. I was sure that if I ever saw him again, I would call him every name in the book and slap his face before I walked away from him for good.

But I could see now just how silly we'd both been. Kids were silly. Everything felt so huge back then, every emotion brand new, every nerve ending rubbed raw by unchecked hormones. I would hate to be judged now for some of the choices I made back then. We'd grown and learned, and we'd both gone out into the real world. I believed we were brought back together for a reason, and I was sick of fighting fate.

I flipped around, straddling his lap and kissing him with all the feelings I didn't know quite how to put into words. His hands gripped my hips and jerked me forward against him as his tongue swirled around mine.

When we were both about to explode just from the friction of our two bodies grinding together, I slid backward off his lap and down the face of the boulder, a five-foot drop, to the little cave it made on the creek's edge. This had been our true hangout, where we could hide from the world, just the three of us.

He followed me down and sat back against the smooth underside of the big rock. I stripped off my leggings while he pushed down his jeans, and then I was on top of him again and we were locked together, our tongues, our bodies. I stared into his eyes as I took him all the way to the hilt. He grabbed my ass, his grip tight, but he didn't blink. We gazed into each other, getting closer and closer, driven by our shared need. I needed to get closer, to feel him even deeper inside me. I dug my nails into his shoulders and bit his bottom lip, then shoved my tongue into his mouth again. He pulled me down onto his cock in a bone-rattling rhythm. He was giving me everything. We pressed together desperately, skin to skin, every possible inch touching, as if we could merge completely and become one.

And then we came together, muffling our moans against each other's shoulders as wave after wave crashed down. It was as if the dam that had been holding back everything we felt for each other had crumbled, and we were drowning in the pain and love and ecstasy.

63.
Lola

"You saw Bob and Tamara?" Hope asked, her eyebrows disappearing under her bangs. I nodded as I attacked a particularly large chunk in my pint of ice cream, carving it out with my spoon.

"I was sure they hated my guts, given that I haven't seen them at all since I came back even though I'm living with their daughter." I glanced up at Hope in time to see a shadow flit across her face. She sighed.

"Yeah," she said. "Things have been kind of weird this past year. It's like our whole family unit fractured when Reid had his freakout."

I put the carton down on the coffee table, stabbing the spoon into it like I was planting a flag. Then I turned to face her.

"I had no idea he took it so hard when Mr. Branson held him back," I said. Hope's heather-gray eyes went glassy as she stared at something I couldn't see.

"He lost his fucking mind. And I really think he might have gone off the deep end for good if you hadn't come along and snapped him out of it, Lols." I dropped my eyes and shook my head, but she grabbed my arm. "I mean it. Even if it hurt him at first, having you back has been the best thing to happen to him in…a really long time."

"I would have been here sooner if that jackass hadn't removed me from his life like a tumor," I muttered, but without teeth. My heart went out to him. He'd always been highly competitive, and ridiculously hard on himself. In high school when I begged him to take a break he would say that the only way to be the best at something was to have impossibly high standards for yourself. I still think it's an unhealthy attitude, but it's one he shares with some of the most successful people on the planet.

"Okay, tell me everything. You saw them. He saw them. He dropped his big news, and…?"

"And they were Tamara and Bob. They hugged him, congratulated him. She made us lunch. If I didn't know all three of them so well, I would never have noticed that something was off."

"Off?"

"Yeah. It's like they don't know how to act around each other anymore. I mean, what made me so comfortable at your house way back when was how you guys all loved each other so much, and there was rarely any tension in the house. Teenagers fight with their parents but even that was pretty mild, at least when I was around." Hope nodded. Her eyes were trained on my face. "But the air between them felt like…" I tried to put my finger on exactly what the sensation had been. Then it hit me. "Like the way your house feels when you've been gone on vacation for a couple of weeks, and you come back and have to air everything out and breathe some life into the place again before it feels normal. Does that make sense?"

Hope laughed, and the sudden sound startled me, but it also helped me breathe a little easier. Discord was normal in my family of origin, but I'd always seen the Wright's house as a safe haven from all that. So I'd been seriously discomfited by the frosty atmosphere there today.

"Yeah, it makes sense," she said. "It's right on the nose. His relationship with them has been vacant for a while. But he told them he was headed to the Prospectors before he told me, so they must be rebuilding the bridge." She sounded put out that he hadn't called her as soon as he hung up with Branson.

"I think he feels guilty leaving you here," I said. It wasn't my business, but I hated to see her taking his slight personally. "I think he's afraid you'll be upset." We locked eyes, and then Hope rolled hers and threw her hand up in the air.

"And letting me be the fifth to find out isn't going to upset me?"

"Yeah, I don't think he thought it all the way through. He texted me an hour ago and said Jamie went nuclear when he found out that Reid told literally everyone else first." Hope smiled a secret little smile that gave me pause. "What?"

"What?" she echoed, wiping her face clean. I frowned at her. I'd long sensed that there was some big secret about Jamie, something no one would talk about but everyone knew. Everyone except me. Hope's cryptic grin made me wonder what she was thinking, but if it was something she felt comfortable sharing, she would have told me already. So I dropped it.

"Nothing, never mind," I said. "Wanna order pizza from that wood-fired place?"

She nodded, her eyes lighting up.

64.
Dallas

From my vantage point in front of the net, I could see the hits coming, and track the puck, better than the guys who were in the thick of it.

We'd been practically living on the bus the past couple of weeks, chewing up the roster and getting closer to the cup with every game. The Ice Hawks were a well-oiled machine by now. With all our key players on the ice, we were downright deadly.

I dropped a knee, easily knocking away a desperate snapshot from the Utah team. My back felt great, and not just because of the adrenaline coursing through me. It was as if Lola's magic hands had kneaded the discs of my spine back into place. I had no idea if something like that was actually possible, but I didn't know how else to explain the sudden, vast improvement.

I was rebuilt, reborn, and ready to get back on the ice in the major league.

Branson had called a few days ago to tell me that if my back held up, my starting spot guarding the net for the Prospectors next season was guaranteed. They'd missed the playoffs by a mile this year with a backup goalie who shit the bed every time the puck came near him. The Ice Hawks, on the other hand, were the talk of hockey radio. Our stands were packed every game, and we just kept winning. I knew how development teams worked, and I knew that Branson had sent us all here to rest and get stronger so he could pack out the Prospectors with fresh, eager, high-talent players next year. Not to toot my own horn, but he'd probably written off this season the second he realized I wouldn't be able to play.

A fight broke out near the other net, and I took the opportunity to slug from my water bottle as the officials swarmed Reid and the poor son-of-a-bitch he was pummeling.

I thought the cagey defenseman was a blow-hard at first, but he'd really grown on me. I was starting to understand why Lola was so fond of him. We were all crammed in on the bus together, and even though we were sleeping most of the time as the driver carted us from one town to the next, the close proximity still forced us all to bond. And our back-of-the-bus shenanigans with Lola helped, too.

We traveled ten hours to Utah for this game, and she spent most of the ride sitting on somebody's cock. Sometimes riding, sometimes napping. The front of the bus was a safe zone for the guys who didn't want to be involved—or might have wanted to be involved but were already otherwise committed.

I held her in my lap when it was my turn, squeezing her and petting her and filling her up. I hoarded her all to myself for over an hour, and she let me. They all did. The team was invested in keeping me happy, especially right now. It was lucky for them that I was willing to share. I enjoyed watching her get fucked, but I loved when she slowed down and let me wrap my arms around her for a little while. When I woke up from a nap still hard inside her warm, wet pussy, I blew my load in minutes and passed her off to Reid, who had been waiting impatiently in his sleeper pod.

She climbed up and disappeared inside with him, and spent almost as long there as she had with me. But she also made sure to spread the love around, giving plenty of attention to Xander and Eric and Huck, too. Patch woke up long enough for a quick blow job. Marcus and Sly spit-roasted her in the aisle and came in, like, less than a minute. I'm not exaggerating.

Still, she wanted more, even when she could barely keep her eyes open.

She was inexhaustible. Insatiable. I'd taken it as a personal challenge to try to wear her out, but I had never even come close. Seeing firsthand how much she craved cock, I understood exactly why she wasn't interested in monogamy. I had a remarkably high sex drive, and mine couldn't touch hers.

I'd honestly be afraid to meet the man who was her match.

On the ice, the shift switched, and I saw Lola press her sweater against the plexiglass, watching anxiously as our guys stole the puck and carried it away.

65.
Will

I felt her before I heard her. Her little voice calling from beneath me. I peeked out of my sleeper and saw her standing there, looking like a literal angel. But I knew she had devilish intentions.

"Can I come up?" she asked, batting her eyelashes at me.

No way could I deny her. I reached down and lifted her easily into my pod. She snuggled up beside me, laying her head on my chest, and I ran my fingers through her hair, holding her tight with my other arm around her.

She skated her fingers down toward my waistband to discover that I was already growing for her. I was exhausted from a week on the road, but we were winning. We were fucking *winning*. Everything we'd been working for was coming to fruition.

Her hand dipped into my boxers, closing around my shaft, and I raised my hips, needing more. It was nearly pitch black in my pod, but I felt her move down my body, and then her lips closed around my tip.

It took everything I had not to yell. Blood rushed to my center, and I realized just how much I needed this release.

She took me down her throat, swallowing around me, her tight little muscles working. Fucking her in any hole was like getting strangled to death by a boa constrictor, and I couldn't get enough.

By now, her relationship with half of the team was only still a secret to Branson. The married guys didn't participate in the X-rated activities that took place in the shadowy back of the bus, but they all loved her, too. From what I'd heard, her sex tips had saved more than a few of their marriages.

Lars announced to the whole bus a couple of hours ago that he and his wife were finally expecting. We cheered for him as he turned to Lola and swept her off her feet into a crushing hug, tears streaming down his ruddy cheeks. She'd earned their loyalty, and they were more than happy to put in their earbuds, pull down a sleeping mask, and ignore us as we worshipped our goddess.

She took me straight down her throat, and I fisted both hands in her hair, holding her there. All other thoughts vacated my mind. I didn't let myself dwell on the fact that most of her boyfriends would be moving to Denver in a few months, and she was likely to go with them. I just let myself get lost in her, accepting the pleasure she doled out to me so generously. She squeezed my balls and stroked my shaft, and pushed herself to take more of me. I wanted to praise her for doing such a good job, but most of the guys were asleep and I didn't want to disturb them, so I bit my tongue. Also, at least for tonight, I didn't want to share her. I wanted to come with her and spoon right here until we fell asleep.

I wanted to wake up with her warm body pressed against mine.

I was getting close, with the devoted attention she was paying my cock. But there was only one place in the world where I wanted to deposit my come, and that was in her pussy. I gave her hair a little tug, letting her know I wanted her to come up and ride me. She obeyed readily, and my cock throbbed and leaked as she slid up my stomach, kissing her way to my neck, then pushing back hard to take my length as she trapped my mouth in a soul-bending kiss.

I swear she rearranged my DNA with that insistent little tongue as her pussy clenched around me and her tits brushed against my chest. I was about to blow whether she was ready or not. But she kept getting tighter, and I raised up off of the thin mattress, grinding my pubic bone into her clit. She let out a breathy, almost silent groan. Then she leaned up, put her lips against my ear, and said so only I could hear…

"Give me your come, Daddy. Please fill me up. I need it so bad…"

My cock erupted like a geyser in her tight slit, draining me of every last drop of pent-up frustration and anxiety. The darkness pulsed blue and purple as I crested, and she clamped down around me, burying her face in my chest to stifle her whimpers of pleasure as she hit her peak.

After that, I got my wish. She snuggled her ass back into my lap, and within minutes, her breathing deepened and evened out.

I lay awake for a while, enjoying the feel of her. I wanted to stay in this moment, this perfect moment, for the rest of my life.

But exhaustion got the better of me, and soon enough, I was dreaming, too.

66.
Huck

We were back at home for a brief stint, but I was still feeling the effects of the road.

On the off chance that you weren't aware, a broken back is a pretty serious injury. Obviously, it's career-ending—especially if your career is "professional hockey player." But it's not just that. Even if you're lucky enough to survive the initial injury and learn to walk again, your body will never be the same.

After weeks on the road, combined with the pressure of the conference finals, my back was in bad shape. Well, "bad shape" is an understatement. My back was completely fucked.

I stumbled into my apartment the night we got back, relieved beyond words to be home, and fell face-first into my bed without even taking my shoes off.

The next morning, I couldn't move. When my eyes opened to see the daylight pouring into my bedroom, I felt another surge of relief. Then I tried to roll over.

No dice.

"Oh, fuck!" I panted as I tried again to push myself onto my back from my stomach. But my arms were weak, and my spine was on lockdown. When I tried to push through the physical block, a thunderclap of pain crashed down from my brain all the way to the tips of my toes.

I couldn't even lift my head to look around for my phone. Tears leaked from the corners of my eyes as I inched my hand toward my pants pocket, praying that I'd forgotten to plug it in.

Yes. My fingers pinched the slim metal casing, and I put every last ounce of strength I had into dragging it out. With sweat beading on my forehead, I pressed the button that would let me give a voice command. I heard the familiar chime that said the device was listening.

"Call Lola," I croaked. I held my breath, waiting to see if it would connect me to the massage therapist or to my Uncle Lowell.

"Hello?" I heard the faint, tinny sound of her voice.

"Lola!" I shouted. "My back is totally fucked. I can't get out of bed. I can't even sit up." She tried to say something, but I talked over her because I couldn't hear her anyway. "I can't even lift the phone to my ear. I can't hear you. But if you can hear me, Will has a spare key to my apartment. If you guys could come over here and help me…that would be great."

Grinding my teeth together, I waited for her response, and then I realized I wouldn't be able to hear it. Eventually, she must have hung up, but just a few minutes later, I heard sounds at my front door. The scrape of the deadbolt. Then, Lola's voice in the foyer.

"He said he was in bed." Two sets of footsteps came down the hall. I heard her make a little noise of sympathy when she saw me facedown and helpless. Will knew me well enough by now to keep his pity to himself, but I could hardly be mad at her when she'd come so readily to my rescue.

She started slow, talking me through the pain as she addressed each spasm in turn. Slowly but surely, my agony lessened. Will fed me a muscle relaxer and some water through a straw, and I could have wept with gratitude.

"Can we revisit the topic of you coming in for a weekly massage?" Lola said primly when she'd massaged my spine back into place well enough that I could roll over and stand to go to the bathroom. Every step was still misery, but the medication was kicking in, and I was numbing out. Back in bed, I stared at the ceiling as she arranged pillows and an ice pack behind me.

"What's the use?" I asked flatly. Bulging discs could be repaired. My injury was different. And I was never getting back on the ice, so what did it matter?

"Maybe if you got regular massages, you would have less chronic pain." She spoke calmly, rationally, appealing to the medical professional in me.

Of course, I knew she was right. She'd always been right. But I couldn't stand to get my hopes up. I'd accepted a long time ago that I would always be in pain. That I would have to fight through agony just to swing my legs over the edge of my bed every morning. I couldn't entertain any other possibility because I couldn't bear the disappointment of learning all over again that there was no help available to me.

Lola eased me back against the pillows, adjusting the freezer pouch and then sliding her hand up into my hair.

"Please consider it," she said. Will was watching us from the armchair, wisely staying out of the discussion. I looked at him for guidance, but he offered none. His jaw was set. He'd been encouraging me for a long time to get some help. "I'll give you a happy ending every single time."

I laughed out loud.

"Fuck. Okay, fine. I'll give it a try, but I'm not promising I'll stick around if it hurts."

"Don't be a baby," Will said, the corner of his mouth lifting in a half-smile when I narrowed my eyes at him.

"I already said I'd do it," I grumbled, crossing my arms over my chest and then hissing and letting them drop when the pressure of the posture tugged on my spine.

"I'm going to hold you to that," Lola said.

67.
Lola

This was it, the last game of the conference final. We'd made it to glory's doorstep, and all the guys had to do was bring it home. I chewed my lip raw as I watched the cutthroat game.

I'd learned that playoff season was different from the regular season. There was no room for error, no fucking around. Fights still happened, but they were more brutal and better justified. The skaters on both sides were laser-focused on the puck, and Dallas was a blur as he moved to bat away an endless volley of attempts. Our guys were sending a lot of shots in, too, and they'd actually managed to score a goal. But the clock was ticking down on the third period, and the clash on the ice was reaching a fever pitch. Sticks and elbows flew as both teams' best players dug in and duked it out for a shot at the cup. As much as it was a physical battle, this was also a battle of wills.

Nate got the puck and rammed it toward the opposing team's goal, and Reid and Jamie cleared a path ahead of him. Lars joined them on the ice as Xander hit the bench for a breather. Lars barreled through the other team's defense like a bull in a china shop. I realized I wasn't breathing and forced myself to inhale.

I needed a hand to hold, but it was an away game, and Hope hadn't been able to get time off from the restaurant to come with us. I was surrounded by the other team's fans, who were growing more raucous by the second. But all my attention was trained on the rink.

Nate lost the puck but brought it back around, pushing hard toward the net, and then the lamp lit up and angry shouts sounded from all around me. I grinned and clapped my hands but stopped myself from leaping up and cheering. Tensions were high, and I wasn't looking to have a soda thrown at the back of my head by an angry Orcas fan.

The Orcas' center was back at our net for another attempt. Dallas knocked it away. They brought it around, and one of the wingers shot again. No good. The clock raced toward zero. I forced another breath into my lungs and held it, crossing my fingers in my lap and my toes in my boots.

Our team had the puck, and now it was a game of keep-away as the last seconds ran out. The buzzer sounded, and the crowd around me screamed their displeasure, stomping their feet and jeering. But the Ice Hawks didn't pay them any mind. They all dropped into a dog pile at Dallas's feet. He smiled down at them dazedly.

I pushed my way into the aisle and then sprinted toward the locker room. I wanted to be there, waiting for them when they came off the ice. The party would undoubtedly rage into the night, and I had lots of ideas for how to celebrate their victory. But more than anything, I wanted to be there when they came through the door.

I beat them, but just barely. They came pouring in behind me. Reid clomped over on his skates and swept me up, kissing me breathless and then pushing me toward Nate and Dallas, who were bringing up the rear.

"These men deserve their heart's desire tonight," he announced, and the rest of the team cheered. Will and Huck came through the double doors and stood there for a second, staring around at all the guys. Then Huck pumped his fist in the air and Will clapped his hands, beaming.

"We're headed to the championship, boys!" Will shouted. The locker room broke out in a resounding chorus of shouting and laughing, hooting and chanting. "Let's give it up for our MVPs, Nate the Great and The Tank!" The noise reached a crescendo that died away when Nate cleared his throat and held up his hand. Everyone fell silent, waiting with bated breath to see what he would say.

"We're all MVPs," was what he said. His usually arrogant face was raw with emotion. "I'm so proud to be a member of this team tonight. Everyone brought their A-game, and we couldn't have done it without every single skater. So cheer for yourselves. You fucking did it!" I stared at him in awe as the locker room erupted once more. A few months ago, I would have bet on Nate the Great to remain an island, more than happy to take all the credit for himself. But here he was, proving me wrong. Somehow, at some point, while I wasn't looking, he had become a team player. A true Ice Hawk.

Will had pizzas and beer brought in, and the toasts went on into the evening, becoming more and more slurred, until the other half of the team retired, stumbling, to the bus. Then it was just us.

Me, Will, Huck, Reid, Nathan, Dallas, Xander, Eric, Marcus and Sly. Patch and Jamie had gone off to bed already, both too drunk to see straight and definitely way too drunk to consent to any group activities.

As soon as we were alone, the guys huddled around me. I dragged my teeth over my bottom lip as Will stepped forward and pulled me against his chest, kissing me hard on the mouth.

"You want to keep this party going?" he whispered so only I could hear. I nodded, looking up at him with a devilish smile. An equally wicked grin split his face, and he raised his head to address the group. "All right, boys," he said. "Our lovely Lola has offered herself up as the prize of the evening."

A little thrill of excited fear rushed through me as men leaned in on every side. Big hands groped my body, sliding over my skin, pulling at my clothes until I was standing naked between them. Nine sets of hungry eyes drank me in, and for a second, none of us were breathing.

Then, the tension broke and they rushed forward, lifting me up, their thick fingers pushing into my pussy, my mouth, wrapping around my throat, my waist, my thighs. They spread me open, and then there was a mouth closing over my clit with suction that made me buck and beg for more.

I looked down to see Xander between my legs, working his usual magic. Hands were gripping my ass cheeks and spreading them apart, and then a tongue was exploring me back there, too.

My eyes flew wide open. This was a new and different sensation. Two tongues, fucking into me at different speeds and depths, both lifting me up, up, up into the stratosphere.

"Look at her. She loves it."

"Somebody get a cock in her mouth, pronto." I recognized Huck's husky, domineering voice.

They leaned my head toward the floor, both tongues still exploring me, and someone stepped in, pushing a billy club against my lips. I looked up to see Sly staring down at me, his face a mask of lust as he fed me his cock. I opened wide for him, letting my head fall back and taking him straight down my throat. He grabbed my head with both hands and thrust forward, shoving himself deeper and deeper, grunting at the bottom of every stroke. I focused on sucking him without scraping my teeth over his sensitive flesh.

The tongues left, and then a cock shoved into my pussy, stretching me, as oiled fingers circled my back entrance and then plunged in.

I was suspended in mid-air, held up by big hands and bigger dicks as the guys had their way with me.

I closed my eyes and stopped trying to keep track of who was inside me. Sly came down my throat and then an even bigger cock replaced him, choking me, fucking my face with force, and unloading into my stomach. Tears gathered in my hairline and my chin and cheeks were wet with my own spit. I felt perfectly in my element, like I was created to do exactly this.

We moved as a group to the bench in front of the lockers and Will sat down, pinning me in his lap and ramming his slicked cock into my ass with earth-shattering force. I gasped, clamping down like a vice around him before he was even halfway in.

He moved his hands from my hips, circling them around my waist. Then he tightened them, forcing me onto his shaft. It was still just pain, only pain. Tears blurred my vision, and I couldn't see what was in front of me as I tried to breathe through it.

"Relax, baby," he murmured against my neck. "You can take it. I've seen you take every single inch of my fat cock." He thrust up into me, still barely moving in my tight hole. Then he brushed his fingertips over my clit, and right away, my body started to uncoil.

I slid down another inch, opening up for him, but he pulled his hand away, and the pain was back. I groaned. Tears spilled down my cheeks, clearing my vision, just as someone knelt between mine and Will's spread thighs and went to work.

I was shocked to realize it was Nate the Great, on his knees for me, tongue-fucking my pussy as his coach stuffed my ass. My jaw dropped as a moan started near my belly button and ripped out of me, filling the room. My first orgasm came on hard and fast. I pushed back against Will. His hands returned to my hips, and he drove me down onto his shaft again and again as Nate straightened up and aimed his dick at my dripping entrance.

"God, yes," I groaned as he slid into my pussy, stretching me beyond my limits. They were destroying my boundaries, training me to take two huge cocks at once.

Nate fucked my pussy, forcing me down onto Will's cock with every thrust. Dallas came to stand beside us, propping one foot on the bench and stroking himself in front of my face. I opened my mouth, locking eyes with him as he gripped himself and aimed the tip between my lips, slamming all the way to the back and pushing when he met resistance until my throat gave just like my ass had surrendered to Will. With that, all three of them were hammering into me. Dallas cupped the back of my head in his hands and held me still as he pumped into me, leaning forward until his tip slid into that tight, rippling sleeve.

"Look at that good girl," Will said, his hand returning to my clit as Nate picked up the pace between my legs. Lowering his voice even more, he whispered, "You want Daddy's come deep in your ass, baby?" I whimpered as I choked on Dallas's cock, and when the goalie pulled back, I took the brief second before he plunged back in to nod. "Fuck," Will gasped, holding me down in his lap as Nate rammed home in my pussy again and again. A moment later, I felt the wetness spreading through me. Will bit down hard on my shoulder, rubbing my clit harder and faster with the pads of his fingers as his cock pulsed and spilled inside me. Nate fucked me right through a second climax as Will started to soften.

"My turn," Nate growled when I quieted down. He threw himself down on the bench beside Will, who passed me over without protest. I felt the coach's come trickling out of me as Nate situated me in his lap, sinking himself into my stretched-out, lubricated ass.

This time, there was no need to ease in. I was ready, and he was ready for me. He lifted me up into the air and then dropped me back down. Up, down, his entire length leaving me and then entering again, spearing me with white-hot jolts of exquisite agony. I moved my hips in small circles and spirals as he buried himself in me. Soon my ass was resting on the tops of his thighs, and I was taking every last inch of him.

Huck appeared in front of me. For a second, he just watched us, his fist working his cock with lazy strokes. Nate grabbed my breasts and squeezed until I cried out. The sound made Huck's dick jump in his hand. We stared into each other's eyes, his ice-blue boring into my chestnut. And then he was bending down, sheathing himself inside me with one quick thrust. I held onto his shoulders, screaming and bucking in Nate's lap, as Huck smashed into me. Nate grunted, raising his hips to support my thrashing body.

"God, what a hot little slut," he said in a ragged voice at my ear. My pussy flooded, tightening around Huck until he groaned. "You love being crammed full of cock, don't you, Lola?"

"Yes! Fuck yes, I love it!" I wailed. Flushed faces gathered around us, watching closely as Huck and Nate shared my body.

Nate pinned me to his chest, resting his forehead against the nape of my neck, panting hot breath down my back. I felt his come joining Will's deep inside me. I rocked my hips back and forth, guiding him back to Earth. Then I braced my hands on Huck's chest and gave him a gentle push backward. His cock slipped out of my pussy, bobbing and glistening between his legs as he eyed me.

I stood up and stepped forward, and then I dropped to my knees on the concrete floor. A second later, a hand reached out, holding a towel for me to kneel on. I looked up to see Dallas gazing down at me, his eyes dark with desire.

I folded the towel and placed it on the floor in front of me, and then planted both knees on it and looked around. At that cue, the guys all stepped forward. Suddenly, I was at the center of a circle of big, hard cocks, all dripping pre-come and pointing directly at me. I gripped Reid and Eric in my fists and opened my mouth for Huck's cock, sucking the taste of myself off of him. He bent double, grabbing my head with both hands, and then he was slamming his cock against the back of my throat relentlessly, again and again until he spilled on my tongue. I swallowed every drop. Wiping his forehead with a stunned look on his face, he stumbled backward and the others closed the gap.

I took Reid down my throat next, still stroking Eric and closing my other hand around Xander's seriously impressive equipment. Dallas hung back, happy to wait his turn. He'd had more of me than anyone by now, and unlike Nate, he'd been a team player from the get-go.

I sucked them like that for a while, like I was on a merry-go-round of dicks. Then, just as my knees were starting to ache, Dallas picked me up. My back was against his chest. He gripped the undersides of my knees, pinning my thighs to my stomach and spreading my legs so the others could get a good look at my soaked, stretched pussy. They stared, pumping their cocks in their fists.

"Reach down between your legs and guide my cock into your ass, Lola," he said. Dallas wasn't much of a talker, let alone one to dole out orders. But when he did, his authority was unquestionable. I did as he said, dropping my hand down to the place where his shaft was resting against my slit. I grabbed him underneath the head and slid it toward my back door. He thrust his hips forward as I pushed him inside.

I screamed with a mixture of pleasure and pain as he skewered me, lowering me slowly but steadily until his dick in my ass was supporting the majority of my weight. I panted, eyes wide open, as my body struggled to adjust to his massive cock.

Xander was bent over between my thighs, licking me eagerly. I ran my hands through his thick black hair and then curled them into fists, tugging him closer, holding his mouth to my clit. He sucked like he was trying to remove it, and at that point, I hardly even noticed the lodgepole that was rammed up my ass. It was just more heaven as I arched my back, taking Dallas deeper when I tried to get closer to Xander's talented tongue.

"Fuck me!" I gasped, yanking on Xander's hair. Always obedient, he sprang to his full height with a blissed-out smile on his face and slammed himself easily into my pussy with one fluid motion. Dallas's grip on my thighs loosened until all of my weight was bearing down on their cocks, which moved in and out of me in a staccato rhythm, taking turns pulling out and pushing in, so I was always full from one side or the other and sometimes both. The underside of their shafts rubbed together between the thin wall that separated them. Xander dipped down to suck each of my nipples, pushing me closer and closer to the edge as they worked in and out of me, deeper and harder, passing me back and forth. I cried out, letting my head fall forward against Xander's chest as I tightened around them, every muscle in my body drawing toward my center.

"Shit," Dallas groaned behind me. "Oh, fuck, Lola." The two of us exploded together as our bodies had learned to do, him swelling as I clenched until I thought one of us would burst. But then he was slipping out of me, stepping away, and Xander was backing me up against the wall of lockers as he increased his speed and power, pounding into my pussy as my body quaked with the aftershocks of my third climax.

His mouth found mine, and then we were kissing. Our tongues wrestling, our bodies grinding together, skin on skin. He was touching every part of me he could reach, worshipping me in the way he did best. When he came with a bang a few minutes later, he kept me pinned to the locker for a long time after he was finished, his face buried in the crook of my neck. He was trembling, his cock still jerking deep inside me.

When he had his legs underneath him again, he carried me back to the bench and set me down, pressing a kiss to the top of my head. Somewhere, I could hear voices bouncing around the shower room as water cascaded and splashed. But I had work left to do. Reid and Eric were standing in front of me. Eric blushed, still shy even after all the times he'd seen me naked.

Reid was as hard as steel, his eyes like twin flames as he looked me up and down. My body was used, leaking, and limp with exhaustion. But I can't explain how much I wanted—needed—them inside me.

Reid leaned down, brushing his lips over mine. I reached between us, closing my fingers around his shaft. Then I looked past him to Eric, waving him closer with my other hand. He stepped up beside Reid, and I sucked the tip of his cock between my lips. He groaned, lacing his hands gently through my hair. Unlike some of the others, he didn't try to guide me. He didn't force me to take more. He just enjoyed my mouth on him, the way I licked and sucked and savored him. He closed his eyes, his long eyelashes casting shadows down his cheeks. Meanwhile, Reid's dick throbbed in my grip. I moved my mouth to him, stroking Eric's wet shaft as I sucked Reid. Eric fucked himself into my hand, moaning low in his throat. I could feel his balls gathering up against his body. I pulled back from Reid and looked up at them, my hands still hard at work.

"How do you want to fuck me?" I asked, looking from Reid's gray eyes to Eric's green ones.

"What do you say, Moose?" Reid asked, turning to his teammate. "You want to keep fucking her mouth or try out that sweet little pussy?" Eric's face flamed bright red, but his voice came out clear and strong.

"I want to fuck her in the ass," he said. Goosebumps broke out across my skin at his show of dominance. We locked eyes, and I nodded.

"All right," Reid said, surveying the scene. "Lola, get on your hands and knees on the bench." I did as he said, balancing on the thin plank of wood. Eric lined up behind me, rubbing his tip, slick with pre-come, up and down my slit, teasing my clit with it before sliding back to press it firmly against my asshole. After the night I'd had, he slipped right in.

"Jesus fucking Christ," he moaned, pushing forward until his hot skin touched mine.

Reid sat in front of me, a leg on either side of the bench, and lowered my face toward his waiting cock. I braced on my elbows instead of my hands, rocking forward to take him down my throat and then back to take Eric up my ass. It was easy for them to leverage me back and forth in this position, Reid ramming his cock down my throat and Eric dragging me back until his stomach slapped my ass and he was buried to the hilt inside me. They went faster, deeper, railing me from both ends, Reid's hands tangled in my hair, much more insistent than Eric's as he plunged between my lips again and again.

Eric's hands fisted around the flesh of my ass, grasping it tightly and slamming into me once, twice, three times. The slapping sound of his stomach against my skin filled the room and then stopped suddenly as he bottomed out inside me and filled me to the absolute brim with what felt like a gallon of come. He pulled away, and I felt it wet and dripping down the backs of both of my thighs, pooling behind my knees as Reid continued to fuck my mouth with the same insistence, never letting up.

I fought to suck in air when he lifted me up by my hair before he rammed himself down my throat again. And again. And again. I hinged forward on my knees, leaning in as he fucked my mouth. Then, when my body was weak, and my knees were screaming, and my throat was raw from taking him, Reid pulled out, used his grip on my hair to tilt my head back, and unloaded all over my face.

Sated at last, he dropped back onto his elbows, his dick softening in front of my nose. And then I heard the slow clapping again, a repeat of that day in the player's gym when everyone had walked in on Huck and Dallas sharing me.

I turned my glazed face in the direction of the sound and saw our audience, every man who had used me tonight, all of them freshly showered and still stark-ass naked. A few were getting hard again.

They licked their lips, all eyes on me like a pack of hungry wolves. I was surprised to find that, for the moment, I had finally had enough. As impossible as it might have once seemed, they had worked together to find my limit at last.

I would take them all again if they wanted me. But when I thought they were descending on me for round two, they lifted me up in their arms instead and carried me to the shower to wash me clean under the warm spray.

Epilogue
Lola

So, we didn't win the cup. We gave it our best effort, but the team from Montana cleaned our clock and kept our lamp lit. Dallas was seething by the end. But Mr. Branson was so impressed by the team's improvement that he had recruited basically the entire first and second lines to join the Prospectors. That included making good on his promise to Reid.

It also included Huck. Apparently, the head coach for the Prospectors was a total asshat and a bad coach to boot. So Branson shit-canned him and hired Huck to lead the Prospectors to victory. He offered the job to Will first, who declined it and elected instead to finally retire and become a house husband.

Huck kept his word and showed up for sessions with me every week, and I kept my word and delivered a happy ending at the end of every massage. After a couple of months of focused work, he told me he had bent over to tie his shoes that morning without pain for the first time in almost a decade.

The guys were pooling their professional athlete salaries and moving into a huge house together in Denver—Nate, Dallas, Eric,

Xander, and Reid. Huck and Will would live in the slightly smaller house next door, so no impropriety could be alleged.

I would go back and forth. Branson had also, I suspected at his players' insistence, offered me a spot as a massage therapist for the Prospectors. So I was headed to Denver, too, to start the next chapter of my life.

"I can't believe everyone is leaving," Hope said, sighing as we put out the food for the farewell party.

"Not *everyone*," I reminded her, glancing at the back of Jamie's head. He and Reid were in the living room having a spirited debate about the merits and ethics of dirty play. Hope's eyes followed mine, and a dreamy grin spread across her face when they landed on the redheaded winger.

Jamie wasn't moving to Denver. He would fill in on the first line and replace Reid as captain of the Ice Hawks. Someone had to stay behind to whip the new recruits into shape.

After a little pointed questioning, I'd gotten to the bottom of his bad attitude and why he never wanted to hang around or participate in filthy fun with the rest of us. For a while, I was convinced that he was secretly in love with Reid, and understandably jealous of me. But then I figured out that he truly was just a loyal guard dog for his best friend.

I was right about him being in love, though. Just not with Reid.

I studied Hope as she carefully arranged the stacks of napkins and paper plates. When I confronted her with my suspicions, she'd been forced to admit that she was head-over-heels in love with her brother's best friend. While I'd been busy slutting it up all season with my various lovers, Jamie had been sneaking into Hope's bedroom almost every night. She told me everything came to a head that night of the surprise dinner party, the night Reid and I finally worked out our drama. According to Hope, the heat between herself and Jamie had been building for a long time, but it finally boiled over while Reid and I worked our shit out on the other side of the house. Those two had been secretly fucking each other's brains out behind Hope's locked door while her brother and I were eating cold leftovers in the kitchen. After that, they never stopped.

And I hoped they never would. Jamie wasn't cold and standoffish anymore. As soon as his secret was exposed, it was as if a heavy weight had been lifted from his shoulders. Now he treated me like a sister, even a friend.

The doorbell rang, interrupting my runaway train of thought.

"Guys, can you get that?" Hope called as she carried a loaded tray of sandwiches to the table.

Jamie and Reid jumped up, fighting playfully over who would make it to the door first. When they got there, they swung it open to reveal the entire team huddled together on our tiny porch. They spilled inside, big man after bigger man. Then, the wives filtered in. And finally, Lars and a very pregnant Jeanine brought up the rear. They both grinned and waved when they saw me.

Lars wasn't the only one who had been grateful for my lessons. Jeanine pulled me aside to thank me one night at Copper's, shortly after they announced that they were pregnant. We ended up talking all night, and Hope and I started meeting her for dinner every week. I was going to miss them both so much when I was gone.

At least I would have two houses full of hockey hunks to keep me company…

We were all leaving the next morning in a moving truck caravan. Pre-season was starting on Monday, and we'd need to settle into the houses before then. I knew that Will and I would do most of the unpacking as the others dove head-first into major league life, but I was going to make them all do a little work before I cut them loose to play.

My guys came to me, one by one, filling in until I was completely surrounded. I'd never felt as safe as I did with their large bodies beside me, when they held me in their warm, reassuring hands.

I leaned against Reid's chest, and he wrapped his arms around me.

When the universe sent me boomeranging back to Casper, I really thought I was cursed. But now I could see that this appointment was the best thing that had ever happened to me.

I could no longer hate my hometown, because it had given me everything I'd ever wanted. And now, it was returning me to the world stronger than ever, with an army by my side.

Together, we could handle anything.

More from the Author

Passing Emma: A Reverse Harem Sports Romance

Team Tiffany: A Reverse Harem College Romance

The Wonderland Ranch Duet: A Dark Reverse Harem Retelling

The Mercenaries and the Movie Star: A Dark Reverse Harem Romance

Triple Diamond Christmas: A Holiday Reverse Harem Romance

A Mountain Man Love Story Series

Burn Down the House: A Small-Town Romance

Printed in Great Britain
by Amazon

46066195R00182